The Occasional Gardener

Nick Hooper

Wordandnote Publishing 2018

Copyright Nick Hooper 2018

ISBN 978-1-9997848-2-9

A CIP catalogue reference for this book
is available from the British Library

Printed and bound in Great Britain by 4edge Limited

Cover design by Sonja Burniston

For further copies of this book, and other books and
CDs for sale go to:
www.wordandnote.com

To Tim Pears for all the help he has given me with my various creative projects over the years

6 am Wednesday 16th September

My life is full of unfinished cups of tea, and it happens again this morning as I prepare to go on a dawn raid in The Avenues. I really don't like going to The Avenues. There's something I can't quite put my finger on, something that makes me shiver every time I go near that part of town. On the face of it, it's a perfectly nice area – safe as houses, and the houses are worth a bomb, I can tell you. I don't think I've ever been on a dawn raid there in all my time here. It's not the sort of area where you'd expect to find drugs. Burglaries yes, but it's the wrong part of town for drug dealers.

Anyway, I'm very reluctant to go there so I've been slow to get up, which is why there isn't time to drink up my tea without scalding my mouth.

"We've had intel that there are drugs at a house in The Avenues," said Ben our new intel officer.

"We'll get a warrant," said Burt, my boss. "But go gently, it's owned by a rich Saudi family and we don't want to cause a diplomatic incident."

I don't want to cause any kind of incident, not if I can help it.

"It's probably a hoax," I said to Burt. "Dodgy intel if you ask me."

Burt sighed. "You may well be right, but we have to follow it up."

So that's it. A waste of time. A waste of a cup of tea. And I'm up and off on a drugs raid on one of the poshest houses in town.

I arrive in time to join my team and I park my car on the gravel drive behind the others. I meet Peggy and we walk up the carriage sweep to this large Victorian house.

Peggy is my right-hand man. We're a team, Peggy and I. She's young and fit and intelligent, and I'm old and not as fast as I was, but I've still got a nose for crime and working things out. Wish I could work things out in my personal life though. I'm supposed to be married to someone called Betty, but it doesn't feel like it. Feels more like I'm married to Peggy, and to be honest, sometimes I wish I was. I can talk to Peggy. We're close. We're buddies.

We walk through an elegant conservatory to the front door and ring the bell.

No response. With all this crunching gravel I should have thought we would have woken up the whole neighbourhood. Maybe the son, who I am told is the sole occupant, is drugged up to the eyeballs.

Give it another go. This time a longer ring – no longer polite – and a big bang with the impressive door knocker.

There's a stirring inside, and the door swings open to reveal a young Arabic man neatly clad in jeans, golfing sweater, and a leather jacket. Not pyjamas, I note – he looks very alert, very awake.

"Mr Said?" I ask, holding up my warrant card. I can't remember his first name, and probably couldn't pronounce it anyway.

He stares at me, as though trying to make up his mind, and then tries to close the door, but I've already got my foot in it. Heavy door though, and I'm glad that Peggy takes the initiative and pushes the door open.

"Mr Said," she says. "We have a warrant to search these premises and…" She reads out the warrant and his rights etc…

He backs silently into the house and we file in.

"Sir, we'll have to search you," says Peggy. He makes as though he's going to resist and then sees Martin, our biggest officer who's come in behind me, and changes his mind.

Martin pats him down and turns to me. "Nothing sir."

"Ok, I'll stay with Mr Said," I say, and the team go off to search the house leaving me to follow the young man, who turns and heads off to what I guess will be the sitting room.

It's an impressive house. The owners have taken from the original Victorian décor, which already had a Middle Eastern flavour, and made it more Islamic. No pictures of people or animals anywhere. Instead there are beautiful intricate designs in blacks and golds. The polished marble floor, too, takes my mind to the temples of the East.

At first glance the sitting room seems to be laid out in a similar way with simple, expensive-looking sofas and armchairs, but as I turn the corner into the room my attention is immediately drawn to a painting that is completely out of place. It's by Seurat, and it's of a woman powdering herself. Last time I saw it, it was hanging in a gallery in London. But that was a long time ago when I was an art student, before I changed tack and became a policeman. I wonder how it came to be here. From what I can remember when I saw all those years ago, it looks genuine to me, and if I'm right it must be worth millions.

But in a Muslim house a picture of a woman doing such a personal thing as powdering her cleavage? It doesn't fit.

I turn to look at the son, who sits carefully down on a sofa without taking his eyes off me.

3

The painting takes my attention again, and I go up to it and look closely at the brushwork. A masterpiece of small brushstrokes making a soft, and slightly fairylike whole. I can't decide whether I like the lady or am repulsed by her. Oddly, she reminds me of my wife Betty – double chin, well endowed, a self-satisfied expression on her face.

There's a shuffling clicking sound behind me and I turn to see the son staring at the ground.

"Mr Said?"

Silence.

"Mr Said, can you tell us where the drugs are?"

No response. He just sits rigidly looking at the floor in front of him as if I don't exist. Well we'll get something out of him down at the station, no doubt.

I turn back to the painting. If this raid's a waste of time, at least I've had a chance to have a close look at a masterpiece. I walk round to the side to try and catch the early morning light from the windows reflecting on the tiny raised brushstrokes, and I notice that the painting is slightly proud of the wall. There's something behind it. I lift the painting off the wall carefully with my gloved hands, and there, set into the wall, is a safe.

I look down at the son sitting on the sofa, his eyes are staring up at me now with such hostility. If looks could kill.

"Mr Said, can you open the safe please?" He looks down at the floor in front of him. Silent.

I put the painting down gently and get my mobile out to ring the station.

"Is George in yet?... great... can you send her up? We've got a safe here, and the son doesn't seem to know the combination."

The son moves as though he's about to get up. I don't want him to make a run for it so I shout for Martin who is six-foot-six and can block any doorway.

The son slumps back down, staring fixedly at the floor as though there's an escape route through the carpet.

I kneel down and look at the painting again. My nose tells me there's something very odd about this – it's so out of place.

Martin blocks the doorway. The son sits perfectly still, and we all wait for George.

It's only five minutes before there's the scrunch of gravel and George appears with a bag full of gizmos, looking slightly flushed from the exertion.

"Open the safe, George," I say. "I don't think Mr Said knows the combination."

George looks at the safe rather like I looked at the Seurat.

"A Phoenix." This is obviously a welcome challenge. "Should be interesting."

As she gets to work with her computer and various bits and pieces, I notice the son getting increasingly fidgety.

"Mr Said," I say. "Can you tell us what is in the safe?"

He doesn't answer but pulls himself forward on the sofa into an almost squatting position, as if ready to pounce on George at any moment. I look at Martin, and he makes to come forward but I shake my head slightly. I want him blocking the door.

I look back down at the Seurat. It's unbelievable that I should be in the company of such a masterpiece. And I'm sure it is – every bit of my early training as an artist screams 'genuine'. I'm just crouching down to have another close look, when I hear a whirr and a click and the door of the safe opens.

George recoils in disgust as the room is filled with an aroma that I normally associate with the mortuary, and, as I drag my eyes from the Seurat and stand up to look inside the safe, there, sitting in pride of place as though it's the most valuable museum exhibit in the room, is a glass jar containing a severed hand preserved in formaldehyde.

I could draw you that pudgy hand with its thick square fingers, and the gold signet ring still on its third finger. The little finger is missing, and there are bits of stringy stuff hanging from the amputation and clouding the liquid the hand floats in.

I could draw you Martin's eyes looking up to the ceiling as he falls over in a dead faint. We never take Martin to the morgue – he always keels over at the sight of something dead preserved in formaldehyde.

I could draw you the 'oooohh fuck' expression on the son's face as he jumps up from the sofa. He looks at us like a startled cat for a moment and then legs it out of the room, jumping over Martin's recumbent body. I run after him into the hall shouting to the others, but I am much too slow to catch up – an old knee injury, and fifty-eight years on the planet are against me. George isn't much better either, being built for safe-cracking, not running.

Fortunately, Peggy is outside on the front drive putting a plastic bag in the van as he whizzes past her. She drops it onto the gravel and runs after him. He turns right, out of the gate, and into The Avenues. I run out and jump into my car hoping to cut him off further down the road. Turning out of the drive I see Peggy gaining ground. She's in training for the police charity marathon, and she can run like the wind. It's quite a sight as she flies down the road – her long fair hair, tied back in a pony-tail, streaming out behind. She's catching up with him and I'm driving down the wrong side of the road to cut him off, the trouble being that I am hampered by the trees that line The Avenues, and I can't see where to pull in.

Then two things happen at once: a car coming in the opposite direction hoots its horn, flashes me and swerves to the other side of the road as I jam on my brakes. At the

6

same time I see the son stop, turn round, and take something out of his jacket pocket. I hear the report of a gun as Peggy falls to the ground in front of him clutching her stomach. Everything stops except the son, who turns and runs down a side path round the back of a block of flats, and disappears.

I wrench the car door open, banging it on a tree, and run over to Peggy shouting for help. Others run in the direction that the son disappeared, but I know it is hopeless. Nobody is armed – it's too risky to go near him.

Where the fuck did that gun come from? We were totally unprepared for this. This is my home town for God's sake, the place where I was born – we don't have gun crime here.

I kneel down by Peggy, who is crumpled up in agony.

"Sir," she gasps, looking up at me.

I can't say anything, I just hold her hand and wait for the ambulance.

5.30 am, Monday 21st September

I've always been an early riser. It's the time when I get up to do the thing that I truly love.

Paint.

I discovered that I had a real talent for art at school, and everyone expected me to become an artist, never anticipating that I would become a policeman. Well I did go to art college, and then bumped around trying to make a living – a bit of teaching here, a bit of bar work there.

But, to be honest, it never took off, and I decided after a few years of living on nothing, that the police force was the thing for me. Follow in the footsteps of my Uncle Andrew – a local police sergeant, and the one adult I could turn to in our rather unstable family. Besides, at that point I'd fallen in love with pretty Betty, and she was never going to marry an impoverished artist – she had far greater expectations that that. Being a policeman in a uniform seemed glamorous back then. Good income – stable life. And I thought that I was going to make people safe – I was obsessed with it.

I didn't make Peggy safe though, did I?

My name even lends itself to being an artist – Arnold Rackham. Not far from Arthur Rackham – the greatest illustrator of the early twentieth century, and one of my heroes. He was a distant cousin according to family history.

I didn't sleep well last night – in fact I haven't slept well since the shooting last week – but I make my way across the landing to my studio, the little bedroom at the back of my terraced cottage, to look at my work in progress. Well, it hasn't progressed at all, and I stare at it, trying to see what it was that I was trying to create. A peaceful dawn landscape, taken from my window – everything in its place. Meaningless now.

I find a brush, look for my palette still covered in cling-film, and then change my mind, and put them to one side. Then I take the dry, half-finished painting from its easel, put it down on the floor, and turn it to face the wall. I carry the palette down to the kitchen to clean it up, and as I enter I hear the familiar thumping of a tail as my lovely old Labrador stiffly gets up off his bed to greet me.

"Hello dog," I greet him.

He walks over to me and nuzzles against my thigh. I call him 'the dog'. The name he answers to is Jip, but he isn't a Jip. He's himself, and I haven't found him a name in all the years we've spent together. He was called Jip when I got him from the rescue centre, and he answers to that name because he was taught to before I released him from his painful early life

"I'll just do this, then we can go for a walk." I lean down and stroke his broad flat head, scratching him behind the ears.

It's still dark outside as I clean the palette with turps and a cloth, and the pungent smell invades the kitchen, taking me right back to childhood when my granny used to paint her beautiful meticulous pictures of local houses. Granny was big in my life then, and I used to love to visit her and watch her work – her strong bony hands wielding the brush so deftly, making tiny strokes, her sense of colour so exquisite. She never minded – always had time for me. She taught me to draw, showing me how to shade the edge of a tree to make the paler middle come forward, fooling the eye into thinking it was three dimensional. Giving me the right pencils, and showing me how to sharpen them with a knife to get the point I needed.

The dog's getting restless, his claws clattering about on the tile floor and his tail beating a tattoo on the table leg. I mentioned the word 'walk', and if I don't get on with it he'll bark and that will wake up Betty, who lives next door now. I always get dressed to paint so I just need to take off my overall – an old white shirt – put on my coat and shoes and go out of the back door into the early-morning air. I reach the gate at the end of my small garden and bend down to put the dog's lead on. As I turn and look back at the houses, I notice that Betty has her bedroom light on. Strange, she never normally wakes up before seven, and it's not even six yet – I'm the early bird.

Betty, my next-door wife. What happened to us? It's a long time ago now, but at one moment we were getting on together, the next she had persuaded me to move next door. In a way it's suited me. She gets on with her life. I get on with mine. We've done so much better than other marriages I've seen fall apart in the force, with all the expense and heartache of divorce. But sometimes... sometimes I wish we could have made a proper go of it instead of living this half-life. Truth is, I don't look forward to having a lonely old age.

The gate gives out onto the common, one of the best features of where I live. Grass and trees extend down half a mile to the town – the rural invading the urban for a change. No chance of building on this sacred ground. I managed to buy two adjacent Victorian cottages when I moved back here. They were affordable then, before the big hike in house prices. The intention had been to live in one and let out the other for secondary income, but life decided differently. Or Betty did.

11

A mellow autumn dawn begins to break as we make our way through gorse and hazel. I love the autumn – a slightly melancholy feel of the decay to come. The leaves will fall off the trees. The wind stirs the world with change, but it's still warm. England's good for autumn – often the best weather, often warmer than the summer. Somehow it feels like a beginning, even if it's the year heading towards its end.

Now, something has come to an end – my peaceful life here. We've been invaded. Not just by gun-toting criminals, but by police from the Big Smoke. The fallout from the shooting last week was immense. Burt, my senior, called me in and ranted on about not being properly equipped, not finding the gun, and then shrugged his shoulders and admitted it was his fault we weren't prepared. We just didn't have the resources to deal with this level of crime in our sleepy old police station. We're a bit of an outpost, almost a remnant from the fifties and Dixon of Dock Green. Before this all happened I could have seen Burt, or even myself, standing outside the old Victorian station dispensing wisdom to the general public. True, neither of us has the rotund stature of Jack Warner, although I'm spreading round the waist now – even me, the tall skinny one.

Anyway, it was poor old Burt who got the rap. An old colleague of mine from the Met turned up with a bunch from Counter-terrorism. They're here because of something found on one of the computers during the search. It also turns out that Peggy was shot by a Russian military issue Yarygin Pya MP-443 "GRACH" handgun, which, with the Arabic connection, makes it look very much like we walked straight into a terrorist operation. So we've got the toughies from Counter-terrorism walking all over us. Burt's in trouble. 'Ran a loose ship', they said, so he's not in charge at the moment – at all, at all. That leaves me as the second in line, and the key witness to boot. Not that I'm actually in charge either.

Dick Grimwode's in charge now. We go way back, me and Dick. Back to my time in the Met when he played 'bad cop' and I played 'good cop'. His speciality was scaring people to death. Didn't actually kill anyone, but being near him was a life-shortening experience, I'm sure of it. Dick has always been skinny with thin hair slicked back onto his bony scalp, accentuating his ghoul-like appearance. But we made a good team then – me using my gentle tactics, subtle even, and him scaring the wits out of our victims. They would usually confess to me in the end, in a private, gentle conversation, with Dick out of the room. Anything to avoid having to see him again.

When I saw him last week I couldn't believe it, he'd gone as bald as a fucking coot. I had to sit down to get over the shock. When he was younger he looked a bit like Dracula – now he looks like Voldemort with a nose. He'd plonked himself in my chair behind my desk, coolly twiddling one of my pens, with me sitting opposite him in the seat that I reserve for my juniors.

"So, this is what you do now." God, how he'd aged. He looked ancient – sounded like he was from beyond the grave.

I stood up, stuck out my hand. "Dick. After all these years."

He didn't respond – he just sat there twiddling my pen, looking at me in that calculating way that I remembered so well. "Commander Grimwode to you, Rackham. It's not as though we've stayed in touch. Better to keep things formal, don't you think." He spat out the words as if they tasted really foul.

I take a deep breath, and the fresh autumn air fills my lungs as I stop at a small road that crosses the common. What have I just walked into? I wonder, as I look at the twinkling lights of our town in the distance. There's so much that I don't really understand about policing the world we live in now – but I still have my policeman's nose, and something smells very wrong about that Seurat. I wish I had Peggy to discuss it with – I miss her more than I'd like to admit, but she's out of it now, lying in a hospital bed. And it's my fault.

There's nothing on the road this early, but I always keep the dog on his lead till we've crossed it, just in case there's some early-morning maniac zooming along, half pissed from the night before.

I let him off and he heads straight for the 'Ups-and-Downs' – an area of craters and bushes where bombs were dropped in the Second World War. Now it's a natural playground for children on their bikes, or on sledges in the snow.

I ramble down towards the town, the odd car coming along the main road on my left, its sporadic drone interrupting the dawn birdsong. The dog follows me, I don't have to whistle, and we turn right by the cricket pitch and through a hedge onto the path by the old drainage pools, and then back up through short trees and long grass to our home.

Back in the kitchen, I give the dog his breakfast and make myself a cup of tea – bag in mug, water, squeeze bag and remove, add milk. It looks very weak. I take a sip. It's cold. How did that happen? I must have forgotten to boil the kettle. That's odd – I don't normally make a simple mistake like that, and what a waste of a teabag and milk. Start again. Pull yourself together, Arnold – do it right this time.

My mind spins back to the time when I was doing up this cottage to rent out for extra income. I'd make a cup of tea and imagine showing my little boy how to hit a nail – the little boy Betty and I never had. In my imagination we'd sit together, father and son, escaping from nagging Mum next door, and be men.

The second tea attempt is more successful, and I sip it looking down fondly at the dog, and relaxing for a moment. He looks back up at me with those trusting eyes, and I'm suddenly pulled back to the image of Peggy lying in a pool of blood. Looking up at me.

"Sir."

The journey in the ambulance – Peggy losing consciousness.

The visit later to see her lying unconscious on her bed after her operation. The bullet damaged her spine and they say she may never walk again, let alone run. If only I'd found that gun. Only a couple of weeks ago I was in the canteen drinking a cup of tea with her, me talking, her listening, as usual.

What has come to our peaceful town? Or has this been going on for a long time right under our noses? Like that perfect lawn that you sit on, only to find it seething with ants' nests just under the surface.

8 am, Monday 21st September

Today I decide to walk to work. I've had my breakfast – boiled egg, toast and cereal – and I decided not to listen to the usual deluge of bad news on the radio. I prefer to be alone with my thoughts this morning.

I come out of the shrubbery at the bottom of the common, and cross the road onto old sensible pavements, opposite the town's only hotel. Along by my favourite Queen Anne house, and then on past the Friends Meeting House. I've always had a soft spot for the Quakers. Difficult to believe in anything when you're in my job, but they are a peaceful happy bunch. An asset to the community. Their scooped front wall shows flint below a brick pattern. The building must be, what, nineteen-twenties. That flint is everywhere in this town, must have been a gold mine for early man who lived in these parts thousands of years ago. Sharp stones everywhere, and chalk to draw with as well.

I walk on and turn the corner before the public hall, then up the hill to the dentist's, and along the street that leads to the road up to the station. All tree-lined like The Avenues on the other side of town.

The Avenues.

I wonder what would have happened if there hadn't been any trees lining that avenue last Wednesday. Would I have got to him first? Would I be the one in hospital, with a bullet through my head and a brain injury? Loose thoughts, Arnold. Loose thoughts won't get you anywhere. Speaking of which, my bladder has kicked in with an urgent message, and I half run the rest of the way to the station, turning the corner past the library and cursing as I automatically make for the original Victorian entrance at the front, and have to scoot round the back through the car-park to the modern entrance, through reception, past Claire, the duty officer, calling "sir" after me, as I dash into the loos to find blessed relief.

I wash my hands and smooth my hair back, finding my dignity, and walk back to reception to find out what Claire wanted.

"Commander Grimwode wants to see you, sir." She looks scared. "He's in your office."

Wondering whether I'll ever get it back again, I walk down the corridor to my office where I find Dick sitting in my chair again.

He shoves a pile of papers over the desk towards me. "He wasn't the son."

I look at the top sheet with a photo of a young man I don't recognize on the front. Dick jabs a bony finger at it. "That's the son. He hasn't been living in that house for months. We don't know who your man is. No-one thought to take a photo of him I suppose?"

I shake my head. "Thought not. And why didn't you search the sitting room? You say in your report that he was glued to the sofa, of course he was glued to the bloody sofa he was sitting on his bloody gun! Hid it under a cushion when he heard you coming up the drive like a bloody herd of buffalo."

"I was looking at the painting. It was out of place. I thought…"

"Painting? You spent your time looking at a painting when you should have been securing the room? Now one of your officers is seriously injured in hospital because you were so…"

"But the painting was so out of place. It didn't fit with the…"

He looks at me across my desk thoughtfully. Then he suddenly bangs his fist down with such force that it makes me almost jump out of my seat. I'm glad I've just had a pee.

"What kind of fiasco are you lot running here? This is a farce. Where did you get your information from? It says in your report, 'a tip-off', not intel. This isn't the sixties, you know. Where's the paperwork?"

"I…I thought it was just a hoax. The caller couldn't be traced. I… thought at best we might find some, you know, dodgy tomato plants, but…" I stutter. "How were we to know what we were walking into?" I spread my hands, scattering the pile of papers all over the floor.

Dick curses under his breath. "Pick them up. It's the only stuff that's of any use so far, and it's got some very important information in it. Take the report home and read it. You know, apply your brain, if you still have one, and come back when you've got something useful to contribute. We don't want you here getting in the way. Goodbye."

"But…"

He waves me away, and I turn and stumble out of my office, nearly colliding with a young woman I don't recognize. "Good luck," I mutter under my breath, and walk on down the corridor past a group of plainclothes that I also don't recognize. They stare at me, as if they've never seen a provincial policeman before. We've been invaded.

Taken over.

No more 'nice cop.'

I walk back down the road that goes up to the railway station, past the post office, the chemist's, the tobacconist's which mainly sells sweets these days – second-class poison. Then I resist the strong temptation to sit in the Railway Arms with a cup of coffee, until I can get a pint. Keep yourself together, I tell myself. Two mortgages and a police pension to look forward to, but if I get forced out now for misconduct, or whatever else Grimwode can think up, I could lose out big-time.

With these sobering thoughts, I walk up the common by the main road, the ceaseless daytime traffic whizzing by, until I realise that this isn't a pleasant way to go home and I veer off across the grass away from the noisy road. The weather is warm, and it looks like it's going to follow the promise of my early-morning walk and be a lovely autumn day.

At one time I would have dearly loved to have had a chat with Betty – make use of her down-to-earth practical mind. But that's all long gone now – I hardly feel I know her any more. She will be at her primary school, teaching her little ones. So it's just me and the dog.

Up the garden path to the back door. The dog wags his tail, pleased to see me – wish I was pleased to see him but I feel depressed, redundant. I let him out into the garden, put the report on the kitchen table, switch on the kettle, sit down faster than intended – creaky knees not so strong these days – and stare into the middle distance just above the paperwork I'm supposed to read.

How dare they? How can they treat me like an irrelevant copper after all my years of experience? That swine Dick. A traitor. No friend of mine. These thoughts race through my mind as I try to pull myself together to actually look at the papers in front of me.

I can't do it. Not yet. I'm too angry. But I can do something else. We might not have a photo of the not-son, but I can remember him clearly and I can draw. It's often my way of unwinding at the end of the day – my private diary of things I've observed – and I observed him in detail.

I decide to come back to the bloody report later when I've calmed down. I go upstairs to my studio, leaf through the sketches I've been doing for my now rejected painting and find my pad at the bottom of the pile, get the right pencils out and start to sketch the 'oooh fuck' face that I remember so clearly. This drawing won't be private, it's all we've got to identify him. So I take my time, careful with all the detail – the shading round the eyes, and the deep hollows below the cheekbones. The dog whines and barks in the garden, but I ignore him – shut him out. Shut everything out as I concentrate on depicting this unknown man as accurately as I can. I remember another angle on the man's face, more in repose and from the side – sharp features, but quite a straight nose. The dog barks more vigorously, but I ignore him and he shuts up eventually, leaving me in peace to finish my work. Three really clear drawings of our man – two from the front with different expressions, and one in profile. It may not be a photo, but it's pretty clear. Much better than an identikit picture. One in the eye for bloody Dick and his oafs.

I put the drawings carefully in three transparent folders, and go downstairs to face the dreaded report. The kitchen table is bare. There are no papers there. I could have sworn I left them there before I went upstairs.

Now, there is a person in my imagination who is forever hiding things from me: keys, reading glasses, wallet, mobile phone. They all disappear at regular intervals, but I always find them – eventually. So with this in mind, I search the house for the papers. I must have put them somewhere safe before I went upstairs. I wouldn't just leave them on the kitchen table, would I? I hunt and I search but there are no papers. And another funny thing – the dog's not pestering to get in from the garden. I open the back door and almost trip over him lying there right in front of me.

He's fast asleep and he won't wake up when I prod him gently with my foot. I kneel down and feel his breathing – he pants with short hard breaths. His eyes are closed. His nose is dry.

"Come on old thing." I shake his shoulder – still no response.

I look around and see the remains of some meat on the ground near him. Where did that come from? Then the dog starts to shudder as if he's having some kind of fit. He's eaten some of that meat – picked it up, but from where? He hasn't been out of the garden – the gate was closed. I know it was. I look down the garden and see the gate swinging open. I look back into the kitchen to the table, and it all falls into place. Someone's been here, drugged the dog and taken my papers.

He looks like he's dying – whatever they gave him is killing him.

I pick his saggy body up with difficulty and stagger through the house to the front door and out into the street. I have to put him down on the hard pavement while I get the rear door of the car open, but then I lay him gently on the back seat. The vet is on the other side of town. I get into the driver's seat, rev up the engine, and break all the rules speeding through the traffic with my little blue lights flashing. I stagger into the reception at the vet's carrying the dog and shouting that he's been poisoned. A young woman, who must be the vet, peers out of the consulting room and beckons me in, tearing her blue gloves off, and telling an elderly lady with her overweight cat that she will just have to wait.

"He's eaten something. I found him like this", I gasp. The dog quivers in my arms.

"What was it?"

"Don't know."

"Stomach pump," she shouts as she helps me get him onto the treatment table. Her assistant comes in with the gear and they get to work taking the contents out of his stomach and injecting him with something. Adrenaline, I guess. He's still breathing – panting quite fast. I grip the bench behind me, everything is a blur. My friend, my solace. Please live.

She looks up at her assistant. "He'll do. Take him out the back and put him in the big rest pen. He might take a few hours to gain consciousness, but he'll be OK."

And that's it.

That's all.

He's saved.

I sit in the car and take a deep breath before driving slowly back across town, still shaking with emotion. No blue lights this time. I just hope none of Dick's crowd noticed.

I have to park quite a long way down the road, as someone, probably a dog walker, has plonked their blue Mercedes in the space I left outside the front of my house. I can see as I walk up the road that in my panic to save my canine friend I had forgotten to close the front door, and I go in with some trepidation, wondering whether the people who took my report might have come back.

Being a small terraced house, the front door opens directly into the sitting-room. All I can see are the signs of my hasty departure – chair shoved to the side, rucked up carpet, and my muddy shoe prints. I carefully take off my shoes so's not to increase my housework, and look into the kitchen. Nothing, though the back door's still open. I turn and go quietly up the narrow boxed-in stairs to the landing.

I freeze.

There is someone up there – I can hear stealthy movements. I could go down and get the poker, but I'm not a great believer in pokers. It's a commitment to violence, and you have to hit the intruder on the head hard enough to knock them out without killing them. A delicate calculation in a brutal situation. I settle for my training, brushing over the fact that I am not as fit as I was, and that the people we are involved with are happy to shoot without warning.

The sounds are coming from my bedroom studio, and I enter, swinging the door back hard in case the intruder is behind it. There's a scuffling sound and then nothing. I look round at the sketches scattered all over the floor – someone's been looking through my drawings.

There's a movement from behind a box full of old scrap paper which makes me jump, banging my elbow on the door as it swings back, and then the room erupts. A small black and white cat, hair on end, scampers frantically round my studio trying to climb up the walls to get away from me. I make a grab at it but it only makes things worse. It heads for the window, which is closed, and it scrabbles up the curtains. There is a tearing sound, as it rips a hole in one curtain and gradually descends to the floor with part of the material still caught in its claws. Seeing this as an opportunity to get hold of it again, I run towards it but it escapes to one side, leaping up onto a book shelf and dislodging my art books which fall onto the floor with a thunderous sound further freaking the cat out. I make another lunge at it, but it's all claws and teeth and I withdraw a bleeding hand as it plunges down to the floor, and runs between my legs and out of the door. I give chase

24

down the stairs – fortunately my bedroom door is shut – and chase it round the sofa, until it dashes under my desk and hides there out of my reach. Feeling foolish and helpless, I kneel down and try to coax it out with a gentle "Kitty, kitty". It knows better than to trust me and stays there – two glinting eyes in the darkness. In the end I go for the cruel option, and get the broom and prod at it with the handle till it flies out straight past me and into the kitchen, and out into the garden. As I slam the back door, my heart beating fast from the built-up adrenaline, I reflect that a cat would never normally enter my house with the dog around – but now he's not there, it's an opportunity for any curious semi-feral cat in the neighbourhood.

I go back up and double-check that my drawings of the missing suspect are still there. The floor is covered with books and papers. Cézanne, Rembrandt, Degas, and Hockney keep company with Da Vinci, Lautrec, and of course Arthur Rackham. The room looks as if it's had a thorough going over by a bunch of hoods, not just a single cat. I scrabble through the ruins, desperately pushing books to one side, and finally find my masterpieces in their plastic covers lying in a heap on the floor, and as I look down I see the gunman's 'oooh fuck' expression staring up at me, and I know how he feels. I've lost the papers that Dick gave me to study. The enemy, whoever they are, now know how the police are proceeding, but I haven't got a clue. I should have given chase, alerted Dick's mob, and left the dog to die.

10.55 am, Monday 21st September

The coffee machine's on the blink now. Betty bought me this thing for Christmas and I have never quite got the hang of it. The coffee is always too cold – apparently that's how it should be, we Brits ruin our coffee by making it too hot. Funny how the coffee seems hot enough when you drink it on holiday in Italy. Anyway, my solution is to boil the kettle and half-fill the prospective cup with hot water to warm it up, so that at least the coffee ends up being warm. Today the machine goes berserk and shoots frothy milk and coffee all over the kitchen worktop. I look despairingly at the brown foamy mess and wonder if the whole world is against me this morning. The coffee left in the mug tastes very watery, but I will drink it anyway as a sort of self-punishment.

I sit down and try to think about my next move. Preferably do something that doesn't cause another disaster, but I can't think clearly about what I'm meant to do. The harder I think, the worse it gets – it's like something has emptied my mind and left a great black void where all my memories were. Who is that man who is causing me so much fear? His name's been on my tongue all morning, and now it eludes me, a bit like that bloody cat. I hunt for some paper and a pen. Now where do I keep it? Desk. That's it. Paper. Pen. Sit. Sip horrible watery coffee.

Still can't remember his name.

I doodle on the paper, and a face begins to appear. Cruel hawk-like nose, black eyes, skull-like head, completely bald, sardonic smile. Anxiety cuts through my body like a knife. Who is he? I know I should be frightened of him. What has happened? My mind's gone completely blank.

I draw another face. This time a young woman with dark hair tied back in a bun. Honest, slightly scared eyes stare back at me. I hear the word, 'sir'.

Another doodle. A comfortable, slightly jowly face of a man in his fifties. Creases caused by smiles. A little overweight, and showing a contentment born of a good long fulfilling life. A friend.

But where have all their names gone?

I go back upstairs and clear up my studio. Maybe restoring order to my room will bring my memory back. I feel better as I read the familiar names of the artists. Stacking the books back on the shelf, putting them in order, calms my strange feeling that my world has fallen apart. Autumn sunlight shines in through the window, and I realise how dusty this room is. Motes of dust fly everywhere as I pick up the paper that the cat has scattered all over the floor. There are my drawings. The Arabic face looking scared and anxious. Big eyes, brown, I remember. Very dark hair. Good even features. Slight build. Five foot eight, I'd say. Golfing sweater, leather jacket and smart jeans. He looked rich. He could have been the son, but he wasn't. I know that because of the papers that Hawk-Face gave me. The name eludes me and I start to get scared. Pull yourself together, Rackham.

I take the sketches downstairs, my room restored to some kind of order, and go into the kitchen. No papers. Then it comes back to me and it feels like a big lump of lead in my stomach. The papers were stolen. Dick. That's it, Dick gave me the papers. I was supposed to read them to catch up on the information so far gathered by Dick and his team. There on the table are my drawings of Dick, Claire the sweet girl at reception, and my old pal Burt who's been suspended.

Well, I'll get suspended – probably lose my job, if Dick finds out I've lost the papers. So I'll have to work out how to make them think I know stuff when I don't. I'll have to do my own investigation. That's it – Inspector Arnold investigates. I like the sound of that. I'll go loco and find things out that the high and mighty from the Big Smoke have missed. Stuff that's right under their noses.

Right.

But first things first. A decent cup of coffee, and then take the drawings into the station, which will help with identifying the missing gunman. I give up on my machine, though I have a sneaking suspicion that I forgot to pour out the hot water that was warming the mug before I stuck it under the machine. So of course the whole lot overflowed. Eureka!

I clear up the mess, find my wallet, mobile phone, and briefcase. Put the drawings in a brown envelope. Lock up the house, and go down the garden path to the common and down to the village, as we call it. I feel better and worse at the same time, as I realise that I must have lost part of my memory for half an hour. It could have been the shock of the dog-poisoning and the cat-invasion, but I have noticed an increasing difficulty in recalling dates and names at the best of times. Not a good thing if you're a policeman. At least I never forget a face, and I can draw it. Still, this is a nasty shock. I'm going to have to keep an eye on myself.

La Capri. I still call it that, even though it's been through a series of different names over the years. When I was a teenager I used to meet friends here, drink grown-up coffee and play the jukebox. It was cool, and we used to meet girls. Well, sort of. We kept in our group and they kept in theirs. Even if there was a couple going out, they would split up into their gangs as soon as they came through the door. Sexual segregation, not like these days.

Anyway it's called the Café on the Green at the moment, and it does very good coffee. Not like the crap we thought was coffee in the sixties. I order a Cappuccino with an extra shot, and an almond slice, and sit by the window considering my position.

Not very good, I think, and I'm just trying to sort out how to get the drawings to Dick without letting on that I know nothing, when I see our gunman walk past the window. Bold as brass. How stupid can you get! He thinks I won't recognize him because he's wearing glasses and has done his hair differently and isn't wearing a golfing sweater.

I'm on the phone to the station. "Shooting incident suspect sighted outside La Capri. Will follow with care." I put my mobile on silent, and discreetly leave the café. There he is, going up the hill past the church hall, and I'm wondering how to stay concealed in such an open space. He's sure to recognize me even if he thinks I won't recognize him. Then two things happen simultaneously – my phone buzzes in my pocket and I switch it on to hear Dick's irritated voice. "Where the fuck's La Capri?" – and at the same time I hear the sound of running footsteps behind me, and someone calling, "Excuse me, excuse me sir, you haven't paid."

My quarry looks round, sees me and makes a dash into the churchyard.

I turn and see a young man, well-built rugby type, running from the café towards me with his apron hampering his movement. I reach into my pocket for my warrant card and flash it at him, while at the same time

30

replying to Grimwode, "Sorry sir, it's The Café on the Green. I've been spotted by the suspect."

More cursing down the phone. Then, "We're coming. Don't do anything stupid. Much though I'd like it, I don't want you getting shot on my watch."

I'm already running into the churchyard, wondering how I'm going to deal with a gunman who has no compunction about shooting police. No sign of him of course. The place is full of tall gravestones, with yew trees scattered about here and there. Still, I reflect, a gravestone makes good protection from a bullet. I cautiously move forward, edging round one headstone, ready to make a dash for another.

I hear a sound behind me, and before I can react someone grabs my arm.

"You haven't paid." It's the rugby boy.

"I'm police, for God's sake." I try to pull him into the safety of my headstone. "Get down there's a gunman in the…"

"Bollocks," he says firming up his grip. "You showed me a Waitrose card. What kind of …" There's a deadly sounding report from somewhere in the graveyard, and he spins round and collapses in a heap on the ground behind me.

3.30 pm, Monday 21st September

"A Waitrose card?"

"Yes D… er sir. I was on my phone to you and I reached in my pocket for what I thought was my warrant card. I was looking at the suspect at the time and I got out my…"

"Waitrose card." He says it in a horrible sarcastic way. He's Grimwode now, not Dick any more. He's a fucking menace.

"Rackham, you're a fucking menace!" he suddenly shouts at me. "Every time you get near a crime scene someone gets shot."

"To be fair sir…"

"Get out!"

"…I did try to warn him."

"I want to think…"

"And I've got these drawings"

"… about what am I going to do with you…"

"…of the suspect, sir"

"Drawings?" He sounds almost deranged muttering to himself, "he's talking about drawings now."

"I'll… I'll leave them at the desk, sir."

I retreat, quietly close the door and walk to the front desk, leaving the fermenting Grimwode to think whatever vile thoughts about me that he can dig up from the cesspit of his mind.

"Claire?" I speak gently to her. She is stuck in the middle of this war zone with no-one to help her. "Can you take these drawings and photocopy them? They are of our main suspect, but Commander Grimwode doesn't seem to understand, so if I could have the originals back in case he bins them? Oh, and Claire?" I give her my sweetest smile, which is very sweet for a bloke. "Could you dig out another copy of the report, I need to look at it now and I've left my copy at home."

While she goes back into the office, I reflect on the day I'm having, and it's not even teatime. Unbelievable. Papers stolen. Dog poisoned. Cat rampage. Memory scare. And now another shooting and the gunman's got away again!

The poor lad from the café will never play rugby again. They rushed him to hospital, while a team of us vainly scoured the graveyard. The bullet shattered his shoulder – couldn't be a worse shoulder injury, but at least he's alive and he can walk. I think of poor lovely Peggy and make a note to go and visit her once I've sorted out the dog.

Claire comes back to the desk with my drawings. "Sorry sir, there are no copies of the report in the office. Commander Grimwode is keeping them in his room sir. Apparently sir," she drops her voice to a whisper and I lean forward to catch her words. "… it's because they suspect it's to do with terrorism sir, it's all classified information sir."

Well it's not classified any more, I think grimly. "No chance I could look on the computer then?" I whisper back.

"No, sir, it's not on the office computer, because it's…"

"Classified."

So that's it. Everything's been tightened up, and I'm snookered.

My phone croaks. It's a text from the vet – the dog is awake and looking better. I can go and collect him. Nobody seems to want me here, and I reflect that while everyone is focused on our trigger-happy Arab, all the normal little crimes are carrying on as usual. Still, time to leave, and walk up to one end of the town to pick up my car to drive to the other end of town, but with no flashing blue lights this time.

"Did I see you going across town with your lights flashing this morning?"

It's a Grimwode acolyte. Dawson is his name, I think. For some reason, ever since Morse died, there seems to be nothing but tall gangly policemen with Adam's apples, and he's one of them. A bit creepy really.

"Just attending to a minor incident. Shooting isn't the only crime that happens in this town you know." I use my seniority, both in rank and in age, to face him down and make for the door before he asks any more embarrassing questions.

While walking back through town, I realise that I'm not in such a bad position. What will Grimwode do? Suspend me? Put me on desk duty? I haven't actually done anything wrong, not when you compare it with what my brethren in the Met used to get up to. Yes, I have lost those 'classified' papers, and I haven't reported it, which is indeed a foul and bad thing, but I bet there isn't anything of much use in them. Background facts about the owners of the house, the son etc. What they said, or didn't say more likely. We know nothing about our gunman – that is painfully clear. I shall root around my local contacts. I have something Grimwode and his team haven't – the fact that I have lived here for most of my life and I know people. Quite a few old friends – well one or two, but at least they're not in the police force.

35

First things first. Get the dog. Visit Peggy. Then start my investigation.

4.30 pm, Monday 21st September

I can hear his bark from reception. He knows I'm here, good old dog. The vet takes me through to the cages at the back, and there he is with his familiar thumping tail, and there am I with a lump in my throat. An emotional reunion.

"Go carefully on what you feed him for the next day or two," she says. "I suggest a high-protein, high-energy dog food, with some extras in it like EPA and DHA. I'll give you a free sachet to get you started."

Hang on, I take those food supplements with my breakfast, along with stuff for my arthritis. Maybe dogs are closer to humans than I thought.

"And," she clears her throat, "you can pay the bill for his treatment at reception."

This is where the similarity ends – there's no National Health for dogs.

"By the way, I think we know what poisoned him. Meat laced with anti-freeze. Very popular with dogs and dog-poisoners alike. Would you like me to send a report to the station?"

"No," I say rapidly. "Thanks. I'll take care of it."

The bill makes quite a difference to my ability to pay my mortgage off this month. Worth it though. Worth every penny.

I take the dog home and feed him the sachet. He looks at me after wolfing it down with a 'why-haven't-you-given-me-this-before' expression, and I anticipate my purse getting even lighter.

It's a twenty minute drive to the hospital where Peggy is. I could put on some music, or the radio with its bad news, but I decide to just drive and think. Friends in The Avenues – well there's Charles. I could have a chat with him – do some neighbourhood sniffing about.

Ah, we're here.

Peggy has a room to herself – I've been in this room to see her twice before, but the first time she was unconscious and the second she was asleep. Today she is sitting up looking over-bright.

"Hello, sir." She looks for words, and so do I.

"How're you feeling?" Crap, I answer to myself.

"Oh much more comfortable now, sir."

Except I can't feel my legs, I add for her, silently.

There's a pause while she looks down at her hands and I look up at the ceiling.

Peggy breaks the silence.

"Oh by the way sir, I have remembered something that doesn't make sense." She moves slightly, and winces from the pain. "The bastard...ow... the man who shot me said something in a language that didn't sound Arabic. Sounded like 'me-move-past-him' or something. It sounded more like it was Eastern European."

"Look, I'm really sorry we weren't prepared for...that I didn't find the gun. It... it was all my fault." I feel myself going hot with shame. "Is there anything I can do?"

"No thanks, sir, they're doing all they can." She looks me in the eye. "Look sir, it came out of the blue. None of us thought to search the house for weapons."

I brought her no flowers, no chocolates. Came straight here without thinking, didn't I. I just wanted to see her, and now I feel a sort of panic setting in. I need to get out of the room.

"I'll pass on your new information to the team," I mutter hastily. "That's really useful – a whole new angle on things." I look at her, torn between wanting to stay and wanting to get out of there. "I'll come back tomorrow. See how you're getting on."

"Thank you, sir."

Please don't call me 'sir', I think as I walk fast down the long white corridors, retreating from the smell – the chemicals covering up the fear and pain that lives in this hospital, and I long for my home and the fresh air of the common at the bottom of my garden. There it smells of life, here it smells of death. But it's all chemicals, the scientist in me says – anyway, you'll be thankful for this place one day. I shudder as I reach the doors, and swing out into the car park.

I stop and look for my car, and a weird and wonderful feeling hits me – a warmth rises from my stomach, and my legs feel slightly shaky. I want to go back now. I want to go straight back and see her again, but something inside me propels me forward and away from her into the car park which is crowded now, with all the early evening visitors. Cars parked on double yellow lines, cars parked on kerbs, the increasing hospital population, and the ever-growing car-driving public colliding in this too-small area of car park.

My car's in the middle of this chaos and somehow I manage to manoeuvre it out to the relative safety of a road crammed with slow-moving home-going traffic. In contrast to the new and unexpected feeling of elation inside me, there's a feeling of tiredness all around. Men and women looking forward to a cup of tea, or a gin and tonic. Looking forward to greeting their latchkey children in this overworked country of ours.

My mobile croaks, but for some reason the hands-free-blue-tooth thing isn't working so I break the law and lift it to my ear.

"Where are you?" It's Betty, and I feel a pang of guilt. We were going to meet this evening for a drink – there was something she wanted to tell me. It had been driven out of my mind by the events of the day.

"Sorry. Got delayed." No you didn't, you completely forgot. "Just coming back from the hospital. Caught in traffic. Be back in half an hour."

"Right." She sounds like she's saying this through clenched teeth. "I'll come round to yours, shall I?" She rings off abruptly, and I wonder what she has to say that's so important.

7 pm, Monday 21st September

I have to park down the road again. That blue Mercedes is still there, parked stubbornly outside my house. Not a dog walker then. Or if so must be a bloody long walk, with a bridge session bunged in, and probably lunch at the local gastro-pub.

Betty's in my kitchen looking at the sticky mess I failed to wipe up properly in the morning.

"What happened here?" she asks, studying me with her intensely blue eyes which, despite heavy make-up, have dark patches beneath them. I look back steadily at her, wondering about that early-morning light I saw in her bedroom.

"Bit of a day." I look away – am I going to tell her the truth? I'm not ready to tell anyone all about my day yet. Especially not the memory blank-out.

"And what's the matter with Jip? He's not his usual self – seems a bit sleepy." True, the dog didn't come to the front door to greet me as usual.

My heart gives a lurch. "Where is he?" I'm suddenly anxious. Was the vet correct in saying he would be alright?

"Out in the garden. I thought he could do with some fresh air." She doesn't understand the dog. Still insists on calling him Jip in spite of repeated discussions on the subject.

I hear a bark at the back door. Good old dog. I open the door and crouch down to let him lick my face. I love him so much. Rather more than I love Betty, I realise.

"What's been going on?" she asks, and I look up at her, which is unusual as she is a good nine inches shorter than me. She's wearing a blue tweed suit with the skirt cut just above the knee. It makes her look rather starchy, more like a secretary than a teacher. I wonder if she can see the relief in my eyes – she's known me a long time, but how well do I actually know her, I wonder?

I get up and go to the wine cellar – actually the cupboard under the stairs – to pull out a good Rioja. Corkscrew, glasses, out to the metal table and chairs in my little garden. Betty follows with a tray of biscuits and cheese she's brought from next door, and I realise I've hardly eaten since breakfast.

"Bit of a day," I repeat, pouring out a generous measure of wine into each glass. "How's yours been?"

"Early years' assembly today. My lot were almost uncontrollable. Lively bunch of kids but…" She waves her hand at this moment in a gesture of resignation – been there before in the yearly round of breaking children in to our ever-changing education system.

"What's that blue Merc doing outside your door?" She doesn't really want to talk about her day either.

"Search me. I thought it was a dog walker."

"People like that clog up our road." We are onto parking – a favourite moan of Betty's and many others in our street.

"Well I'm sure it will go soon, then I'll nip back in and claim my spot again."

We lapse into silence, gazing out onto the common. The view of trees and bushes hides the town beyond, giving an impression of rolling countryside. The houses screen the noise of the traffic too. Just a low distant drone.

42

Is she going to tell me why she's here? Should I kick things off with a description of my day?

Silence.

I munch a biscuit with cheese on it. The cracker feels dry and sticks to the roof of my mouth. I take a swig of wine to help it down.

I look at Betty as she gazes intently down the garden, and I wonder: do I have any love for her anymore? Or am I actually just scared of her? We've rubbed along for so long that I can't really remember the reason why we're together. You know that quip about two houses and the perfect marriage? Just now I wonder if this is the perfect un-marriage. Here's this woman that I've supported all my working life, and I can't even talk to her about my worries – I'm not even sure that I trust her. We've lived at one remove from each other for too long. It's been convenient – my police colleagues' divorces proved expensive and painful, but at least they moved on. It hits me that, if I'm honest, I resent paying her mortgage. Surely she should pay her own, she's been a teacher for more than twenty years.

Anyway, it was she who wanted to talk to me about something, so I try to get her started. "You said you wanted us to talk...?" I can't look at her. I just stare down the garden.

"I'm worried about..." Her voice is quiet, husky.

"Yes?"

"There's something..." Her voice shakes slightly.

"Tell me." I should be able to get this out of her – whatever it is. I'm the policeman after all – I'm used to getting things out of people. But somehow I can't even look at her.

"Arnold." The teacher is back, all firm and clear. "Look at me."

43

I turn and look and I don't like what I see. Her face is cold and rigid. Pinched. There is no love there at all.

"We can't go on like this."

"Like what?" I feel a mixture of outrage and relief.

"Like this." She waves her arms about, gesturing towards our two gardens side by side. "I mean, how can we go on like this? Don't you want more?"

Oh it's me is it? That's the problem. "Well I…"

"I mean, isn't it time we tackled this?"

"Tackled what? I thought you were perfectly happy." I'm paying your mortgage – I nearly say it out loud.

"Well I'm not." I see tears in her eyes now. Some signs of emotion. Is it me? Should I offer her more? I put my hand on hers.

"Is it because we never had a family?"

She shakes her head and looks away. It feels like she's summoning up the courage to tell me whatever it is, and suddenly I feel sorry for her.

"Do you want to go out for a bite?" I don't know what else to say.

She abruptly takes her hand out from under mine. "No, I've got marking to do. Better get on." A teacher's version of 'I need to wash my hair'. I look at her face – it's rigid, cold, inscrutable. There's definitely something up, and I wonder how long she's been like that. I have seen so little of her recently.

So that's it, we've nothing more to say – or miles too much. She gets up stiffly and walks off down the garden, through the gate, and up to her back door, treating me to a cold smile before disappearing into her house.

7.45 pm, Monday 21st September

"How's tricks?"

Charles, my oldest and probably my closest friend in the town, is propping up the bar as I walk in to The Engineer for my steak-and-chips-and-pint deal. Old stained wood, inviting-looking bottles, and a variety of hanging tankards makes our local a comfortable place for a man who likes to drink from the early evening till closing time. Charles is as wide as he is high. God knows how he stays alive – I dread to think what his innards are like, but he seems a wholesome enough human being on the outside, with a capacity to charm, listen and be interesting on any subject under the sun. He is truly a mine of information, and in the past he has told me stuff that has helped me solve an investigation. He's not a grass – he's way too successful in the property market to be that. But he is my own personal provider of 'intel', and I trust him more than some young whippersnapper that the force has recruited. Especially now, after Peggy. I just think of him as a wonderful man that has made his pile and is happily drinking and eating it away – sometimes in my company.

"Hell of a day, Charles. You wouldn't believe it if I told you." And I'm really tempted to, I reflect.

"Go on. Spill the beans."

"Can't spill all of them, Charles. You know me: policeman. Need for…" What – secrecy? I shrug. I need to talk. "Someone poisoned the dog."

"No!" Charles is outraged. "The dog? I was surprised he wasn't keeping us company like he usually does. Is he…"

"…and you heard about the shooting last week?"

He nods.

"Well, someone took a pot-shot at me in St Nick's graveyard today. Missed me and got the waiter at La… the Café on the Green."

"Jesus." He gives a low whistle, and looks me full in the face. "I heard about that. It was you, was it?" He lowers his voice. "I heard someone from the police didn't pay their bill and Luke gave chase, and that they showed him their Waitrose card. So it was you." He chuckles – not unkindly, more conspiratorially – and then rumbles into a fruity fit of coughing.

So it's out. Everyone knows about the Waitrose card.

"Luke's just come down from uni – Oxford rugby blue. Otherwise he would have known who you were. You've been going there for long enough."

Nearly half a century, I reflect.

"So… er… the dog?" Charles looks worried.

"Oh, he's alright. Got him down to the vet in time. Pumped him out. Right as rain now." I hope.

"Saw you speeding through the village with your blue lights flashing. Was that to do with the dog?"

Is there anything this man doesn't know?

"Did you hear about his shoulder? I mean the waiter." I change rapidly back to rugby-playing Luke. "Seems the bullet hit him right in the joint – never play rugby again." I feel responsible for that as well. Be near Rackham and have a life-changing experience – for the worse, that is. That's two people now, who could have been me.

46

"Listen, it doesn't sound to me like it was your fault. You weren't to know Luke would do that, and that bloody gunman... I can't believe this is happening here, and you in the middle of it." Charles's usually red face has gone purple with outrage.

There's a lull while the landlord takes my order, but I stay at the bar with Charles. I need his company, and I want to find out if he knows anything.

"So what else?"

I thought the first two things were enough to make a bad day.

"Stray cat got into my house and nearly wrecked my studio. Unbelievable what a small animal can do."

"And...?"

He knows there's something else, he can sense I'm fobbing him off.

"Saw Brian the other day," he says, changing the subject for me.

"Funny you should mention him. I bumped into him quite recently at a school reunion party. Changed a lot, hasn't he?" Changed so much that he didn't want to know me, even though we were best friends when we were kids.

"Yes, he's moved back into The Avenues." Charles says this as though I should be really interested, but I'm not. I'm just pissed off with the memory of a man who spent all evening avoiding talking to me.

"How's life been in The Avenues since you moved there?" I change tack, to cover up my annoyed feelings about Brian.

"Oh, quiet. You know, genteel – that's why I moved out of the town centre. But people are a bit rattled by all that stuff last week. Police going from house to house asking questions. Not nice for the respectable folk in The Avenues." Charles smiles into his pint. "Got interviewed by a gook – all Adam's apple and elbows. Nasty piece of work. Not local. Hey, but you know all this – you're police."

I look down to avoid his eyes – he doesn't know I've been pushed out. "I used to like dropping into your flat in the high street. The Avenues, you know, it's so out of the way," I say to change the subject.

"Well, you should come and visit me – see round the new house. Have supper." Charles looks at me intently. "Pushed you out have they? Bunch of goons from Scotland Yard?" So much for my attempt to change the subject. "I heard there's a real terror in charge – Grim something-or-other."

I pick up my glass to find it's empty. Following the Rioja I had earlier I'm beginning to loosen up. That's the end of my steak-and-pint deal, except I haven't had my steak yet. I look at Charles's personal glass tankard which is nearly drained.

"Another pint?" I make a decision. "Look Charles, you're right. They have come in and taken over. It's bloody awful – they're trampling everywhere and putting people's backs up, including mine. So... The Avenues... anything?"

Charles wheezes a bit, contemplating his empty glass. A dreamy expression crosses his face followed by a hard, almost fierce look in his eyes.

"Bloody foreigners."

"Beg your pardon?" I never had Charles down as a racist.

"More and more houses going to overseas money. Bought mine just in time. Prices going through the roof." He looks up straight into my face. "Used to be I knew plenty of people in The Avenues, at least on nodding terms. All those houses I did up... Now..." He spreads his hands, and in doing so deftly catches hold of the pint that barman Joe has just poured him. Taking a sip, he grimaces and grunts, apparently satisfied with the taste.

"And now?"

"Now, The Avenues are peppered with rentals. People come and go. Houses are split into flats. All those lovely Victorian mansions ruined. The whole neighbourhood is going downhill."

If he could spit on the floor, he would, but decorum gets in the way.

"Look…" He's about to tell me something, but he thinks again. "Come to think of it, the house you raided last week, that was one of mine." Charles, the nomad, lived in houses and did them up to sell during the eighties and nineties.

"So you know it better than anyone."

"Well… it's a while ago – one of the first I did. 'Hazelbank'. I remember the basements, I think there were five of them. You know how the house is a storey lower at the back – that was the coach house, and then there were storage rooms and a coal cellar, and a couple of good-sized rooms down there. All a bit dark of course, but quite an asset as extra storage. That was a big house." He has that dreamy look again. "The biggest."

I didn't see much of it myself, just the sitting room and the hall. "Do you think there might be more to the basements than Grimwode's team have found?"

He leans in conspiratorially. "You should take a look for yourself," he wheezes. Then leaning back he gazes at me in a satisfied way, and sips his pint.

My steak arrives, and I munch away as Charles regales me with a story about a sailing trip he did in the Med. Our 'intel' conversation is evidently over, and I need to get back home, check on the dog, and have a think.

"Give my love to the dog," says Charles, as I leave.

4.55 am, Tuesday 22nd September

I wake up. It's early, and I'm glad to be out of the dream I was having – dark cellars with terrifying things hiding in the shadows. I crept from room to room trying to escape the encroaching darkness, desperately trying to find my way out – my worst childhood fears coming back to haunt me. And there was something else – a horror which I forgot as soon as I woke up. Something in my memory, in my past, that lies buried.

Then reality hits me with a jolt – lost papers, poisoned dog, Waitrose card, pushed out of my job, and something I need to tell them at the station but I have forgotten what it is.

I get up and wearily stomp downstairs, my knees aching with the promise of osteoarthritis. The thump, thump in the kitchen tells me that the dog is still in the land of the living. I give him a cuddle and let him out, and then try to remember what I was told the day before. I find a pencil and paper while the kettle heats up, and start to doodle. Dark rooms appear on the paper – shadows and doorways. Was this my dream? Or… Charles. I was with him last night and he talked about basements – must be why I dreamt about them. That's one thing beginning to come back, but there's another. I start to draw a man – he's in his fifties – he has his back to me. Brian, that's it, Charles said Brian had moved back to The Avenues. It didn't hit me at the time, but now I wonder what he's doing there, and why he didn't want to talk to me at the reunion.

I dismiss the thought because there's something else nagging at me – something more pressing. I draw another man. A young man. He's got a gun in his hand and he's saying something.

Shit, I have forgotten all about Peggy. For a moment the shock and grief get me again, just like when it happened. On my watch. My raid. My fault. I wrench myself away from the table and make my tea, stirring mindlessly – my eyes unfocused. Sit down. Look at the drawing. He's saying something.

That's what it was – I forgot to pass on what Peggy told me about his language. Can't really remember it now. Something to do with him going past her? Definitely not Arabic, she said. She, she, she…

I go through the routine of dog walking, breakfast, showering in a kind of daze. I've got to go and see Peggy again, but I mustn't visit too early so I sit there waiting for time to pass. I can find nothing to do or to fill my mind as I watch the clock slowly grind round to an acceptable time for me to leave. It's as though Betty is there just behind me, and I have to convince her that I only need to see Peggy on police business. That's it, I will find a way to get those words out of her again and then – gulp – go and pass them on to Grimwode and Co.

But, who am I kidding? There's something deep in my stomach that has nothing to do with police work, and in spite of all the fear and anxiety hovering around me, I feel strangely elated. Everything hits me vividly as I walk down the street: the blue of the Mercedes still parked outside my door, the red of the Victorian houses, the smell of the early air, the sound of a bird singing.

I drive carefully to the hospital, watching the sleepy emerging traffic commuting in the opposite direction. No hurry, no hurry, I say to myself. But every bone in my body wants to be there, to be with… No, I can't feel like this. She is over twenty years younger than me, and I'm supposed to be married. Take a deep breath, pull yourself together, Arnold.

At reception I ask if I can see her on police business. I don't show my Waitrose card this time, and a nurse takes me to Peggy's room. "She may still be asleep," she says.

"Don't worry, I can wait." I try to sound calm, though my voice sounds a hundred miles away. And I'm in the room, and there she is asleep.

She has a smile on her face, even in the repose of sleep. Her face is thin and fine-boned with a slightly aquiline nose. Her fair hair is always tied up at work, so it's only now that I can appreciate its length and luxuriousness spread out on the pillow. As I look down at her I feel this huge sense of loss: my youth – where did it go? That time of being in love? Those laughing girls? When all I could feel back then was… nothing. I don't feel nothing now as all this uninvited emotion floods into me making my legs go shaky again.

I sit down, trying to compose myself, to think myself back into Arnold Rackham, respectable police inspector – pull yourself together, Arnold, this girl's young enough to be your daughter. Betty comes into my mind, uninvited, and I remember her words, 'We can't go on like this.'

As I gaze down at Peggy, I see her eyes open – she looks at me with a puzzled frown.

"Sir?"

"Peggy, how are you feeling? Shall I call for the nurse?"

"What time is it?" She flinches as she moves.

"Seven… thirty. Peggy, I …"

"Thanks for coming, sir... shouldn't you be at work?"

There's a knock at the door and the nurse comes in.

"How are you feeling, dear? We will have to get you sorted in a bit. Would you like a cup of tea?" She doesn't offer me one.

We both nod, and she goes out to the trolley.

"I need to talk." I feel so weak saying this. I should be letting her talk – she's the patient.

"Sir?" Oh damn, we're in work mode again.

"Listen, you don't need to call me sir. You can call me Arne or something..."

Nurse comes back in with the tea in a paper cup. Bound to be tepid. I offer it to her.

"You have the tea s... I don't feel like it." Silence. She smiles – she can't say Arne.

I take a sip of her tea, and it is tepid. "So, I've been sort of knocked off the case – pushed out, you know." I pause – I'm sort of lying. "Actually," I clear my throat, and take another sip, "I've lost the report. It was stolen from my house. They poisoned the dog."

"Your dog?"

"Yes, look, he's alright, but I'm up shit creek and I haven't the faintest idea what's going on. And..."

"And?"

I look down at the floor in front of me, suddenly fascinated by the grey and brown pattern of the carpet. Where does it repeat?

"I keep forgetting things."

"Things?"

"Like I can't remember what you told me yesterday about the bast... man who shot you. He said something."

"Oh 'mirupafshim', I looked it up s... It's Albanian for goodbye."

"My God, Albanian." I type it into my phone. "I'll pass it on to the..."

"No need."

"What?" Oh what have you done Peggy? Landed me in more shit?

"I contacted the station when I found that out. I didn't let on I'd told you when they didn't seem to know anything about it. Didn't want to get you into trouble."

"So you knew."

"Well, I knew the boss had been suspended, so I thought you might not be their number one favourite s…"

"Peggy." I love you, I say to myself – you're a star.

The nurse comes bustling in. "Sorry, we'll have to sort things out now."

"Fine, I'll leave you to it." I wrench myself away determined to keep my stupid emotions at bay. "What I said about forgetting things…" My eyes meet Peggy's, and I know she understands.

"Better go now… but… thank you," I say. "I'll come back this evening if you like."

"Thanks." I can't tell from her face whether she's wincing as she changes position for the nurse, or whether my suggestion is a bad one

"See you."

"See you."

9.30 am, Tuesday 22nd September

The blue Merc is still there, sitting outside my house, and I feel an irrational twinge of irritation. Where is that person who has seen fit to park in my space, and just go off on some kind of jaunt with their friends?

Careful, Arnold, this is a public street, I remind myself, as I have pointed out to others in my road who have complained angrily if anyone parks in their 'space'. I shrug it off and go into my house, get the kettle on to warm the mug. Switch the coffee machine on. Do it right this time, Rackham.

I check the phone. Nothing. I feel relief to start with, then unease creeps in. Have I been sacked? Am I in big trouble? Or are they just leaving me alone?

I look at the coffee pods all stacked neatly on the shelf above the machine. 'Intenso', or 'molto intenso'? Blimey, it's like a piece of music. That reminds me that I meant to listen to the Bellowhead CD that I bought before all this crap came my way last week. I put it on and the unique sound of Boden's voice accompanied by his extraordinary arrangements percolates through my cottage. I love folk music, I'm a real old folkie at heart, and given the chance, I would sneak off to all the folk festivals around. The music takes me away from my emptiness after leaving Peggy in hospital – my feeling of isolation. It takes me into its own realm of weirdness and surprise. I find myself sipping a decent coffee to the creepiest song I've ever heard. Boden sings about the rancid sound of the accordion, the alcohol, the decay in Amsterdam. And suddenly I feel quite sick. I have got to get out. I call the dog, get him on the lead as he wags his tail at this unexpected adventure, and we're out of the back door and down the garden to the common before the song has finished.

We take a different route this time, crossing over the main road and into a little hamlet with its own green. We take the top entrance to the park – once a grand house and grounds, now public parkland and an agricultural experimental station. I walk down the avenue of old trees, looking up at their thick, twisted branches that have known so much time. The autumn wind is in my hair, and I let the dog off to go sniffing in the bushes that line the verge. The dog is following his nose and I am following mine. As I turn a corner and walk down the hill towards the swimming pool and play park, I realise where I am going. There is an uneasy feeling in my stomach as I turn left by the pool and through the empty car park, and enter the realm that I have always avoided if I could help it – The Avenues.

The first road isn't quite The Avenues proper. The houses aren't so big, and a number of them have been turned into flats. No trees line the road, and the cars, parked nose to tail all the way down, show the absence of garages and driveways.

I cross a road and I'm in The Avenues proper. 'Hazelbank' is on the right, a little way down. Police tape is still up blocking the entrance to the driveway, and I pass it hoping that there are no police 'colleagues' to notice me. I glance through the gateway and the house looks deserted, all the clues sucked and dredged from it, while on every side the neighbourhood seethes with possibilities – nasty creepy things. I shiver as I walk down the hill to the place where Peggy was shot. I expect to see a patch of blood still there on the pavement, but there's nothing – not even for the dog to sniff. We turn left and walk up another tree-lined road to the old-people's home on the corner. I've been called out there a couple of times to go and find some lost old waif or stray and bring them safely home. I wonder if I will end up there, and then reflect grimly that I would never be able to afford it.

Grand Victorian house follows grand Victorian house. So much space to hide things and people. So much wealth, so much secrecy.

I come to one house that stands out amongst the others. It's large and Victorian like its neighbours, but the dilapidated state of the fence and gate, the peeling paintwork on the windows, the overgrown front garden with weeds sticking up through the gravel carriage sweep, all tell a tale of neglect. I pause and consider this wart amongst beauty spots, and imagine what the neighbours are saying: 'Bringing the standard of the whole road down. Tut, tut.'

Out of the blue, something stirs in me – a memory – and I feel an involuntary shudder go down my spine. Have I been here before? There is something here I wanted to forget – something I buried. Pictures of being a boy at embarrassing tea parties with a young woman and her elderly mother start to appear in my mind. It begins to come back to me. I was with other boys, and none of us knew what to say. Matron, that was it. Matron at our school was young, but not particularly attractive. Slightly overweight with a flaccid face and a high over-gentle voice that, I felt, concealed something else. With long dark hair, she was sugary-sweet. Creepy. Why did we go to her tea parties? It was like a dare between us, or so we believed. Actually we were too frightened to refuse. So we would lose a Sunday afternoon sitting in her large clogged-up chintzy house, trying to make conversation but lapsing into silence.

It could have been this house – it was a very long time ago. As I gaze at it, trying to remember, I see an elderly figure drifting about the neglected garden. Curiosity takes me into the front drive, but she disappears from view round the side of the house. I wander aimlessly to the front door, leaving the dog tied up by the gate, and I notice that some small attempt has been made to tidy up the drive. The larger clumps of grass have been pulled up and flung to one side, and a huge thistle has been uprooted leaving loose earth and gravel behind. By the front door a climbing rose has been deadheaded, the shrunken blooms scattered about the ground like so many sad victims of some tribal head-shrinking ritual.

Wondering what on earth I'm doing here, but compelled by something I don't understand, I wander round the side of the house to the back garden, which must once have been laid to lawns and a pond, with an apple orchard at the end. Now it is a jungle of grassy hummocks – dark mossy corners. Tall reeds stand up from the dried-up pond rising above the mess of rotting foliage, and the trees are laden with cankers and rotting apples.

This is the place. I remember it now. They must have had a gardener then. The picture in my mind is one of ordered beauty, slightly at odds with the strange taciturn occupants. I remember Matron looking at us with an odd expression – a bit like a cat contemplating some small, cornered animal. Meal or plaything? Her mother presided from her throne at the end of the table, grand and old enough to demand awe from us little ten-year-old boys, but her eyes seemed vacant as if she was somewhere else leaving her body uninhabited.

As I round the back corner of the house I suddenly come across the elderly lady hacking at a huge bramble with a pair of secateurs. She has her back to me and hasn't noticed my presence.

I clear my throat. "Excuse me."

She half turns. "Yes?" There is no surprise in her eyes.

"I'm a…"

"But they came last week."

"Just following…"

"Don't I know you?"

"Inspector Rackham. I'm making..."

"Rackham. That's it. Never forget one of my boys."

Her eyes widen. The slack skin round her face has turned into long shrivelled jowls. She has coated the wreck of her face with pale powder, turning it into a ghastly mask. But they are the same eyes – cold, predatory, and I realise, green.

"Miss Witherspoon." The shock of seeing the past meet the present like this makes the words I was going to say vanish from my mouth.

"Cornelia. Do call me Cornelia. Would you like a cup of tea?"

I'd rather stick my head in a bucket of cold vomit, but the policeman in me overrides my repulsion. "Are you sure?"

"Gunman running about on the loose. Need all the protection I can get," she mutters to herself. "Arnold," her voice suddenly turns sugary-sweet, "yes, you must be Arnold. You're a police inspector now, aren't you? Do come in, I think I've got some cake." She says this to me as if I'm a little boy again, and cake would be really exciting.

I suppress a shudder, and follow her through French windows from the ruin of her garden and into her house. There is a smell of damp and decay as I enter, and something sweet and unpleasant that I can't quite identify. The autumn light struggles through grimy windows half covered with dusty drapes. I take in the wrecked version of the cluttered drawing room that I knew as a boy. The once-polished occasional tables covered in dust, the sofa and chairs showing stains and wear, and the floor mostly obscured by old newspapers yellowed with age, and magazines – *Harpers and Queen* keeps uneasy company with *The Lady*.

"Come through to the kitchen." This is more like an order now. What gingerbread house have I got myself into? As I pass the door to the dining room I get a horrible shock as I glimpse her mother sitting in there staring out at me with those other-place eyes, just like she did all those years ago. Then I realise it's a life-sized photo, with a hardboard backing, propped up against the wall.

The sickly aroma gets stronger as I follow her down the corridor towards the kitchen. We enter to the buzzing fanfare of flies, and I see the cause of the smell – a huge bowl of rotting apples is set on a large table in the middle of the room. The brown fungus-covered carcasses are turning to liquid and dripping onto a tablecloth that was once white and is now covered in brown stains. Flies and sleepy autumn wasps buzz round the remnants, drunk with the fermented juices. Right now I swear I'll never touch cider again.

"Here we are. Do sit down." She talks as if this were all perfectly normal, as she totters around filling the kettle and getting the china teacups and saucers out of a glass-fronted cabinet that has seen cleaner days. I look round the kitchen searching for a chair that hasn't got piles of papers or clothes on it, and spy one at the other end of the table. I perch on it, discovering too late that there is a sticky substance just where I put my hand.

" So, Miss With…"

"Cornelia, please."

"Have you noticed anything recently? New faces, people you don't know, unusual traffic?" I know it's hopeless. Why am I here?

"I don't know anybody these days. It's just little me on my own, minding my own business."

What business is that? I wonder. "So nothing unusual? Nothing at all? Any detail can help us."

"That poor girl." She pours water from the kettle into a small pewter teapot. "Do you take sugar?"

"No thank you."

"You should always take sugar at times like this. Shock you see, it's good for shock."

She really is stark raving.

"Now where is that cake?" She potters off into some dark horror of a corner. I dread to think what she will find, and more to the point, what I will have to eat. I decide that I will not eat anything that has been in this kitchen.

"Really, don't worry about the cake. I had a huge breakfast, and I have to watch what I eat – coeliac you know. Can't eat wheat, or any of that stuff." Am I lying effectively? Obviously not, it doesn't seem to make any difference.

"Ah, here we are. A cream cake I made… I made… oh not long ago."

Did she say green cake? It certainly looks green in this lugubrious light. I feel a lump in my throat, and a loosening of my bowels. The power this woman has over me is frightening. I struggle to gain control of my feelings of repulsion and fear. This is ridiculous. Here I am, a grown man, a police officer no less, reduced to a quivering wreck by a mad old lady who probably has half my strength or less. But there is something – a compulsion. I'm a rabbit in the headlights. A small boy caught up in something he doesn't understand. The past is reaching out to me. Something buried. Amidst all this trying to remember, there is something I have tried to forget, and I have managed it. Now something is seeping through – something vile.

"So how are Paul and Stanley?"

Electric shock. I take a sip of her tea. Tepid, sweet – some other flavour in there.

"They're fine, thank you." No they're not – one dead, the other clinically depressed. I'm going to have to make my escape. I take another sip of my tea, there is definitely something odd about the taste.

"They were such treasures, your little brothers. We used to see a lot of them. Here's your cake." She hands me a chunk of something cheesy-smelling on a dirty plate, and I think of my brothers and how I should have protected them. How I should have been there for them. It's all starting to come back. My parents saying it was alright for them to come here, but how they would return from their visits glassy-eyed and distanced from me. No proof, no proof at all, nobody said anything, but something was going on here. Something very harmful to young boys like my brothers.

"Stanley in particular. I remember how pretty he was. Could almost have been a girl."

I hear the dog barking.

Enough. I can't take any more of this. I'm going to find you out, Cornelia Witherspoon. I'm going to investigate you, and if I'm right, you'll spend what's left of your disgusting life behind bars.

More barking.

I find I'm saying, "I'm sorry, I have to go now. My dog…" But as I try to rise to my feet, it seems that my legs have parted company with my body. I lurch dizzily out of her kitchen and down the corridor to the sitting room feeling terribly sick. I have to get out into the garden, get fresh air. I stumble out of the French windows and across hummocks of old grass, my head spinning faster and faster. I want to get away from the house but I can't turn the corner, and just head in a diagonal towards a dilapidated fence and a weedy flowerbed. I stagger the other way and find I'm making for the pond. Something is wrong with my eyes – everything is closing in on me – my vision is getting narrowed down to a point of darkness. I stumble into the pond and the ground comes up to meet me. I scrabble desperately with my hands at the clay soil that borders the dried-up pond, trying to escape the evil that is pursuing me and I come into contact with something that feels like a small bundle of bones. I hear heavy breathing above me and roll over onto my back to see, in a halo of light surrounded by darkness, the distorted sight of my pursuer with a meat cleaver raised above her head. There is a bark and a scream, and the fearsome vision topples over sideways.

Silence.

Then barking.

Then sirens.

Then…

We are all sitting round sipping her tea and eating her cake. Sickly sweet Victoria sponge with that icing that feels more like skin and hard gelatine than the nice crumbly icing that my mother makes. Four boys perched uncomfortably on her sitting-room furniture. Silence has fallen and she presides over our small group who are wondering why we are here – her mother, it seems, scarcely alive in a wing-backed chair by the fireplace. There's Terry, Barnaby, Richard and me all from the same form, Matron's favourites, all privileged to be invited to tea. It will be 'such fun' she said.

'She's such a good kind person,' Mummy said. 'In her free time she goes up to London to help with the homeless. I'm sure you'll enjoy yourself.'

I pick at a crumb on my grey woollen short trousers. Why do I have to wear itchy wool when all the other boys have nice smooth Terylene? I'd much rather have worn my jeans but mummy said I must be smart in my best clothes for tea with Miss Witherspoon and her mother. Mrs Witherspoon senior made meringues for a royal wedding.

'It's bound to be a wonderful tea,' my mother said.

It is not. It all looks good but tastes wrong. Neat sandwiches chopped into triangles with the crusts cut off all filled with rubbery cheese and tongue, and smothered in bright yellow piccalilli. I hate piccalilli. Then the cream buns made from tasteless pastry and UHT cream. The meringues are bought from the shop and they are the best thing, but they had to be smothered with fake 'squirty cream'.

"My dad's in Vietnam," blurts out Barnaby in his gentle American accent. "He's in the air force. He says we're bound to win. The Commies haven't a chance."

There is an awkward silence.

"How nice," says Matron in her sweet sing-song voice. "But it must be hard having Daddy away so much." She clasps her hands over her knees and I notice she has painted her fingernails a bright red. I glance up at her face and see her mouth like a gash across her chalky white complexion, painted with matching red lipstick. Who is this all for? I wonder. Does she have a bloke? Do they...? I shy away from wondering what they might do.

Richard has broken the silence now. "My dad's in the civil service. He goes up to London on the train and reads The Telegraph. He says communism is bound to fail." We are getting into politics now. Richard blushes as he imparts this important information. He blushes easily – he has light ginger hair and a very fair skin. His eyes always seem red-rimmed as though he's been crying.

"And what does Daddy do in the civil service?" That sing-song voice. Is she really interested?

Richard blushes deeper. He doesn't know. "I'm n... not sure," he stammers. "He doesn't like to talk about it at home. Says he likes to keep it separate."

"Bet he's in the secret service," pipes up Terry. "Sorting out those Commies."

Matron doesn't like this interruption. I can see her eyes harden as she looks sharply at Terry. "And what does your father do?" No sugary-sweet voice here – all hard-edged.

"My dad's in chemicals." Terry is completely unfazed. "He makes pots of money and likes to drink champagne in

68

the drawing room. Sometimes he lets me have a sip. And he's got a Rolls Royce." Yes, we all know your dad has a Rolls Royce, and we all secretly want a drive in it. But it never appears anywhere near our school. His mum drives him to school in a much humbler car.

I can see the focus turn to me. What does my dad do? My dad's an alcoholic. Mummy said so. He's a draughtsman when he's not in hospital being treated. I feel the shame and disgrace showing in my face, which is bright red before I've even said anything.

There is an awful pause as I wait for Matron to ask me the question. My bladder comes to my aid, and I put up my hand.

"Yes, dear?"

"Can I be excused?" I haven't the foggiest where the loo is.

"Of course, dear. Shall I show you?" Am I mistaken or do I see a gleam in her eyes. She gets up with alacrity and I jump up off the sofa remembering not to clutch myself, much though I feel like it.

"This way." I follow her down a corridor, past the stairs, through a doorway and into a dark passage. She opens the door to the toilet and turns on the light.

"There you are." She stands in the doorway and I have to push the door to, trying not to slam it in her face.

I unbutton my stupid flies and feel the blessed relief as my bladder empties into the bowl. Is she still out there? There's no hand basin and I must wash my hands. My mum's always telling me to. And what am I going to tell them when I walk back into the room? I am taking my time, trying to think up a story about my dad, when I hear the door open, feel a movement behind me and a warm soft hand slides down to my crotch. She's come in and she's rubbing my penis. My little penis gets stiff, it can't help it and I feel strange. A mixture of panic and thrill. I feel her

69

breasts against my head, and I hear her breathing faster. I just don't understand what's going on or whether I like it or not.

"That's nice," she gasps, "isn't it. If you come again I can show you something. Something really exciting." I am finding it exciting now, and frightening at the same time. I want her to stop, and I don't want her to stop. Suddenly I feel a searing pain, she has grasped my scrotum in a vice-like grip.

"But you mustn't tell. You know what happens to boys who tell. This must be our little secret."

The pain stops, I feel sick and faint and I stay still and silent like a frightened rabbit. I will never tell, but I will never come back.

11 pm, Tuesday 22nd September

'*Come back, come back, come back*' echoes round my
head as I struggle to wake up. I feel terrible - it feels like
someone has scraped my stomach out with a rusty shovel,
and my throat is horribly dry. I try opening my eyes and
find that I am looking down a tunnel at a distant white
light. As I stare, the tunnel broadens out and a face
appears. It's a woman's face – I recoil for a moment, and
then realise it's not her. Not Matron. It's not anyone that I
recognize.

"Sir?" she says gently, and turns to someone behind
her. "He's come round."

Immediately there's a rustle and a nurse comes into
view. No face, just a body, and I flinch. She takes my
wrist, pauses, and then bustles off leaving me with the
woman who's looking down at me – she's young and
healthy-looking with red cheeks. I shift my gaze to a clock
that's slowly ticking just behind her.

"Sir? Can you hear me? We need to talk to you. There's
a team in the garden and they are digging up… bodies." I
hear the words '*Something really exciting*' still resonating
in my head. I shiver.

"Bodies? How long... have I been..?" I manage to
croak.

"Twelve hours."

"Twelve hours?"

There's another incursion of nurses, two this time, and I'm hauled up into a sitting position.

"He needs a drink. See if he can hold anything down," says one of them, as if I'm not actually there.

A cup is put to my lips and blessed fluid passes down my parched throat. There is a pause as the liquid drops down and hits something uneasy somewhere in my stomach.

"Please," I manage to gasp.

"You can have a bit more water, but we must take it carefully. You don't want to be sick again."

Water? I thought it was nectar from heaven.

"Can he talk now?"

"Just a short while. Then he must rest."

Sleep? I don't want another of those dreams. I want the safety of company.

"Sir. I've called Superintendent Forester, he should be here any moment. We've had to bring in a new team to deal with this. I'm WPC Gail. You were saved by your dog who knocked down the suspect and barked until a neighbour came to see what was going on. We don't know what she gave you, but you have been really ill. We found you holding the bones of a human hand. They're digging up the whole garden."

You bet they are, and my life too. I'm thinking this wasn't a dream I just had, it was a memory. A buried memory. I need a counsellor not a Superintendent.

At least my vision is improving – I can see the WPC if I don't look straight at her. The tunnel has enlarged enough for that, although the odd black patch floats in every now and then.

She stands up.

"Ah, Rackham, Forester." A grey suit comes into vision. I squint at this new person, his face is slightly out of focus but I can tell he's medium height, medium build, medium everything – he could be a bank manager. "It seems you have stumbled onto something really big. Can you tell us what made you visit the suspect? Any information will help at this stage." Superintendent Forester settles into the WPC's chair, leaving her to stand behind him ready to record any pearls of information I am able to give at this stage.

"I was in The Avenues and I came across this house that I recognized. The old woman was in the garden... gardening." I can't do this, my mind's all jumbled.

"Go on," he sounds patient, but he looks tired and he's beginning to twiddle his thumbs in a distracting way.

I try to pull my thoughts together. "I thought I knew the suspect and she recognized me... actually she recognized me first... I think."

"Go on." Twiddle, twiddle, twiddle.

"She was matron at my school. She seemed a bit... you know... batty, er weird... said she was frightened of the gunman."

"Yes?"

"She invited me in for tea. It tasted funny. I had to get out, I felt really ill. I fell in the pond and saw her standing over me with a meat cleaver... my dog... I think I'm going to be sick."

"Sir." She's quick with the bowl as I puke up the tiny contents of my traumatized stomach.

A nurse comes in. "You'd better stop for now. He needs time to recover." She takes my wrist as if it's the divine route to my stomach.

"That will do for now, Rackham." Forester stands up. "We can hold her on the information you've given us."

"But what about the bodies? Surely..." I croak.

"Oh, she denies everything. She says someone else put them there when she wasn't looking."

2 pm, Wednesday 23rd September

"Twenty?" Peggy's eyes widen in disbelief.

"And three dogs. The last dog was quite recent, probably caught digging up her secrets. The pathologist thinks they were girls in their early teens buried during the nineteen-sixties and early seventies."

Fifteen hours and a couple of wonderful meals later, including watery porridge, Heinz tomato soup, and raspberry jelly with vanilla ice cream, oh and a ham sandwich, I'm up and about and have found my way to Peggy's room. They want to keep me under observation as they're not sure what the poison was – apparently she had quite a lot of choice in her kitchen – but I am determined to leave. I have an important visit to make.

"Peggy, I want you to keep this under your hat." She nods. "I need to see my brother Paul. Witherspoon mentioned him and my other brother Stan. I'm sure they were involved in some way all those years ago and I need to get to him before the news breaks. My other brother…" I always find this hard to say, "killed himself."

She reaches out and puts her hand on my arm. I feel her warmth surge through me – the best healing I've had for years.

"Were you involved too?" She takes her hand away.

"Yes, I think so – I can't really remember."

I don't want to tell her about my dream.

"She was matron at our school and I went to tea there, and there was something very wrong about it all. I can't remember what it was, but I never wanted to go back." *'Come back, come back,'* wasn't that what I woke up saying?

"Did you... see anything... back then?"

"Bodies? No, nothing like that." *'Something really exciting'* comes into my mind again, but I don't say anything.

"You know sir, I mean... Arne. Ouch, shit, sorry," she winces as she shifts her body. "I mean, shouldn't you see a counsellor?"

"No doubt they will offer one after they have fully debriefed me." I shudder at the thought. "I want to see my brother first. I want to know what was going on..."

"When you didn't come back last night, I wondered. Look, you've been really ill, are you sure you should...?"

"I've got to go."

"Please... take care of yourself," she says with a grimace. She watches me, with those lovely eyes, as I leave.

I think how life used to be so simple and empty. Now it's full and complicated.

3.45 pm, Wednesday 23rd September

"You should do something about it."

The blue Merc is still outside my house, and as I get into my car, which is parked down the street, Mike something-or-other comes out of his house and grumbles that I'm taking up his space.

"Don't worry, I will report it once it has been unattended for long enough."

"It's been unattended for long enough already. You should do something now, or I will." He's obviously got nothing better to do at half past three on a weekday afternoon.

"OK, OK." Does he think I'm a bloody traffic warden? "I'll sort it out." Honestly, parking. It's like dominoes – one car out of place and the whole street's up in arms.

I'm out of here. I'm going to the seaside to see my brother. I managed to sneak out of hospital, get a taxi home, turn off Bellowhead which was still doing the rounds on the CD player, wolf down some yoghurt, pick up a couple of bananas and my pyjamas.

I close the car door against any more rhetoric from Mr Grumpy.

Next stop Crickhowell for steak and chips.

Black shapes float across my vision as I pull out onto the main road. It's only just over twenty-four hours since I was poisoned.

Is this wise? I ask myself. Of course it's not wise, but what choice have I got? I've got to see him. If he hears the news, he could do anything. He's been ill with depression for so long, and I never really understood. In and out of hospital, given this drug and that. Still, at least he has his music – really talented singer-songwriter. Should have been much more successful, but depression always got in the way. But some of his songs! One or two have done really well over the years – been covered by some really famous singers. It's what has kept the wolf from his door. As I think about him, I realise I have a twinge of jealousy. He went the whole way. Became an artist. Did what he was made for. And I became a policeman. For why? To make people safe. A safe job to make people safe. Safe, safe, safe. But it's not safe at all – the entire ship that I've spent my life in is creaking under the strain. And now I'm having trouble remembering things.

I switch on the car audio to distract myself from this negative train of thought. It's one of Paul's CDs, and it's like I'm hearing it for the first time. The lines hit me with new meaning as I pass through small towns on my way west. One in particular catches my attention:

'Like the occasional gardener, I let the weeds grow,
Now I look in my garden, and what do you know?
They're everywhere…'

I drive on into the gathering gloom, listening to my brother's wisdom. The black shapes have been replaced by a headache, and I'm feeling really tired. This is such a bad idea, driving in this state. I pull into a layby, turn the engine off, and close my eyes.

Suddenly, I jerk awake. The car clock says I've slept for half an hour, but what woke me up was the thought that I hadn't phoned Paul to let him know I was coming. How do I know he'll be in when I arrive? What state will he be in? I press Paul's name, and listen to the phone ringing.

Come on, come on. I imagine him lying on the floor. He's heard the news. He's taken an overdose.

"Hello." Paul sounds irritated.

"Paul, it's me. I'm coming to see you."

"I know, you phoned me hours ago. Did you have to get me out of the bath?" he pauses, and his voice drops. "Are you OK?"

"Oh, oh sorry. I just wanted to give you a progress report. Just passed Monmouth. I'll stop for some food in Crickhowell. I'll be a bit late."

"That's OK. You told me you'd stop for a meal on the way. I never go to bed early. You know that. Are you sure…?"

"I'm fine." No I'm not. "See you about eleven."

How did I forget that I'd already phoned him? I was so sure. Still, he sounds well. Maybe he'll be the one that copes.

My way to Crickhowell is smooth, and I'm soon sitting in the old wooden bar of The Bear, slowly eating steak and chips, and hoping my stomach will cope. I love this place. It's always been my stop on the way to see Paul. Reliable food and service, though they never recognize me. Just another traveller passing through.

The road's easy for a while, but gradually gets slower as I head for the coast. He's chosen a lovely spot to live in, has Paul. His house looks out over the bay, the crashing sea his solace. The smell of salt and seaweed, the cry of the gulls. He lives on the edge of this island, and I have chosen to live plumb bang in the middle. Does that sum us up? Where we live?

It's pitch black as I drive carefully down the steep lane into his village. Parking is always a problem. There is space down on the beach, but you have to watch the tides. I slowly wiggle down the winding streets. Honestly, I still don't know where it's safe to park. I see a row of parked cars and look for a gap, but there's nothing. In the end I find a small car park on the road out of the village. It's empty. No flocks of holidaymakers this time of year. I take my torch and walk carefully back to the huddle of houses. The moon is up, and the lights twinkle invitingly, but I am wobbly on my feet, and feeling the effects of the poison still in my system. I need to stop, I need to sleep – but I must talk to him first, and I'm not looking forward to that at all.

His house is at the end of the path out of the village, perched high above the sea. The narrow stony track takes me there, and I struggle the few remaining yards up the steps to his front door. The black patches have returned in front of my eyes, and it's all I can do to bang on his door, and wait slumped against the porch wall for him to answer.

9.15 am, Thursday 24th September

I awake to the sound of the sea. I'm lying in bed in my pyjamas, but no idea how I got there. Paul's spare room is sparsely furnished – an old pine chest of drawers, a straw seated chair, and the double bed I'm lying on. But, with its bare floorboards and small faded rug, it feels comforting, like the old Victorian house has enfolded me protectively in its arms and lulled me to sleep by the sighing sea.

I hear the sound of tinkling cups, and footsteps on the stairs, and Paul comes in holding a tray set with tea cups, a boiled egg and toast, a pot and jug, all in that old china he rescued from our parents' loft when we were teenagers. He looks every bit the ageing superstar. Bronzed and muscular, handsome and tall – he and Stanley shared the good looks in our family, even though they weren't identical twins.

"I've done you an egg, thought you needed it. You were such a mess last night, we managed to get you to bed – you kept trying to talk to me, but nothing made any sense. Have a bit of breakfast, and when you're ready we can talk. I'll just go and get a paper."

"No, no." My throat is horribly sore and my voice rasps. "Mustn't go. Stay here." He must hear the news from me, and not read it in the papers.

Paul turns from pouring my tea, his mouth half open as if to say something. He gives me my tea and then turns back, pours a cup for himself, and sits down on the chair.

"So."

"I've been poisoned." How to start?

"Poisoned? You should be in hospital!"

"I've been in hospital. Better now."

"You look awful…"

"No, it's not the poison. I'm recovering from that. It's," the moment has come, and I feel horribly sick, "it's about Cornelia Witherspoon."

"Cornelia Witherspoon, you mean…"

"Matron, yes."

He shrinks into the chair. His bronzed happy face turns gaunt and stone-like in front of my eyes. I've got to do this. We've got to get through this.

"I came across her by accident."

"By accident?" He sounds angry.

"I was investigating something else in The Avenues, and came across her house. It's a right mess, and there she was in the garden, and she recognized me and invited me in for tea."

"And you went?" Judas, his look says.

"It was disgusting inside the house. Mess everywhere, you remember." Shut up, says my sensible self, and get on with it.

Paul looks distracted, as though he's forgotten something. He gets up to leave the room.

"No don't go, please. I've got to tell you…"

"Andy's downstairs. I'd better tell him to leave us to it. He might come up at any moment." Paul's looking scared now. He leaves quickly and I hear the mumble of conversation, then a door slam. Paul returns looking angry – tears in his eyes. "He can't bear being excluded, I… we need to introduce…"

82

"Look, Paul," I need to master this situation. "You may want to share this with him. It's going to come out anyway."

"What?"

"She tried to murder me. She poisoned my tea and chased me into the garden with a fucking meat cleaver. The dog saved me, and we found bones."

"Bones?"

"Sorry, Paul, this is all coming out wrong. We have found twenty corpses of teenage girls that were buried in her garden between forty and fifty years ago."

"So it was true." His face looks blank.

"That must have happened during the period when you and Stan used to go there for tea. What happened, Paul?"

"I wasn't making it up." I see a glimmer appear in his eyes.

"But what happened? I had this dream when I was in hospital, more like a memory. She did something horrible to me, and I never went back."

"We weren't making it up. It was true."

"I am so sorry. I should have protected you. I should have gone with you. I should have stopped the whole thing. I should have told." I want to cry but I can't. "I'm so sorry, Paul." I can't go on – my voice is cracking up.

Paul stands up. He's like a giant as he walks across to me. "You, you couldn't do anything. It was them. Those bloody psychiatrists. Give him drugs for his fantasies. Help him get over them. Face the truth – it's all in his mind. Nobody believed me."

"Was it something to do with those girls? In my dream I heard her voice saying about something exciting she could show me."

Paul takes a deep breath. "She took us down to the basement and showed us a girl. She was naked – just lying there on a table. She must have been dead. We thought she was dead. We felt so guilty, because we colluded with her, because it was so exciting. That's what she said, and we believed her. It was exciting, it was our big secret. Us little boys with so much power. But really we were frightened. 'You'll end up like that if you tell,' she said. We believed she could kill us and make us disappear with a click of her fingers. We could never tell, and we had to keep going back or it would look suspicious. Anyway, nobody would believe us. Nobody did believe me in the end after, after Stan died."

"Did she... abuse you?" I whisper.

"Yes."

"I think she may..."

"Arne, we've had this all these years." He's kneeling by my bed now, holding my arm and weeping.

"I knew something was going on, I should have done something."

"You've supported me, been there for me."

"No I haven't, if only I could've remembered what happened. Then it would all have come out. And you have been carrying this all these years. Why didn't you tell me?"

"If you hadn't believed me, it would have finished me. I couldn't take the risk. Don't you see?"

I did, and I saw how much gets buried that should be in the open, that should be dug up and exposed to the sunlight, like bindweed roots that shrivel and lose their power when lying on the hard earth.

My younger brother, the one who survived, is kneeling by me, and he has saved me. The good policeman wants to dig things up, find out the truth. The policeman that I was, the bad one, wants to bury things – keep them safe. I wanted to keep him safe – my brother. I thought I was going to have to protect him from those unearthed bodies, but it was me I was protecting.

Paul stands up, stretches his arms wide as though they are wings he's trying out for the first time. He looks fresh – different. I am worried that he will have a reaction – fall into deepest depression, try to do something terrible to himself.

"Are you up for a walk?"

10.30 am, Thursday 24th September

The sands stretch into the distance. Peaks of rock, strangely slanted, poke out here and there creating knife-like silhouettes against the skyline. The warm autumn sun falls on our backs, but there are no holidaymakers to play under it. Just us and the gentle waves slowly getting closer to the shore.

I wish the dog was with us now, chasing balls and waves – it would take the intensity of our mood away. Should have brought him along, but that would have meant more lies to more people – Betty, who thinks I'm still in hospital, will feed him, and Anne, who lives a couple of doors away, will take him on walks with her two collies – an arrangement that has always been in place in case I'm called away. Actually, I suspect that Anne does the lot – Betty hasn't got much time for my dog.

"So what now?" Paul asks. "Are you going to tell them?" I see a dangerous glint in his eyes. Not quite balanced.

"Just now, I don't know what to do." I shrug, and begin to feel sick again, in spite of, or maybe because of, the boiled eggs and toast.

He stops in front of me and turns round to face me. "Will I be seen as culpable? Will Stan? And what about the others? Will they come out of the woodwork, or will they keep quiet? I just imagine standing in front of a jury having to explain, no, confess, all the horrible things I was involved in. I don't know whether I can do it. Don't you see? I could end up in prison."

Panic is showing in his eyes. I look into them, trying to connect with him. "I don't think there's any chance of you ending up in prison. You are definitely a victim in all this. But the rest…" He's right. It will be horrific.

A thought strikes me. "But won't it be great to shout to the world that you were right. That you weren't mad – having fantasies."

And think of the other victims, I say to myself, but I can't say that to him – I don't like using moral blackmail, especially on my own brother.

He turns and walks on. The long flat sands are soaking up our fear. Our feet are bare, and every now and then a wave comes in across our path and caresses them with cold, refreshing water. We walk in silence to the end of the bay, where the sharp, barnacled rocks and disintegrating cliffs come down to meet us. An unpleasant dark yellow liquid streams over our feet – probably something dead in the rocks, and we turn and walk back in the opposite direction washing our feet in the cleansing waves.

Then I remember. Wanting to wash my hands. Cornelia Witherspoon coming into the toilet. I feel the pain in my crotch and almost double up. There's a rock sticking up out of the sand, and I sit on it and put my head in my hands.

"Arne…? Arne what is it? It is the poison? Should I…?" I look up to see Paul getting out his mobile phone.

"No, it's not that. I've remembered… what she did to me… what she said. That there was something really exciting. And then she hurt me, and I never wanted to go back. But I let you two go there – my little brothers." It feels so bitter, so unredeemable.

"You were… what? Ten years old? Frightened. No dad to turn to. Mum was running ragged. Our world was not a safe place." Paul turns and looks out to the incoming waves.

"Oh shit, shit, shit, I don't know what I'm going to do if Forester askes about my experience with Witherspoon. If that happens I'll try and keep you out of it. That's what you want, isn't it?"

Paul nods, his face still turned to the sea.

"There's just not enough time to think. If you tell them about me now, won't it all happen very fast? And there'll be no going back. I'm not sure I can do this, Arne." His voice is steady. Not the voice of a man near breaking.

Here I am caught in a net of my own making. If we don't tell, it will be on our consciences for the rest of our lives. If we do it will open up a can of worms the size of which we cannot guess. I will not sacrifice my brother to the law, but I am not sure if I can go along with this. I seem to be repeatedly finding myself on the wrong side.

The thought comes to me: I became a copper to protect, to make people safe. But who was I trying to protect in the first place? My brothers.

"We'd better get going, the tide's coming in. And I'm going to have to get back and face all of this."

Paul takes my hand and helps me up.

"I mean, what's going to happen?" he asks. "Are the papers going to get hold of this? Where will it all end? And will anyone benefit from knowing that I was involved?"

The sea is pushing us closer to the cliffs and rocks. It has covered the smooth sand, and now we have small pebbles under foot which make us hobble from time to time like two old sea-birds.

"And what about Stan?" Paul asks.

I am thinking the same thing. If that gets looked into…

"The way he died. The way Mum and Dad wouldn't talk about it. Do we want to know?"

No. I don't want to know. Not now, not after all this time. An experiment that went wrong, Mum said. But it sounded more like suicide – he was found hanging. Would that all be dredged up? The papers, keen for lurid details – innuendo, suggestion turning into facts in peoples' minds.

"And then Dad drinking himself to death."

"I'm not sure that was connected," I say. "He was being treated for alcoholism all our lives. It could have just been that his liver…"

"But the timing."

"Dad was nearly sixty by then. It's not surprising."

We start picking our way amongst the rocks. Little pools with tiny creatures darting away from our feet. We are giants in this pool-world – I wish I didn't feel so small in the world that I have to go back to.

"Are you seeing anyone for..?"

"No, I haven't had any counselling or therapy for some time now." Paul looks down at his feet, treading carefully to avoid the sharp edges of rock. "But there is someone. Someone I used to go to. I can't tell Andy. Not yet, anyway. Have you got anyone?"

I feel a warm glow: my brother cares for me. I'd always thought of it the other way round – I was the carer. But now I find that has changed, and we are equal. Together in this tragedy.

I shrug my shoulders. "Sort of," and I hope Peggy is there for me.

We pick our way up to the coastal path and put our socks and shoes on. The unpleasant feeling of the damp grittiness on my feet, as we trudge up the hill away from the sea, makes me yearn to be back in those days of innocence and family that was torn from us too long ago.

3 pm, Thursday 24th September

Andy turns out to be a tall good-looking man about ten years younger than Paul. The lines in his face show that he has seen a lot of life – not all of it pleasant, but he has a genuine smile that lights up the room, and makes me want to smile back. It strikes me that, of the two of us, Paul is the one with the sorted out life. He has a good stable relationship: love, friendship, and, I guess, sex.

Sex. God's little joke, someone said. But it's not little, and it's not a joke. Old man Freud got it right, even if he was a bit black and white in his Germanic way.

I'm thinking all this through as I drive the long way home. Away from my brother, away from the sea. Back to trouble. For lunch, Andy cooked us a beautiful gentle soup made from autumn vegetables and herbs that helped to settle my poison-scoured stomach.

After that there was little to say – Paul and I both knew that he couldn't be put in the witness box. The intrusion on his already intruded-on life would be too big a price to pay. Cornelia Witherspoon will go to prison for the attempted murder of a police officer. You can't put that kind of poison in someone's tea by mistake, and there were the contents of my stomach and the contents of her kitchen cupboard to prove that she'd done it. As to the bodies, that will be an on-going investigation, which will take a long time. All those dental records going back fifty years. I suspect they were girls picked up in London from her 'good work' with the homeless.

Why did she do it? What made her so warped that she would kill and molest in that way? And what has it done to me and my brothers? It's affected me, I'm sure of that. Put me off sex for a start. I thought I was lucky to have such little libido. Other men seemed to be getting into continual trouble because of their sex-drive. To be honest, I sometimes thought it was an excuse. But now I realise it's such a complex thing – sex. It pervades every part of the human psyche. It's at the root of so much trouble, from the pub brawl, to the gang-land shoot-out. From the peeping Tom to the celeb molester.

Looking back at my marriage, I realise that I was not much of a lover. Betty didn't seem to need sex much, which was just as well since I certainly didn't provide it. At the time it seemed a peaceful and easy solution. Now I am beginning to wonder.

As I drive on I find I'm in unfamiliar territory. I don't recognize this road at all. I got so caught up in my thoughts that I'm lost now. A sign says city centre. What city centre? I feel panic rising in my chest. Where am I? I follow the flow of traffic which is getting slower. Buildings on every side. Cars crammed in a slow-moving stream. I've got to stop but there's nowhere to pull over. I signal turning left, but get hooted at – it's a no-entry street. Finally I see a 'P' sign and find myself crawling up through a multi-storey car park. Floor after floor is full – no spaces.

Panic spreads through my body. My hands shake, my knees shake, and I can hardly control my feet. I see a space in a dark corner – just room to squeeze in. Stop the car. Sit in darkness.

Where am I? What am I doing? What's this thing I'm in? There must be something to tell me – my mind's gone completely blank. Calm down, breathe, a voice in my head says. But I'm terrified.

I search for clues, but it's dark and I have to feel all around this unfamiliar thing I'm in. I'm sitting on a chair, but something is stopping me moving properly. I feel to the left and find another chair, and as I push my hand across it I come into contact with something small and oblong. Maybe this is a clue. It's light, thin and hard, and as I raise it in front of me it lights up. This small thing has a picture of a tree on it – a tree with brown leaves. I feel I should know this tree, but for the moment all I can do is hold it and look at it in the hope that it can help me. The light goes out and I nearly drop it. My thumb touches the smooth front, the thing lights up again.

"CROAK-CROAK!"

I drop it in a total panic now and it lies there by my feet. "Croak-croak", it goes again and I make a grab at it, hitting my head on something hard but I manage to lift it up again. Then it croaks again. It's alive, this thing. I have to stop it croaking! I rub it with a finger and the thing lights up with lots of little pictures. An instinct tells me to jab at one with a red dot on it and a tinny female voice starts talking to me. I lift it to my ear. I don't like the sound of her – she has no warmth or emotion in her voice.

"Welcome to your EE voicemail. You have ten new messages. First new message, received yesterday at 7.29 pm."

"Rackham! Where the hell are you? The hospital say you left without signing out. Ring me!"

"To listen to the message again press 1. To save the message press 2. To delete the message press 3. To r.."

I press 3 I don't like that voice – I want to delete it. But there's something oddly familiar about doing this.

"Message deleted."

"Next new message, received today at 8.30 am."

"Sir, this is DC Gail. Superintendent Forester asked me to call you and ask you to come in and see him as soon as you get this message." (I can hear voices in the background – "he's gone AWOL… see if you can find a counsellor, try…" and the voice becomes mumbled. Then… "urgent, say it's urgent…" "It's urgent you contact us sir, as soon as you get this message."

I press 3 again in a panic.

"Message deleted."

"Next new message, received today at 9.03 am."

"Hello, Inspector Rackham? My name is Valerie Redman. I've been asked to contact you by Superintendent Forester to set up a meeting. I am a police counsellor, and anything you wish to say to me will be in the strictest confidence. Could you please call me on 0778….."

I like the sound of her voice – it's warm and encouraging so I press 2.

"Your message will be saved for – seven – days."

"Next new message…" But I can't bear the sound of that voice any more so I switch her off.

I switch her off! I am looking at my phone – that's how I knew what to do. I do it all the time without thinking. I am sitting in my car in the dark! What the fuck am I doing?

A huge surge of relief comes over me as I reach up and switch on the internal light. Where am I? How the heck did I get here? I rub my face with my hands and feel sweat and tears. I've had another of those things. This is worrying, but hardly surprising considering the circumstances, is it?

So where am I?

There's a tap on my rear windscreen. A man wearing a blue uniform is trying to attract my attention. I wind down my window – my car is parked so close to the next one that I can't get out.

"I'll have to ask you to move, you're blocking a pedestrian exit." He's not angry, just matter-of-fact.

"Can you tell me where I am?"

He looks surprised and peers at me in the gloom, "You're in Emlyn Street car park."

"But where? What town?"

He looks astonished. "Newport."

Now I know what happened, I was so wrapped up in my own thoughts that I failed to turn off for Monmouth, and ended going all the way down the dual carriageway to Newport.

I switch off the internal light, start up the engine and back out, muttering an apology to the car-park attendant. I see him staring at me as I drive back down to the exit. Then I have the joy of finding my ticket which I dropped on the floor, finding a machine and getting out of this hellhole. I follow the signs for the M4 and head home to what I know will be trouble.

5 pm, Thursday 24th September

I hate driving on motorways. I know, they're the safest roads etc. etc. but no soul. I don't think well when I'm on them, or certainly not positively. The thought of what I'm going to face when I get back is getting me down. I'm going to have to stop and phone in. And tell lies.

I stop at some nameless concrete horror that is advertising all the usual chains, and have the inevitable skinny chips and something that might have been animal once. Then I settle in my car to go through the rest of the messages and phone in. They are asking me to make contact, as I expected, but the tone is gentle which surprises me.

Finally I pluck up courage and get through to the station.

"Hello sir, I'll put you through to Superintendent Forester," a relieved-sounding Heather on the desk.

"Rackham. Where have you been? We've been really worried about you. The hospital said you weren't ready to travel."

"Sorry, sir. I just had to get away." I don't want to give too much detail. "I was so upset, sir. I just needed…space."

"Well, we've spent a lot of time trying to track you down, and we've found you a counsellor."

"I know sir, she's contacted me…"

"You realise how important you are. You're the chief witness in the Witherspoon case. We're trying to keep it under wraps but it's bound to come out soon… then the bloody papers…"

"Sir, I'll be OK now. And I'll see the counsellor as soon as I can."

"Good. Now just one more thing. One of your neighbours reported a car that's been abandoned for some time. A blue Mercedes. Outside your house apparently. Do you know anything about this?"

Welcome home! Bloody neighbours. I thought I was Delft china – now I'm a bloody dogsbody.

"No, sir. Shall I look into it?"

"If you would."

And that was that. No yelling, rapping of knuckles. Just a sort of half-hearted concern, and then back to business as usual.

Back on the motorway I'm digesting the factory food with the feeling it's just sitting there not doing me much good. Just filling a space. But my mind's gone into overdrive. Papers, two cases, counsellors. My home town must be so full of police that they've probably taken over all the public buildings – the church even. We're rapidly becoming the crime capital of the UK.

And I thought it was such a quiet, safe place.

I plough round the M25, stopping and starting in the longest circular queue in Britain, and finally get onto a normal road home.

It's dark by the time I get to my house. I've had to park even further away – it will be good to get that Merc sorted and have my space back. I'm such a hypocrite.

I open the front door and the dog rushes at me, wagging tail, slobbery tongue – the full welcome. Then as I start to close the door, he squeezes past me and runs out to the Merc. He's sniffing round the boot, tail wagging. Then he starts to bark. I go to pull him back and quieten him down, but as I near the car I become conscious of an unpleasant smell that seems to be coming from the boot. Shopping left too long and gone off no doubt. But where are the owners?

I can't deal with this now. I'm exhausted from my long journey – I'll deal with it tomorrow.

Dragging the dog back into the house by his collar, I shut the door and sit down in an armchair. The house feels cold and empty. I live here – this is my life, but surely there should be more. There is so little here to say who I am – what I do. True, there is my folk CD collection, and upstairs there is my studio with its art books and my sketches. But the house seems very sparse, almost empty. As if no-one lives here. At this moment I feel totally alone. If I am honest with myself, Betty left a long time ago, Peggy is just wishful thinking, and I am out on a limb as far as the police force is concerned. At this moment all those friendships I thought I had feel very shallow – surface deep.

I can't face this, I need to get out. Take the dog for a walk, go to the pub. Beer is meant to be calming for the stomach, so they say.

We walk down the common in the gathering dusk, watching the lights from a distant street get nearer. The grass is fairly even underfoot, so I can beam in on the road where the pub is. I can see the decorative lights from the back, and it gives me a surge of hope. Maybe I will find company there. Charles will still be there, propping up the bar. I could talk to him. Perhaps we could keep off police business, just talk.

We enter the pub to find it full of youngsters. I really can't tell whether they are under-age or not. The girls are loud and probably look much older than they are. The lads are mainly spotty, but there is a culture of fitness which gives them a muscular look, again making it difficult to calculate their age. I wonder if they've all been ID'd. I remember enjoying a drink in this very pub when I was sixteen and nobody turned a hair. But the beer was weak then, and there was Babycham for the girls. Anyway, I haven't got the heart to check, I'm off-duty and even though the noise level is irritating, I leave it and make for the bar, dog in tow.

"Malcolm Smith-Rogers has gone missing. Hasn't been seen for a fortnight." Charles shouts this bit of unwelcome police business across at me.

I order a pint of something light and then change my mind and go for a stronger beer, thinking that this will probably be better for my digestion.

Who the f... is Malcolm Smith-Rogers, I think. Oh, I've got it. "Malcolm Smith-Rogers? Wasn't he headmaster of Betty's primary school? Long time ago when she started?" I recall a plump, cheerful man in his forties. Plenty of curly hair going grey. About five foot seven. Blue twinkly eyes. Charming.

"Yes, that's him," Charles wheezes gently. "Not that he's a headmaster anymore."

"Well, he'd be retired by now, surely."

"Got out of teaching years ago. Set up his own business doing God knows what, but he must have made a tidy sum. Lives in The Avenues."

Like you Charles, I think, with a twinge of envy. "What makes you tell me this now?"

"Thought you wanted to know what was going on in The Avenues. Well, there's one thing for you. Hello." He bends down and scratches the dog behinds the ears. "Looking better?" The dog wags his tail. He likes Charles.

"You were saying about Malcolm Smith-Rogers..." I sip my beer carefully. It has a slightly metallic taste. Actually, nothing tastes quite right at the moment. I wonder if it is wise to drink beer after all. "Come on, Charles, there must be more. I mean, why has he gone missing? Has he been reported missing?"

"That's just it," Charles looks uncomfortable. "His wife hasn't done anything about it. Just carried on as usual. But being as he lives across the road, I noticed. Then I bumped into her today outside Waitrose. She's worried, but she hasn't said anything to the police."

"Maybe he's gone off on a jaunt somewhere. Maybe he's got a mistress, and he's gone off with her."

Charles goes red in the face. "What's going on at Cornelia Witherspoon's? Police tape everywhere. Nobody's saying anything, but they seem to be digging up her back garden."

Something Charles doesn't know.

"She can't be connected with the shooting, surely." He's trying to get me off the subject of Smith-Rogers.

"Look Charles, I can't talk about that. You know. But why did you tell me about Smith-Rogers in the first place?"

"I assumed you knew."

"Knew what?"

"About Betty."

"What about Betty?"

"I saw her yesterday so it can't be that."

"Be what?" I'm not sure about this beer idea. I'm beginning to feel distinctly queasy.

"Are you OK Arnold? You look very pale."

"No actually, I need the loo." I turn and make my way through the milling crowd of youngsters to the gents', hoping there's a spare cubicle. I find one and shut the door. The bowl looks uninviting, but as I lean down closer I realise I can't do it. I just can't be sick in that. I feel a sweat break out on my forehead and I start to shake. Dizziness overtakes me and I have to sit down on the toilet seat to stop myself from falling over. As the spinning subsides, I begin to wonder what I am doing here. Why didn't I simply go to bed? I'm recovering from a serious poisoning. Why do I think I can just carry on as if nothing has happened?

But that's how I am, so, grasping the door handle, with renewed determination to find out what's going on, I stagger to my feet and make my way back to the bar. Charles has gone, disappeared, leaving me with an uneasy feeling that there was something I should have known about long ago. The dog has fallen asleep under the bar, and I have to nudge him awake to get him to move and come with me out of the pub, leaving my pint mostly un-drunk and definitely unwanted.

Back in my street I look at that bloody blue Merc as I near my house, and a mad determination takes hold of me. I walk back to my car, take out the large wrench from the spare tyre kit and return to the Merc. This should be interesting!

Levering the wrench under the lip of the boot I put my full weight on it. For a moment, nothing happens, then with a crunch of broken thin metal the lock begins to give way. They don't make Mercs as tough as they used to, but they didn't used to have alarms like they do now. This one goes off, its repeated beeping echoing round the neighbourhood. The indicators flash, and by their light the boot lid slowly rises to reveal the body of a man in the early stages of decomposition. A bloody stump where his hand used to be is uppermost as though to protect him in a useless gesture. The smell is overpowering, and I reel back in disgust, colliding with someone who has come up behind me.

"Arnold. What are you doing here?" It's Betty. "Oh my God! Malcolm!"

Then she begins to scream repeatedly, her voice rising in a crescendo of pain. I get my phone out and press 'Grimwode.' After a pause during which I wonder whether to comfort Betty, or just let her get on with it, I hear his voice. He sounds furious.

"Yes?"

"Dick," I shout above the noise of car alarm, wife screaming, and the dog now barking hysterically. "I think I've found the body that belongs to the hand."

9.50 am, Friday 25th September

I awake to streams of light shooting through the gap in my curtains, slicing into the shadows on my bedroom wall, and illuminating motes of dust which dance above me as I stir under the duvet.

It must be late – I've slept in after a very late night, but I'm feeling good, Leslie Bricusse. Yes, and it's a new dawn.

I wake up to the fact that my wife who coolly lived next door, taking my money to pay her mortgage, has been shagging a dodgy ex-headmaster. And for how long? How long has this been going on right under my nose? Amidst my anger I feel relief – this is the end of years of a cold half-life together. Or not together, actually.

But now, as I awake to this sunny day, I realise there's someone to fill the gap. The gap that I never knew I had, and I'm going to see her, and I'm going to hold her hands and look into her eyes, and tell her everything.

As I stare at the autumn sunlight, I realise that the dark specks have gone from in front of my eyes, and that my stomach feels in the right place. I feel cleansed inside and out, and I stretch luxuriously, the soles of my feet touching the end of my bed and my hands reaching the wall behind me.

A new dawn.

Oops, forgot the dog. He'll be desperate for a pee. He's never disgraced himself yet, but he's not as young as he was. Speaking of which, I need to go first - my bladder gives me urgent messages as I sit up.

The dog barks impatiently as he hears me moving towards the bathroom, and quick as I can, I relieve myself and get down to the kitchen to let the poor old thing out.

I watch him make for the first shrub, and I think of what is behind me and what is ahead. Things are coming out of the shadows – things I have hidden from myself, and now they're here and I have to deal with them. But I feel alive – more alive than I can ever remember feeling.

The kitchen clock says it's after ten and I realise my own internal clock is up the Swanee. It feels urgent now to get on and move things. I go into my front room and peek out through the curtains. There's still some activity out there – I can see at least one SOCO pottering in and out of the tent that now shrouds the blue Merc. There's been such a buzz of activity, following my discovery last night, and I'm hoping I can sneak out through the cracks without anyone noticing.

The dog has done his business and I let him in and give him his breakfast. I shovel down some cereal which I am pleased to note my stomach is happy to accept, have a shower and get dressed quickly, and walk rapidly out of my front door turning down the street towards my car, hoping nobody will notice me.

"Sir."

I grind to a halt.

"Commander Grimwode asked me to tell you that they will be interviewing your er…"

"Wife?"

"This afternoon at 2.30."

"Thanks."

106

I turn and smile at him, seeing his worried face, and wanting to reassure him that it's OK. Actually, it's the last thing I want to do – to watch my wife pouring out her soul to my comrades having kept it from me for so long. Look ahead Rackham, I tell myself, and I smile at the SOCO, and walk to my car to find it still unlocked from last night. I catch a glimpse of something on the back seat as I get in, but I'm in too much of a hurry to look at it now. My mind is full of Peggy, and what I will say to her, and imagining her lying there – her smile, her eyes.

This time in the morning the hospital car park is half-empty. People are busy with their lives, leaving their loved ones and relatives to the boredom of a hospital ward. Well, I will cheer Peggy up. I will support her. I will be there for her. I will…

I walk past the front desk and down the main corridor. All very white and clinical, but suddenly the whole space is transformed. There's a café with chairs and tables put out in a random pattern. There's a shop, and in the shop there are flowers. I buy the big bunch in the corner, and go up to her ward feeling like I'm walking on air.

I go through the doors and turn the corner towards her room, then screech to a halt. There's someone in there – I can see a dark shape through the frosted glass. It's a woman. My first thoughts are that it must be a WPC come to get more information from her. Why can't they leave her alone? I say to myself angrily. But was I going to leave her alone? No, I was going to dump my life in her lap. I sigh, and walk away to sit down in the little waiting area where I can watch to see when her visitor leaves.

The clock hand moves slowly but relentlessly round and I feel my impatience building. My mobile buzzes in my pocket making me jump. Leave me alone, I think, as I switch it off.

After what seems like hours, but is in fact ten minutes, I decide to go in and use my senior police officer guise to flush this intruding WPC out.

I give a gentle knock and walk in to see a woman holding both Peggy's hands – there are tears of emotion in her eyes. The woman, who is facing away from me, lets go of her hands and turns. Her face shows signs of tears, but she is angry now.

"What do you think you're doing?" she says.

"Hannah." Peggy looks torn. Embarrassed.

"Sorry, I didn't mean…" My world has suddenly got a great big hole in it.

"Hannah, this is Inspector Rackham. He's in the force with me. We work together. I told you about him."

Hannah is slightly mollified and reluctantly extends a hand, her face shuffling itself into a smile of sorts. She has a striking face. Her long dark hair frames a complexion full of lines and tiny muscles. She has dark eyes – almost black, that make her look ferocious. I would say that she has dyed her hair and that she is in her fifties. So Peggy has someone. Though what sort of someone is yet to be seen, but I feel nothing but jealousy just now. And I get the same vibes coming back from Hannah.

"Hannah's an old friend." Peggy's being the grown-up while we two oldies do battle with our eyes.

"Look, I really must be going." There's an edge to Hannah's voice – I think she was planning to stay longer and I've flushed her out.

"I'm sorry to intrude." No I'm not.

"That's fine." No it's not.

She gets up and gathers her bags.

"See you… soon." They exchange a look, and she's gone.

"Sorry." That's the third time. Will you ever stop saying sorry Arnold?

"It's fine." Peggy collapses into her pillows with a sigh. She looks drained. All my plans for telling her my feelings have gone out of the window. There seems to be a line drawn between us. A line I didn't see before.

"Nice flowers."

"Yes I... Look, if you'd rather be alone."

"No, don't go. Tell me what's been going on. What happened with your brother?"

"He was in a good place and coped with what I told him, but he won't tell his story. Even though it proves that he hasn't been imagining it all these years, he doesn't want to be dragged through the courts. Hounded by the media. He says that in a funny way he feels culpable – keeping it all secret when he was a boy, out of fear. Anyway, we've got her. And he is strong. He's in a relationship now, and he's happy."

"What's she like – his girlfriend?" She's slipped into an assumption about him, and I've slipped into the opposite about her.

"He's lovely – a great cook." I look at her, but she doesn't seem at all embarrassed by her mistake. "Quite a bit younger. I think he relies on Paul for emotional support, but Paul's happy with that. Funny, in a way I think it makes him feel strong – not the one who's always relying on other people. I used to think I was the one who supported him. But this time..."

"You need support. Anyone who's been through what you have..." Is it just good, good Peggy who cares, or is there more in her eyes?

"They've found me a counsellor. I must make an appointment, but... can I trust her?" I look at her. "I can trust you." I can feel my cheeks getting hot.

Peggy just shrugs, and then winces. How much pain is she in? I decide to soldier on. She needs to hear my story, and leave hers for now.

"On the way back, I had another memory thing. I was in my car in a car park in Newport and couldn't work out where I was, or what I was sitting in, or what the strange thing that went Croak-Croak was." I start to laugh. It sounds so ludicrous, and now I can see the funny side. "A car park... in Newport..." It's no good – can't go on. Peggy's beginning to smile for the first time. I want to reach out and hold her hand as I get myself under control.

"But seriously..." I burst into laughter again, and this time she joins me. I can see that it's physically painful for her to laugh, but we're both caught up in this chemical reaction – there's nothing like a good laugh to relieve tension.

She stops suddenly. "Horse riding."

"Horse riding?"

"They said I could always do horse riding. Now that I can't... won't... be able to run. Fucking horse riding." She explodes. "Sorry, sir, but..."

"It can't be like that. You'll walk again, I'd stake my life on it."

"The thing is, because the bullet grazed my spinal cord, they say there might be permanent damage – it may never repair."

Never say never, I think. But I say nothing.

"I used to ride when I was young. My foster parents had a pony – I loved it." Her eyes go inner as she thinks back to that time. I get the feeling it was a good time with these people. Where are they now?

"Tom and Gina. They were quite old when I went to them. I wish they were here now. Still, they're not, are they?"

I look down, not being able to meet her eyes. She shifts uncomfortably.

"Could it be stress that brings them on – your memory lapses?"

"I didn't notice having this kind of trouble before the… you were shot." I grasp at straws. "Maybe it's just that." I'm sure it's more.

"You should see someone. Do some tests or something. What about this counsellor?"

"Trouble is, I can't have anyone finding out – it would be the end of my career. You're the only person I've told." I look down at the flowers in my hands.

We pause, both caught up in our thoughts. She reaches out and gives my arm a squeeze and withdraws her hand immediately, looking straight into my eyes.

"There's more, isn't there."

"Betty's been having an affair for God knows how long. Right under my nose." I say this through clenched teeth. I feel so angry now. "And I'm supposed to be a detective. Couldn't even spot that."

"Oh." Peggy looks away – it gives me a feeling that she suspected as much.

"Last night I found this body in the boot of a car outside my house. It was Malcolm Smith-Rogers, her old headmaster. Betty went berserk. It was his hand we found in the safe."

"What?"

"Grimwode's cronies are crawling all over the car right outside my front door, and I've got to go and watch Betty being interviewed. I'll hear all about it along with the rest of the force. Crap detective – crap husband."

"You're a good detective – you see things that other people miss." She slumps back into the pillows and whispers, "and… and you're a gentleman… she's a stupid woman."

I look at her. Gentleman? Perhaps too much the gentleman.

"You're good at working out what people feel." I flinch.

"I didn't work that one out though, did I? My own wife."

Silence then as our eyes meet, I wish I hadn't said 'wife' like that.

Peggy looks exhausted. Time to go.

"Look, I'll see you in a bit, and let you know how it's all going." I cover my confusion of hopes, dashed hopes, and embarrassment, by finding a jug to put the flowers in.

I manage that, I manage a smile, and I leave.

11.45 am, Friday 25th September

I sit in my car in the car park. I left her with my head full of more questions than answers, and now I'm wondering what all this love thing is about. I can't get her out of my mind. I don't want to – she's the warm bit of my life. But who's Hannah? Is she Peggy's lover? Am I just a foolish old gooseberry?

I turn to look behind me before I leave my parking space, and something catches my eye. There's an envelope on the back seat. It was there when I left my house, but I ignored it. Now I pick it up and tear it open. Forensics would be aghast at my carelessness, but I don't care. I have a feeling I know who it's from, and as I open the sheet of paper I see a plan. It's Charles' plan of the house in The Avenues, and it shows the basements.

It's started to rain in The Avenues as I duck under the police tape and walk up to the front of 'Hazelbank' for the first time since my disastrous drugs raid. I march up the gravelled drive to the theme from Indiana Jones going round my head – I won't be stopped by one of Grimwode's goons, or anyone else for that matter.

A uniform toting a machine gun is standing by the front door, and he speaks into his radio without taking his eyes off me as I approach.

I hold up my ID.

"Sir. Are you part of the investigating team sir?"

"I certainly am Constable er…"

"Barker sir."

He knows I'm not one of his invasion squad, so I enlighten him a bit more.

"I was involved in the original raid. I'm Detective Inspector Rackham." How paper-thin and pathetic this sounds to me, and I'm sure I see a glint of amusement in his eyes. But Indiana Jones continues going round my head reminding me of my determination not to be stopped.

"I want to gain access – I have new information," I say pompously.

"If you can wait sir, I've just contacted Sergeant Brown. He should be here in a minute sir."

So I'm to get the guided tour from someone called Sergeant Brown. In my mind I conjure up this burly figure – a man you can trust. Scottish, bluff and rubicund.

In fact he turns out to be small and thin with a worried look on his face as he appears, as if by magic, from round the side of the house.

"Sir. Are you part…?"

"Yes, I'm part of the investigating team. Now can you let me in? I need to look at the basements."

"I can't get through to the Commander to check sir. Can you wait?"

"No I can't, Sergeant. I have a meeting with him later today and I need to get on with this now."

Reluctantly he gives way, and he leads me round to the side of the house. I hadn't realised, since I had only been in the front, that there was a sloping gravelled drive hidden by a tall evergreen hedge that led to the rear of the house and the basement area. We walk down the side of the house to find a couple of police vehicles parked in a courtyard in front of large green garage doors. I guess that in Victorian times this would have been where the coach was kept, and I can see other doors to the side that would probably have been the stables. The house looks tall at the back with its extra basement floor, and the whole courtyard area is surrounded by high walls making it completely private.

We go past another armed policeman and through an entrance to the left of the garage doors. As I put on the inevitable blue gloves and shoe covers, the smell of damp, petrol and old bricks greets me, and I am surprised at how old this basement area looks. Charles evidently didn't do much restoration here. The light is inadequate but Brown switches on police floodlights to illuminate the first large basement.

Stark damp walls greet my eyes as I look around. At this point I'm not sure what I'm looking for, so I let my eyes wander, taking in the details of each nook and cranny, stain and cobweb.

"The owner kept vintage cars here. We found an old Bugatti, and a nineteen-thirties Lagonda. Impounded now." Brown looks wistful – I guess he loves old cars like those, but can't afford one on his police pay. To me they're cars that break down. Beautiful, yes, but they serve no other purpose.

"Can you show me where these doors lead?" There are three doors leading straight off into the darkness ahead of me. The left-hand one looks half rotten.

"That's just a coal store on the left." We go and peer in. The little room has no window and a low ceiling. Brown's flashlight shows it has been swept out – no doubt every morsel of coal dust has been taken away for analysis, but it still smells strongly of coal.

"Anything behind here?" There's no sign that they've attempted any excavation at the back of the store.

"Goes straight into the hillside. All these rooms run into the slope, but the other two go further."

115

We go to the middle door, and I recall Charles' plan: this must be the big room nearest the front of the house. It has a bit of natural light coming from a small window that I guess looks out onto the sloping drive by the side of the house. It has a dank smell, and I can see stains of encroaching damp on the walls, and places nearer the floor where the paintwork has bubbled up.

"This was evidently a storeroom. You've read the report sir, so you'll know what we found here."

I nod sagely, wondering what else I don't know and how I'm going to find it out. I look at the wall at the back for signs of disturbance – there has to be more than this, though there was nothing on Charles' plan.

Brown follows my gaze. "There's nothing behind there sir. Just mud and rock."

I take a risk. "So you excavated then?" I can see no sign of it.

Brown gives me a curious look. "We used sonar. Didn't want to disturb anything. It's all in the report sir."

"Yes, yes of course. I'd forgotten. Sorry." I go to the back wall and reach out a gloved hand. "Do you mind?"

"Go ahead, sir. Forensics have finished there." He has a slightly superior look on his face which says 'you won't find anything that we haven't'.

I rub my finger along the wall. It's greasy and slightly gritty as though it's been covered with a mixture of coal-dust and oil. I sniff at my finger. Yes, I can smell coal and petrol.

The whole room from floor to ceiling seems to be covered in this residue. "Any idea how this all got here?"

Brown shrugs. He's not going to give me any more information.

And why? It's covering something up – making it difficult to find traces of anything else, including cracks where bricks may have been removed and put back again.

There's something behind these walls – I would swear to it.

"Can we see the next room, Sergeant?"

He leads the way out and into the main basement. I feel the oily residue under my feet, and I can see that it covers the walls there as well. Brown opens the third door and I peer into a small room lined with wooden slatted shelves. A new smell comes through – a smell that makes me want to gag – the smell of rotten apples.

"This is the apple store sir." Brown states the obvious. He isn't going to tell me more and I'm not going to ask him.

There is no window to this room, and the light from the police spotlights casts sharp shadows into the corners making me think of recent dreams – feared things in dark places. Rotting apples rest on shelves that line one side of the wall – small furry dead things – pulling my mind back to Cornelia Witherspoon's disgusting kitchen.

I shudder. "Any chance you could move one of those spotlights so that I can get a clear view of the walls in here?" I seem to remember an unclear bit of shading on Charles' plan that was somewhere around this area. It would be good to have a closer look.

"Sorry, sir. Not without permission."

He clearly isn't going to help me if he can possibly avoid it – 'them and us' situation.

I fish out my mobile, which is useless as a phone behind all these stone walls, but the flashlight is bright enough for me to search along the back wall for any sign of disturbance to the bricks. The oily dirt makes it impossible to be sure about anything, but I take in the whole picture of that back wall. I want to be able to draw it when I get home.

I jump and bang my head on the low ceiling as I feel something moving against my elbow. It's Brown trying to see what I'm up to. "Forensics haven't finished here yet, sir."

"I can see that." I clamber stiffly out of the apple store, careful not to disturb any of its mouldy inhabitants, and into the large open space of the main basement. Claustrophobia sets in making me want to get out and leave the cloying smell of oil enriched by the sickly odour of rotten apples. I move quickly past Brown and out of the building, noticing a flicker of alertness on the face of the armed guard as I pass him.

"Sir?" Brown is behind me. "Have you finished?" I take off my blue plastic shoe covers and gloves and hand them to him.

The rain has stopped and I look round at the house, taking in the proportions of the building, and wondering what lies concealed there. There is something – I know it. I can feel it in my bones.

My phone croaks and I look down to see that there's a message from Grimwode. Putting it to my ear I hear his piercing tones. "What are you doing there, Rackham? You're supposed to be at the station. We've had to pull the time for your wife's interview forward, and we can't wait around for you for ever."

I curse and look down at the time of the message – ten minutes ago.

"Sorry," I say to Brown for some reason, and I run for my car, calling the station as I go.

1.15 pm, Friday 25th September

A wave of stale sweat, stale tobacco breath, and cheap aftershave greets me as I enter the observation room. I can make out two other people in the darkened room, but I don't recognize either of them.

"Have I missed anything?" I whisper to the nearest figure.

"No… sir. She seems to be very upset."

I bet she's upset. I'm upset too, in fact I'm fucking furious – but scared too. Scared of what she'll say. I don't want to be here, listening to my private life being dragged out in front of a group of strangers.

In the interview room Betty is sitting at the table with a box of tissues, wiping her tear-stained face and dabbing at her eyes. Seated by her side is a hard-faced young woman dressed in a dark pinstripe suit, the solicitor I assume, not taking much interest in Betty's emotional outburst, but examining her nails with determined concentration. The woman sitting opposite Betty seems much more interested, and is offering Betty another tissue with a look of concern on her face. Her blond hair is tied back in a bun, and she has that look of earnestness that young women detectives attain as they try to push their way up the male-dominated ranks of the force. Grimwode is there. I can only see the back of his head, as he has got up from his chair and moved round – no doubt restless and impatient. He must have scared the shit out of Betty when she first saw him, and that gives me some mean satisfaction.

"Mrs Rackham." A voice I don't recognize – a deep purring cat-like sound, gentle and reassuring.

"Mrs Rackham, can you tell us about your er... relationship with Malcolm?"

I hear a badly-suppressed snigger somewhere near me in the observation room. Enjoying the show are you? Bastard. But I am wondering where this purring voice is coming from. I look round the interview room – there's no-one else there. In my imagination there's a god-like figure seated in a booth somewhere speaking over a microphone.

"Mrs Rackham, we need to know who has done this to Malcolm. If we are going to find his killers, we will need all the information you can give us." Grimwode has moved round to sit down in his chair opposite Betty. It is his voice, a tone I never heard when we worked together. The jagged edges of Grimwode smoothed out into a gentle cream – it gives me the creeps, even more dangerous than his snappy hit-you-hard mode.

"Why don't you start at the beginning?"

This brings about a fresh stream of tears as Betty thinks back to how it all started.

"I thought I loved Arnold, but when I met Malcolm... I realised what... what love could be..." Fresh tears. You never loved me – so now I know. Cry your heart out you fucking traitor. I grip the table behind me. In the dark my knuckles glow white.

"Go on," croons Grimwode.

"I met him when I started at Gravel's Primary School. He... he was headmaster. He was so kind to me..." More sobs. I bet he was, the bastard.

"So we started seeing each other."

"How long ago was this?"

"I think… I think…"

"Yes?" He sounds really interested.

"Twenty years a… ago." Bitter sobbing.

Twenty years ago. Twenty fucking years. All that time you'd been screwing him, and I never knew. I thought you were faithful. I trusted you. Looked after you. Thought of myself as a faithfully-married man.

"How about more recently? Did you continue to see each other?" Purr, purr.

"Oh yes. We were going to…" She looks nervously at her solicitor.

Her solicitor seems in a world of her own – her and her nails.

"Go on."

"W… well, Malcolm said we could go away. Leave all this mess."

So sorry it all got spoiled for you.

"When was this?"

"He's been talking about it for the last few months." She's speaking as though he's still alive.

"Tell me, Mrs Rackham, why didn't you just leave…" Grimwode clears his throat. "… your husband." Hey that's me. "You had no children did you? Surely you could have gone off with Malcolm any time you wanted."

"I wanted to, but Malcolm said he couldn't leave his wife. She had all the money, you see. And then she was ill – having an operation. He wanted to be with her till she recovered. And then there was the…"

Grimwode suddenly perks up. "Yes?"

For the first time Betty's solicitor shows signs of life. She looks hard at Betty and shifts in her chair.

"He… had this deal that was waiting to go through."

"So after being headmaster at your school…" Grimwode looks down at the papers in front of him. He evidently hasn't had time to be briefed properly.

"He left all that years ago. He's in scrap metal now." He *was* you silly cow.

"So he had a big deal, did he? Was that what would give him enough money to take you both away?"

The solicitor looks like she's about to interrupt. But thinks better of it.

"Yes. That's it. You see, Malcolm wasn't just a scruffy scrap metal merchant. He went all over Europe. Smart hotels. Sometimes I went with him."

So that's what those residential courses were. 'Shag me in a posh hotel' courses.

"All over Europe." Grimwode's voice is hardening up slightly. "Did you get to meet any of his, ah, business partners?"

"Yes, well it struck me as strange you see." The solicitor is definitely taking an interest now.

"Strange, why?"

"Well, they weren't Malcolm's types you see. They were… tough. Tattoos, that sort of thing."

"Really?" Grimwode acts surprised, as if tattoos and scrap metal couldn't possibly go together.

I am getting drawn into this interview. The policeman in me takes over from injured hubby – there is definitely something dodgy about Malcolm's friends, and the solicitor is getting visibly twitchy. At the same time another part of me is letting go of my anger with Betty. After all, I've fallen for someone else. Doesn't this all just release me? Permanently? Free me up to finally move on from this sham of a marriage?

"Yes. They weren't very nice. I used to go off shopping when he had his meetings."

"So you didn't get to hear what they were meeting about?"

"No, but.. there was one man we saw quite a bit of."

The solicitor clears her throat.

"Yes?" The purr is back.

"He… he was different. Nice man. Came round and had drinks with us. Brian. He came from around here as well and we had lots in common. I liked him, he was a gentleman." Brian? My old so-called friend? No, it can't be the same person.

"So, did he talk about this deal? The one that was going to give you a new life?"

"I think she's told you enough." It speaks. The solicitor's sharp-edged voice shatters the safe warm atmosphere that Grimwode has been creating. "I won't have my client being drawn in to incriminate herself. Don't you think she's been through enough?"

Enough? I thrust myself forward wanting to give the solicitor bitch my side of this sordid tale, and succeed in banging my head on the window that separates us. Everyone in the interview room jerks round and stares at the mirror.

"Now unless you are going to charge my client with something, I think we should leave." The solicitor stands up, and leans over to Betty grasping her by the elbow.

"Sit down, Miss…" The old edge is back. Grimwode is in command mode.

It has no effect on the hard-as-nails solicitor. "Mrs Braithwaite. Now unless you have any legal reason to keep us, my client and I are leaving."

"We would like Mrs Rackham to see some photos." He's almost pleading – I can't believe it.

"We're leaving. Now." She almost drags Betty to the door, and is out, leaving a thunderous-looking Grimwode staring into the space that they had occupied.

123

2.15 pm, Friday 25th September

"Rackham. My office."

I stagger out of the observation room suffering from a mixture of disbelief and claustrophobia. All I want is to get out of the bloody building.

The two goons that had been in there with me shuffle past silently on some mission of their own as I walk shakily towards Grimwode's office. No doubt in their minds the title of 'cuckold' has been added to 'incompetent policeman'.

"Close the door." He's standing with his back to me, looking out of the window. A snake of schoolchildren in their green jackets is making its way into the town library opposite, worlds away from the place that Grimwode and I occupy.

He turns, and I can see the fury in his face. "Who the fuck banged on the one-way mirror?"

I'm not going to answer that one. He knows it was me – there must a red patch on my forehead, it's still stinging. Instead I say, "Betty knows something."

"Of course she knows something, that's bloody obvious."

"Why did you let her go? Couldn't you have…"

"Her solicitor was correct – we had to charge her. Anyway, I want to see what happens next. I want you to keep an eye on her."

"You're kidding, Dick, I don't want to be anywhere near her."

"You'll do what you're told, and don't call me Dick. Now get out of my office."

"It's my office actually. All this front of being the great commander, but you can't even get past a junior solicitor."

Grimwode's face turns white, red patches appearing on his neck. If I wasn't so angry I'd be petrified. "It's not your office any more, Rackham. You're suspended. Sergeant Brown said you were snooping round The Avenues house without my permission. He said you didn't even seem to have bothered to read the report. You broke into a car without proper procedure. You left the area without telling anyone. And now you won't even do the simple job of keeping an eye on your wife. Mind you, you didn't do a very good job of keeping an eye on her for the past twenty years, did you."

How low can you stoop?

"You know what, Dick, I think you're just taking it out on me because you screwed up the interview and allowed that solicitor to put one over on you. If you take my advice you'll keep an eye on that one. By the way, have you looked at my drawings of the gunman yet? I thought not – well they might be a good lead. I can draw, you know. Used to be an artist, remember? And up to this point you haven't got very far, have you?"

I turn and walk out, slamming the door behind me before he has the chance to say 'get out'. For some reason the phrase 'handbags at dawn' comes into my head and I start to giggle. It's no good. I walk through the station, tears of laughter running down my face. It all seems so ridiculous – two old men behaving like overgrown schoolboys.

The shock hits me as I walk out of the station doors into the bright flash of cameras.

"Inspector Rackham, can you tell us how you're feeling after your ordeal?"

"Can you tell us what she said?"

"You've lived here all your life – how well did you know her?" At first, in my confusion, I think they're talking about Betty. Then I realise it's Cornelia Witherspoon. The questions stumble over each other – impossible to answer, even if I wanted to.

I make for my car, surrounded by a posse of press. Get in, start the engine and drive off slowly. So someone has leaked the Witherspoon story. Now my tear-streaked face will be all over the papers. I drive through the town back to my house, wondering how long it will be before they discover where I live, if they haven't already. My head's spinning as I park near the Merc with its SOCO team still ferreting about.

One of the men gets out of the car and hails me over. "Sir, can you take a look at this?" He shows me a small piece of tissue paper attached to a bit of bubble-wrap.

I shake my head. "Sorry. I'm off the case now." And I walk slowly to my front door, hoping that the press don't find me. I want to shut the whole world out just now. I am wrecked – completely wrecked.

It's like I'm in slow motion as I open the front door – reality shifts, everything feels unfamiliar. I look at the chair and sofa with bewilderment. There's an animal making odd noises – is it dangerous? I'd better be careful. Slowly I make my way through this strange room to a doorway into a kitchen. What was I just thinking about? Everything's gone blank in my head, like I can't turn back and see it. It's disappeared. I start to panic – I'm lost in this strange place. There's a chair. I sit on it. Feel the hard wood cold beneath me. The table has got paper on it. I can draw on that paper. I know I can draw. Something tells me this is what I must do. My hand reaches inside my jacket, and I feel a long thin hard object – that's a pen, isn't it? I take it out and look at it in astonishment. How did that get there? I reach for the paper and start to draw.

The face that begins to appear on the paper is smiling. It's a man in his fifties – rugged friendly features.

I jump as something nudges at my thigh. It's that animal again. I push it off and continue with my drawing.

The man has no hair on his head but a good beard. His smiling face stares up at me and I begin to hear a sound in my head. 'Brr,' it goes.

The animal's back again – the heavy weight of its head is on my thigh, and it's making a beating sound as its tail hits the table leg with a regular rhythm.

BEAT, BEAT. BEAT.

For some reason I stop being frightened. This animal is friendly – it means well. The face I have drawn is friendly too, and the word 'Brian' comes into my head. If I could draw it in colour I would make his eyes a warm brown. Gentle – trustworthy. And I look down at the animal and I see warm brown eyes looking up at me – I can trust this animal too.

My mind begins to relax – things start to come into focus. I search around in my memory, and instead of seeing a blank, I see a word forming. DOG.

This is my dog. He has come to rescue me. Lovely, good dog. I scratch him behind his ears – I know he loves that, and we look at each other. Man and dog. The most reliable partnership in the world. Then I remember I have a wife. Not reliable at all. Then I look at my drawing. Brian. She said 'Brian' a short while ago, in that horrible interview. It's all coming back to me now – I wonder if it can possibly be the same Brian. Suddenly I have an urge to take it and show it to her.

I go out of my kitchen door and into the garden, the dog following me wagging his tail. I look over the wall that

128

separates our two cottages and notice that her back door is open. She emerges holding a suitcase with something pressed against her ear. She sees me and quickly puts the thing into her pocket, shuts her door and walks briskly down her garden. I have to run to catch her at her gate. She won't look at me and makes to walk straight on, but I catch her arm and put the drawing right in front of her face.

"Brian?" I whisper.

She looks at me then, her face full of fear, wrenches her arm out of my grasp, and almost runs down to the road that crosses the common where I catch a glimpse of a car waiting for her. A woman gets out. It's too far away to be sure but she sets off another visual memory in my mind – nails. She looks at her nails. I hear a voice in my head – angry, bullying: 'I want you to keep an eye on her,' and I begin to run down towards the car. I have no idea what I'm intending to do when I get there, but both women get in quickly, slamming doors and the car drives off leaving me standing by the road gathering the pieces of my life together.

I could swear her eyes said 'yes' when she looked at my drawing.

3.30 pm, Friday 25th September

I'm back in my kitchen, sitting at the table, making a most unusual list – this will be my quick way back into my memory the next time one of these lapses happens. It's a series of drawings with titles by them. So:

Young woman looking down at her nails with expressionless face – *Solicitor Mrs not Miss*

Angry-looking man with hawk-like nose – *Dick Grimwode*

Middle-aged woman looking up appealingly with tearful blue eyes – *Betty my wife.*

Very plump pleasant-faced man in his late fifties – *Charles, my drinking friend*

Man with pudgy features, eyes glazed in death – *Malcolm, Betty's lover*

Labrador with big soft eyes and a broad head – *The Dog, my true friend*

Old woman with loose cheeks sagging down to her scraggy neck – *Cornelia Witherspoon – tried to poison me*

Man with long face carved into beauty by life – *My brother Paul*

There's someone missing. Someone important to me. I feel pain. I move on.

Worried-looking man with thin face – *Sergeant Brown*

A series of dark rooms showing the detail of the walls. This takes a large sheet of A3 all to itself – *The basements at 'Hazelbank'*

Man in his forties with broad pleasant face and thinning hair – *Superintendent   Forester – in charge of the Witherspoon case.*

Shit. He set up for me to see a counsellor. I look at my watch. Was I meant to meet her today? After Betty's interview? I hunt around for my mobile phone, and find it under my first drawing – *Brian.*
There's another voicemail on my phone, it must have come in before Grimwode's but I missed it. It's the counsellor offering me an appointment this afternoon. It's too late now and for some reason I'm very worried. Forester will be angry with me. Then it comes back to me – I've been suspended. Dick did that, but does Forester know? Does anything matter now? Or shall I just walk away from it all?
Still there's something nagging at the back of my brain. How did I miss that call from the counsellor? It must have come in when I was at the hospital.
Hospital? I start to draw a face.
Her face.

Peggy's face. I take more trouble over this one showing her smooth skin, the details of her long eyelashes. The slight smile that always inhabits the corners of her mouth. She should have been first on the list, but my last visit to the hospital has left me the feeling that she has someone else. So I don't draw the other woman's face – the one that was with Peggy – I don't want to remember her.

Then, going out into my front room, I ferret around in my desk for some Blu Tack. I stick my drawings up on the kitchen wall, making a gallery of my memories. I just hope I can get back here if my mind chooses to empty itself again.

I decide not to put up the drawings of the basements – I need to find Charles' plans, and have another good look at them to compare them with the sketches I've made. I have a hunt round the cottage, half-heartedly hoping to find the plans. The dog follows me, I think he's hoping for a walk.

It's still light outside – plenty of time for a good long walk, so we go out along our familiar route. Down the common towards the cricket pitch. A path I've walked so many times before. But now this world feels unfamiliar. My memory has come back but everything seems changed. Security gone – uncertainty everywhere. I look on my phone and find the counsellor's number. I walk down as far as the cricket pitch, and standing under the eaves of the pavilion with the smell of wood and autumn, I make the call.

"Hello, it's Inspector Rackham. Sorry I missed your call… Can I see you soon…? Yes, the sooner the better… yes, that would be perfect… yes, I'm an early riser. 6.30 tomorrow… thank you for fitting me in."

She sounds like she understands the seriousness of my situation. Warm, earnest – there is an urgent undertone to her voice, and I so need someone to talk to.

As I look down across the cricket pitch to the town beyond, I notice a small group of people making their way in my direction. Press? I don't wait to find out, but turn and walk briskly to the main road, now busy with work-weary drivers. I take my chance, grab the dog by his collar, and run across in front of a lorry which toots furiously at us as we gain the bushes on the other side of the road. Looking back I can see the posse making its way to the cricket pavilion. Am I becoming paranoid? Was it just a group of cricket enthusiasts coming to inspect the pitch? I don't wait to find out but scramble through the bushes to a narrow track that will take me to the park, and from there to The Avenues.

I look at the dog, and he looks at me. I wonder what he's thinking. Maybe he's saying, 'Now Arnold, you know what happened last time you took me to The Avenues. We don't want a repeat of that, do we?' I sense a reluctance to go on in the direction I'm taking him, and he slows down and stops by a bench conveniently situated for the elderly walker in need of a rest at the top of the hill that leads down to the main park and leisure centre. I sit down at this vantage point and look through the trees that line the path down the hill. Memories of my childhood flood back into my mind. The park hasn't changed much in fifty years. True, there's the new sports centre but otherwise it's the same. I remember going down the hill on a rickety old go-kart made from planks and old pram wheels. Sitting in front of me was Brian. He was always the leader in our games and adventures. This time we came to grief halfway down and he scraped his knee. But Brian, always brave, made nothing of it, wanting to continue to the bottom and then start all over again.

What happened to him? I met him a couple of years ago at a school reunion. One of those odd events where everybody looks around at the people they were at school with, and tries to recognize the boy or girl in that middle-aged face. Brian was easy. He still had the essence of his character showing through his ageing skin. Cheeky, brave, the friend everyone wanted. But he didn't want to be my friend that night, and he disappeared before I had a chance to catch up with him.

I remember someone saying he had come back to our town and was living in The Avenues. What is it with The Avenues? It seems to have attracted every dodgy character into its leafy groves. I'm assuming he's dodgy of course, because Betty brought his name up and she obviously wasn't meant to. I should try and catch up with him as soon as I can. I text Charles to ask if he knows Brian's address. After a minute of staring in an unfocused way at the trees, I jump back to reality as Charles' text comes back with a loud beep.

37 Hawkshaw Avenue. Good old Charles – we're on our way.

If I'd turned right instead of left when I found Cornelia Witherspoon and her dead bodies, and gone down the hill towards the town, I'd have walked right past his house. Now the sign 'Marshalls – To Let' greets me before I see the house. It is set back like all the bigger Avenues houses, with its gravel drive in front of a pillared porch. I ring the bell, with the growing feeling, as I peer through the stained glass set in the front door, that it's useless – that he has gone. No answer. No sign of life. I go round the side to the back garden and peek in at the windows. In stark contrast to horror and decay of Cornelia Witherspoon's rooms, these are neat and soulless. Modern functional furniture. Dark colours, shiny leather, square lampshades, and a sparseness that shouts 'rented'.

"Excuse me, are you looking for someone." The voice seems disembodied at first until I make out a thatch of grey hair and a pair of round spectacles peering over the fence.

"Brian O'Connell. I was hoping to find him here."

"Oh, he left a week ago. Don't know where he's gone. The estate agents might have some contact details. You are?"

"Just an old friend trying to catch up." I decide not to show my police identity – I don't want anyone giving Brian a clue that I'm on to him.

"I say, your dog's doing its business in the flowerbed." This person is definitely not going to go away. "Are you going to clear it up?" Outrage.

There's nothing here except this nosy busybody. I hear him muttering about irresponsible dog owners as we beat a hasty retreat.

We quickly walk back through town as I hope to catch Marshalls before they close. I get there to find that I'm too late, but I see my reflection in the glass door of the estate agents and am shocked at how dishevelled I look. It's all catching up with me – shooting, poisoning, bodies in car boots, betrayed by my wife. Some people may be made for this, but definitely not me. All my clothes seem to be sagging off me and I look like I haven't slept for a week.

I put my back to the glass door and slide down till I'm crouching, my hands hugging my knees. The dog whines and wags his tail, nudging me with his cold wet nose. He is hungry, it's his suppertime and he's worried.

6 am, Saturday 26th September

I wake up with a jerk, suddenly aware that I am meant to be somewhere. My watch says six and usually I get up easily at this time, but I've had a restless night – I just couldn't get Betty out of my mind, and when I did sleep it was full of those recurring dreams about dark basements and being chased by someone.

Confused, I go downstairs and find my picture gallery in the kitchen – the drawings I made of people so I could remember who they were. I can't find the person I am looking for – I know it is a she, but the only face that rings a bell is Forester's. Then the penny drops and I remember that it was he who had recommended a counsellor. I find my phone, and there it is: six thirty, Valerie Redman, 3 Leyton Crescent.

I rush up to the bathroom, splash cold water onto my face, scrabble around for clothes and keys and am in the car with five minutes to spare. Then I realise I've forgotten to clean my teeth. No time – I hate being late – so I floor it down to the centre of town, narrowly avoiding a cat on its early-morning stroll, and arrive at 3 Leyton Crescent three minutes late.

She must think I am a mess when she opens the door – stinky breath, hair sticking out from restless sleep, but she doesn't say anything. Just looks me straight in the eye and lets me in. I could be anybody – she could be anybody, and for a fleeting moment I feel all my trust fly out of the window.

The house is modern and airy, and she leads the way down a corridor to a plain uncluttered room with a window looking out onto a neat rear garden. The room has two chairs and a divan bed. Nothing else. No pictures, no ornaments – a stark place for the mind to discover itself.

"Would you like to sit or lie down?"

I look at the bed with mounting fear. Lie down in a room with a woman I don't know? After my experiences, I want to be able to make a swift get-away.

"I'll sit." My voice is gruff with sleep.

She sits down opposite and looks at me quizzically. "Have you ever had counselling before?"

"No. Never. Never needed it."

"Well, there are a couple of things you need to know. Firstly, the session lasts one hour, and unless something unexpected comes up at the end we stick to that and you leave. Secondly, within that hour you can say anything you want. It is your hour and it is completely confidential. Nothing leaves this room."

I stare at her, uncomprehending for a moment. One hour. How can I fill that hour? How can I tell her everything in just one hour? Where do I start? Then it strikes me: confidential. "You mean that you will not pass anything I say to the force, to Superintendent Forester?"

She shakes her head. "This is just between you and me. If you thought your boss or anybody else was looking over your shoulder, how could you possibly be completely open?"

"I see." One hour. The time is ticking away – the sand is pouring through the sieve, and I feel a rising panic. Where can I start?

"If you're finding it hard to know where to start, just tell me how you're feeling right now."

"Panic." I feel the blood rush to my face. There, I've told you.

"What is the panic about, do you think?" She looks completely calm.

There's a silence, and I feel my precious time sliding away. I need to ask her about my memory. She might know something about it. I take a deep breath. "I keep getting these memory lapses." I say it so quietly, I wonder if she hears me.

She looks down. I look down. The carpet has no pattern – nothing to follow.

"When did they start?" She heard me, and I feel a huge sense of relief. It was out now, not just with Peggy, but with a professional – someone who can offer expert advice.

"After the shooting."

"The shooting?"

She doesn't know. She hasn't been briefed about me. I find that reassuring. "One of my officers was shot during a drugs raid."

"So are these lapses related to stressful moments?"

"Yes... no, I don't know." I've been permanently stressed, but was I particularly stressed driving back from Wales?

"Can you describe what happens?" She looks at me with those grey eyes. She feels safe to me at this moment.

My mind goes blank.

"My mind goes blank."

Panic.

What else?

"I can remember if I draw." I think back to the time when I couldn't draw – when I was in the car in Newport. "I can't work out what anything is. I was in my car. I didn't know what it was, or where I was. And the mobile phone – it was strange to me. I was so shocked when it made a noise that I dropped it. That was when I first heard your voice, on my er… voicemail."

"So you don't know where you are, what things are? Does this happen in familiar surroundings?"

"Yes. It's happened at home. I didn't even know what my dog was."

"Your dog?"

"Yes. He's been with me for a long time. I know him better than anyone else." How pathetic does that sound?

She looks thoughtful for a moment. That blank carpet – what colour is it? Fawn?

"Does this happen suddenly or is there a gradual build-up?"

"Suddenly. It's completely confusing."

"And how long does it last?"

I realise I have no idea. I've never checked a clock or a watch. When I was in it, it seemed like an age. Afterwards it seemed like a moment.

"I don't know. Half an hour, twenty minutes, an hour. I can't be sure."

"And do you have any warning that it's going to happen?"

"None at all. Suddenly I can't remember anything." I feel so bleak at that moment – I look at her for support. She is looking down at that carpet, trying to capture something in her memory. Thinking.

"It sounds like it might be some form of..." She stops. "How many times has it happened?"

"About five, I think."

"And how do you feel afterwards?"

"Washed out. Worried."

"And you're sure you had no previous signs of this?"

"I've always had a bad memory for names, but it's never worried me. Just annoying. But… but… no. Nothing else. Except… recently I've been remembering things that I covered up, you know, buried. Like I found out…"

"Yes?" She looks at me intently.

"When… when I was poisoned by Cornelia Witherspoon it uncovered memories for me. Bad ones. I began to realise why I became a policeman."

She looks at me with a puzzled frown on her face. "I know very little about what happened to you before you walked through my door. Can you tell me?"

So I do. There isn't time to go through everything in detail, but I feel it all so acutely in that room. I am allowed to feel. I dare to open up to her, and by the end she has a good sketch of the picture that was my life of the past couple of weeks.

She tells me it is time to go, and as I get up to leave she says, "I think it would be good if you saw a consultant. There's a memory clinic I can recommend. Would you like..?"

"Could it be dementia?"

She looks at me for a moment, "I don't know."

I feel this lead weight in my chest. Dementia – when you put a name to it, it sounds so final. "It will be kept private won't it? I could lose my job."

"It will be an entirely private matter. Shall I talk to them, and get you their contact details?"

I nod.

"And I'll see you next week. Same time?"

I nod again and leave the room, the hall, the house, and stumble off over a large semi-circular patch of grass on the other side of the road, forgetting I had brought my car.

In the middle of the green is an old yew tree. I touch its papery bark, peeling a bit off absent-mindedly, and then I press my hands against it hoping to suck in its ancient wisdom. It must have been in this place for hundreds of years, and here I am facing my end already.

Not fair.

Impossible.

Unfathomable.

I'm so angry – so sad.

I don't know how to deal with this.

I stand by the tree for some time, and gradually become aware of a gentle rain, almost a mist, coming down around me. It isn't touching me – the branches of the yew shelter me, but suddenly a drop of cold water goes down the back of my neck. I shiver. Pull myself away from the tree and walk stiffly through the chilling drizzle to find my car.

7.45 am, Saturday 26th September

I get back to my car to find my phone croaking. A message. It's from Forester. "Can you come in and see me at ten?" His voice sounds non-committal. What does he want? To know what my counsellor said? Or has she already betrayed me? I feel a shiver of paranoia. Can I trust anybody?

I drive back home, eat my breakfast, and walk the dog. Have a shower. Dress in cleaner clothes, and just sit shivering in my front room until it's time to go. The rain has hardened up into spiteful javelins of cold water, and as I run for the car with a raincoat over my head, I discover that there is a small posse of press staked outside my house with cameras at the ready.

"You must be really cut up…"

"She was your matron at your old school wasn't she..?"

"Did you have any suspicions when you were young…?"

They crowd round me with their umbrellas, nudging each other to get a better picture. I hope that their lenses and cameras will get soaked – blurred pictures of an old copper trying to get into his car. Pathetic fallacy. Hah!

And where is my faithful posse of fellow policemen to protect me? I have no mates, I realise, except possibly poor old Burt, my suspended senior. As I sit in the car – damp trousers, spoiled shoes – it occurs to me that I haven't been much support to Burt. I've treated him like a leper, and now I'm one as well. I drive slowly away from the dismal crowd of journalists, through the town, and up to the police station. The car park is full, so I reverse round the corner and park on a double yellow line, make a dash for the entrance, and sit in a soggy pile outside Forester's office – Burt's name is still on the door.

Forester pokes his head round the door. "Come in Rackham, come in. You look soaked. Filthy weather. Like a tea or coffee? I'll get Lucy to get you one. Lucy!"

"Thank you sir, a coffee would be lovely."

Lucy appears at the doorway. Red-haired, jaunty. I don't recognize her – another youngster from the area murder squad, no doubt.

"White, no sugar please." I sink into the chair opposite Forester's desk, a chair I have sat in so many times in the past when talking to Burt. Comfortable times they'd been. But now I sit in damp clothes, the vapour of drying cloth smelling a bit like wet dog, waiting for Forester to deliver the final blow to my career.

"Seen your counsellor yet?"

Is this an opening ploy, or does he really not know?

"I saw her this morning sir." Wait and see. Don't give anything away.

"Go well? Was it helpful?"

"Yes, sir."

Forester frowns, strokes his chin thoughtfully, and gets out of his chair. He walks up and down in front of the window, then stops as Lucy comes in with my coffee. As I look at it in horror, I realise I've made a mistake. A scum floats on the top of what looks like dirty washing-up water, and the unmistakable smell of weak instant coffee floats up. I'd forgotten that some people still called this coffee. Should have gone for tea.

"The Witherspoon case. Nobody's come forward with any information." He sits down and looks straight at me. "You knew her. She was your school matron. There must be something. Surely other boys would have talked about her – given a hint that there was something wrong, something they were keeping secret."

For the first time I realise that there is a camera suspended from the corner of the room pointing straight at me. This is a debriefing, not a cosy chat. So I'm not being sacked, I'm being squeezed.

"No sir, nobody talked about her dark secrets," I reply, truthfully. "We all thought she was a bit creepy, that was true, but…"

"Yes?"

How far to go? How much to tell him without giving my brother away.

"Well, we used to get invited round to tea."

"Yes?" Forester looks horribly interested.

"And we'd just sit round and try and make polite conversation. It was embarrassing."

"Can you give us the names of the other boys."

"But I thought I'd already submitted a report." I start to feel confused.

Forester is evidently trying to conceal a lot of impatience. "We've been hanging on, waiting for you, giving you time to recover, but you haven't submitted anything. We need to move this case on. Forensics are happily churning away with the mass of data they have from the bodies, but we have no other witnesses apart from you."

I try a diversionary tactic. "But what about the people in London? The charity she worked with?"

"The people who knew her are all dead. She was quite young, remember."

145

She seemed old to me then, but I realise she must have only been in her thirties.

The other women involved were all elderly then – the rich and worthy doing their bit.

"And nobody else noticed what she was doing. It's unbelievable." Forester studies me for a long time. There is something in his look that makes me feel very uncomfortable, as though he's trying to peel my skin off and see what's inside me.

"WPC Gail reports that while you were asleep, recovering from the poisoning in hospital, you said Witherspoon's name, and then something like 'I won't tell, but I'll never go back'. Now that makes me think you know more than you're letting on." His voice hardens. "I've talked to Commander Grimwode who says he's suspended you for insubordination. You're in trouble already, Rackham. Now are you going to cooperate, or am I going to have to throw the book at you?"

I look at him, trying to weigh up how to keep this situation under control. All these years I had a friend on the other side of the table, but now...

"Listen, Rackham, we've been very patient with you. You go off AWOL, God knows where, and we handle you with kid gloves because you've had such a hard time. But we need to know what you could have told us in the hospital, and I'd like to know where you went for twenty-four hours." He doesn't actually get any closer to me, but it feels like it. His face seems to loom huge in front of me.

"Witherspoon abused me in the toilet, sir."

There.

It was out.

I can tell him the truth about the abuse, but I'll have to lie about where I've been, and I'm not sure how good I am at lying.

"She hurt me, and told me I must never tell…" I am back there, in that horrible place – that's the way to tell the truth. What shocks me is how ashamed I am. I can't look Forester in the eye, and I feel myself going deep red.

"So that was all?"

"No, sir. She said something. Something about there being more. Something exciting if I came back."

"And?"

"I never went back."

"And you never told?"

"No. I was too frightened. I was only ten years old. Besides, in those days nobody would have taken any notice. People abused children with impunity then. It wasn't considered so important as long as they didn't kill them." I find myself getting angry. That fury is catching up with me.

Forester doesn't seem to notice. "So tell me about the set-up. How did you come to be in her house?"

He knows this, I realise. He's just fishing for more clues. We could be here for hours going round and round the information.

"She would invite four or five boys round for tea on a Sunday afternoon. We all felt we had to go, and our parents thought she was safe. They thought she was a saint, with all her charity work in London with the homeless." My voice is getting harsher with bitterness.

"And was there anyone else there apart from the boys?" Calm Forester doesn't give a damn about my feelings.

"Yes. Her mother. She just sat in a chair, bolt upright, and never said anything. She could have been dead – she hardly seemed to move. I never saw her get out of her chair."

"So there was the mother, the boys, and Witherspoon. You weren't aware of anyone else?"

"No, sir."

"And did she abuse you more than once?"

"No, sir."

"Do you know if she abused the other boys?"

"No, sir."

"So nobody said anything?"

"No, sir. In those days you didn't tell."

"And how many times did you go to the house?"

"I've been trying to remember. Four or five. Could have been more."

"And that's all the information you can give us?"

"Yes, sir."

"Tell me one more thing. How did she hurt you?" I could swear I see the hint of a smile cross his face.

I pause. "She squeezed my... er... testicles, sir." I can feel it as though it is happening right at this moment. I know I must have gone pale – Forester looks amused for a moment and then, seeing my face, thinks better of making light of it.

"We need you to go through the lists of boys at your school, to see if you remember who else was there at those tea parties."

Thinking that's the end of it, I start to get out of my chair, but he ignores me and walks up and down in front of the window again.

"Bloody cowards. These men who must have been abused by Witherspoon when they were boys, why don't they come forward? The case has been given plenty of publicity in the last couple of days, and no-one's come forward. They're culpable now. Withholding information from the police."

So that's how the press knew! Forester told them. I stand up. I've had enough.

"I haven't finished with you yet, Rackham. Where do you think you're going?"

"They're not cowards, they're not guilty. They're victims!" I feel my voice getting louder. "Have you any idea what they might be going through? Has it entered your tiny mind, that this coming out now might push people over the edge? You've no idea, have you? Sitting in your safe office with your safe life. You haven't been near that dark side, the Cornelia Witherspoon side. Can you imagine what must have gone on? These people want to bury these horrific memories, or, at the most, want to talk to someone in private. But you expect them to come out and be put through the mangle of public speculation and voyeurism. Do you know what has happened to victims in the past, after the police and the press and the lawyers have got their hands on them? Eh? How many suicides? Do you want that on your hands? Witherspoon will go to prison for the rest of her life simply because she tried to poison me – attempted murder of a police officer."

Forester looks down at his desk for a moment. "So we're not going to get much cooperation from you…"

"I'll look at the names for you." Anything to keep him away from my brother. "But to be honest I think most of the boys in my form went to tea at Cornelia Witherspoon's one time or another."

"But you were a favourite, weren't you Rackham?" Forester's voice takes on a nasty edge. "Pretty boy, were you? Well my 'tiny' mind has a suspicion you're concealing something. My 'tiny' mind, which has very much been involved with the dark side. I've seen more murders than you could possibly imagine in your safe little local cop life."

"Do you want me to look at those lists or not? I'd like to leave now."

"Sir. Leave now, sir," he says. I'm getting through his armour now. He's reddening, his hands clenched.

"Now… sir."

"You're suspended Rackham, but don't think of going off on one of your jaunts. Come in later to see the lists, and you can tell me where you went as well. I've finished with you for now."

No, I've finished with you, I think as I turn and walk out of the door.

Then a thought strikes me.

Claire doesn't know I've been suspended. I ask her to let me have the Witherspoon report as I leave the station. She says she'll let me have the secure link. I want to know more about the charity that Witherspoon used to her own ends.

4 pm, Saturday 26th September

Burt lives in a new-build estate out on the west side of town. Green fields all around and tasteful vernacular architecture. Quite a nice pad for a policeman these days, but I wonder if it's doing Burt much good now. His wife, looking thin and worried, answers the door with a 'where have you been?' look, and reluctantly lets me in. Burt always said she was the strong one that held their life together. Now she looks crumpled, as if something has collapsed inside her.

"Burt, here's Arnold to see you," she calls from the hallway.

Silence.

She shrugs her shoulders and opens the door to the lounge. "He's in there."

Burt's sitting by the French windows, looking out into his garden. There is a bottle of whisky on a little table by his side. He doesn't turn round. At first I think he's watching the robin that's searching for food just outside on the grass, but the robin flies off as I approach, and there's no sign that he's heard me enter the room.

"Hi, Burt." I reach for a chair and sit down to look at him. He is staring straight ahead. For him I don't seem to exist. Only the glass in his hand exists. He puts it to his lips as I watch, and sips the sweet alcohol.

"Burt. I've been suspended," I speak softly. "I came to see you for help."

He makes a sound. At first I can't tell what it is. Then I realise that he's whispering through clenched teeth. "… all my life. I've given all my life. I've given all my life…"

"Burt. I've been suspended." I reach out and touch him on the arm. He jerks round to look at me, and spills his whisky.

"Bugger." He looks down at his trousers. "Bloody waste. You've been what?"

"Suspended for insubordination."

"Insa… insa…" He can't get his mouth round the word, and begins to chuckle. Then the sound turns to a horrible cry as he starts to weep. "Now you… now you know what it's like."

"We're like lepers."

"S'right. Like fucking lepers. Gave my life to the force and nobody's been to see me. You're the first. I thought this was a lovely town. It's full of fucking criminals, and I didn't even know. My patch, and I didn't even know." He starts to sob and whine again. It's an eerie, ghastly sound.

"Burt… Burt…" I grab his elbow and shake him. He looks at me as if he's seeing me for the first time.

"W… what?"

"Burt. We've got to do something. They don't know their fucking arse from their elbow. Trampling around missing every clue. You've got to help me. I'm on to something, I'm sure."

I suddenly have a picture of myself. An elderly copper holding the elbow of another elderly copper. Both in deep shit. Both off their trollies. Anyway, I can see that I am going to get nothing from Burt.

"Brian." He says.

I jump. "What?"

"Brian. He came to see me. Said he had some infor…infor…" He can't say it. "Bout the shooting."

"When was this?" I must have sounded a bit sharp as Burt starts to cringe.

"I dunno, I dunno, f… forgotten." He lapses into silence, and resumes his scrutiny of something out in the garden.

"So Brian…" I hope to gently jog him back into the present.

"He… he said summing 'bout tart…"

"Tart?"

"No. Art. You know 'bout tart Arn… Arnol'. You sh… should 'ave been n'ere. Thieves they were. Thieves. Gone to Lonnon now. Should 'ave… should 'ave toll summon." He looks around uneasily. "Sacked now. Make no difference."

"No, Burt. Not sacked. Suspended. This isn't the end. We can still do something." I try to get his attention again, but he is back – trapped in his own world, sipping his whisky and gazing into the garden.

I gently get up and leave the room. His wife is waiting in the hall, anxiously rubbing her thin hands together. "See?"

"How long's he been like this?" I follow her into the kitchen.

"A few days. He wouldn't talk about it for a bit and then he started drinking." She looks at me angrily. "Spent my life with him wanting to see more of him, and when I do, I get this." She gestures towards the lounge.

"But he must see someone. Have you called the doctor? Looks like he's had a massive breakdown." He could die from that amount of alcohol, I'm thinking, but I don't say it.

153

"They'll take him away. Section him. I want him here. I don't want to lose him." Her frozen cover melts and she starts to weep.

"Clara." I reach out to her then. Daring to bridge a gap that had always been there. "Get help. I'm in… difficulties as well, but at least they've given me a counsellor. I'll ask her. But please, find a way to stop him drinking."

"I'm scared he'll hit me. Then it will be the end of us."

"No… surely…"

She looks at me, tears streaming down her face.

"Clara?" I don't want to bring it up but I have to ask. "He said he was visited by someone called Brian. Said that there was some information…"

A curious expression forms on her face. She smiles, but her eyes look wild. She turns away for a moment, keeping me waiting. Then whirls round on me with a sudden force. "So! Is that all you want? Information?" She spits the word at me. "You don't care about Burt at all, do you? You're like the rest. Now get out!"

"I'll see what I can…"

"Get out," she shrieks.

I realise, at that moment, that they are both breaking down. They hate the world with a fury that means they will never ask for help.

4.45 pm, Saturday 26th September

I drive home and find that the Merc has gone at last, so I can park outside my house. I run the gauntlet of a couple of journalists, who are standing outside my house in the drizzle, and slam the door in their faces. My phone is ringing, and I pick it up – it's Valerie Redman with a number for the memory clinic. I take a deep breath and call them. It's private, probably horribly expensive, and being Saturday, the office is probably closed, but I need to know about these terrible moments when I lose everything, and I can't risk it getting out. At the moment I feel like I'm being scrutinized from every side.

I feel a mixture of relief and panic when a woman's voice answers. Neutral accent, but kind and encouraging. "As soon as possible?" She pauses. "There may be a space on Monday for an assessment. Someone will call you back."

Monday. The day after tomorrow.

I open up my laptop.

An email pings in from Claire, with the link.

I spend twenty minutes scanning through the report, and checking up on the charity that Witherspoon worked for. All gone. No leads there. But there must still be women around who knew her. Street girls who'd escaped her grasp. But would anyone survive on the streets that long? I do a search online, and discover that a sizeable

155

proportion of people living on the streets of London are over the age of fifty. There might be someone who knew her, maybe even a child of one of the charity workers. But it's all so long ago. If Forester's team had found someone, it would be in the report. If I tried looking for someone in London who knew Witherspoon, it would be like trying to find a needle in a haystack. The trail is dead, there's no use in looking any further – I know, I've been in the force for long enough.

I close the laptop, put on my coat, and take the dog out for a walk, going out the back door to avoid the journalists. The drizzle has settled in for the afternoon. We ramble round the common, rooting in and out of bushes, dells, ponds. Looking for something but having no idea what it is. The common extends up beyond my cottage and we roam up and away from the town. There is a public golf course where golfers and dog walkers share the land in an uneasy contract. I don't like having small hard balls coming in my direction at a hundred miles an hour, so I tend to avoid it. But today, nobody is out hitting balls in the wet.

After an hour of aimless wandering, I sneak in round the back of my cottage, get the dog his dinner, and go down to the Engineer for mine. There is hardly anyone in there, and they aren't serving food yet, so I settle down with a pint, looking out at the gathering gloom and drizzle, and wondering if this will be the night that Charles won't appear for his regulation bar-propping. There is music playing but it changes, irritatingly, from decent oldies to factory pop. My mind follows it for a while, and then I shut it out. What am I going to ask Charles? Is he going to slip away to avoid giving me answers? Is he avoiding me now? How much does he know, but just isn't telling?

As I turn these things around in my mind, I study the table in front of me. There are deep dark grooves in it where countless generations of wax, beer, and varnish have solidified to make a smooth resting place for any food or drink that gets trapped there. I dread to think what festers there, in the cracks between the seemingly clean and beautiful old oak grain that makes up the table's surface.

"Did you find Brian?" Charles' voice is close by my ear and makes me jump. I must have drifted off.

"No," I splutter. " He... he..." I can't get it out. The dog's already into his Charles-welcoming routine – wagging tail, ears up.

"Fancy another?" Charles points to my nearly empty glass, and walks off to his regular seat by the bar. I follow him, deciding, there and then, that my food-cheated stomach will soon be filled with the ham and eggs special that has appeared miraculously on the blackboard by the counter.

"I'd go for the scallops – they're on offer." Charles loves his sea food.

Somehow the slimy origin of shellfish doesn't appeal to me right now. My stomach is still delicate after its recent ravages, and safe comfort food is my yearning tonight.

"I think I'll go for the ham, egg and chips."

Charles scowls and hands me a pint of something dark brown. "Try this. Brewed in someone's garage. Nectar it is."

"Yes, no, thank you. Brian had left the house you told me about. Looked like rented accommodation. How did you...?"

"I went to a meeting there about a month ago. Art appreciation. He knows his stuff does Brian."

A month ago. When I lived in a safe world. "How come I didn't get to hear of it?"

"Oh." Charles clears his throat. "It was, you know, for people who could afford to buy art…"

Poor policemen obviously don't come into that category, even if they have studied art. I wish I could have been there. "I didn't know you were into art to that extent, Charles."

"I'm not, really. I got invited, so I went out of curiosity."

"And Brian was offering something, was he?" This is getting interesting.

"Well, not exactly… he was talking about the quality of copies and prints that you could get on the internet. Amazing the disparity – what people will fall for."

"Copies." I remember the Seurat I saw in the lounge the day that Peggy was shot. That was no copy – that had to be the original. "So Brian's an art expert these days? I never knew what he got into, but I thought it was accounting."

"Well, he seemed to know his stuff, but why the interest in Brian? You used to know him at school, I know, but…?"

"His name came up in relation to Malcolm Smith-Rogers. I am pursuing my own line of enquiry. I've been suspended, so…"

Charles looks down. He knows. "Playing local detective, eh?"

I pause, not sure whether this little exchange is going to help. "Look Charles, anything you can tell me about Brian will help. You've nothing to lose, have you?"

"No. Not at all." He chuckles. "I got his address at the meeting – the one I passed on to you. Interesting that he moved on so quickly. I also got a phone number and email you can have, but that's all. In the end, I decided not to go any further with his art scheme – it didn't seem worth pursuing, and he was so much more interested in the people who already had collections. The last I saw of him, he was leaving with one of them."

"And who were all these lucky people, who could afford to have such good quality art on their walls?"

"I don't know, but I remember getting into a conversation with someone about that BBC series on art. Have you seen it?"

I shake my head. "So you don't remember anything about the people who were there. Surely you remember a name, somebody you knew?" His memory is something I would rely on, more than that of any policeman I have ever known.

"No. They were all new to me. The Avenues have changed so much recently."

"What about the person he left with?"

"Oh, I don't remember his name – bit of a chav."

Charles, you're such a snob sometimes, I reflect. "So you didn't catch the name?"

"Oh, no. I just heard him talking to Brian. Seemed less snobby than the others. Probably why he went off with him."

"And that was the last you saw or heard of Brian?"

"Yes." Mysteriously, Charles has managed to finish his pint of nectar, while I have scarcely started mine.

"My turn," I say, leaning towards the bar lady. Charles is my friend. At this moment, I reflect, he is probably my only friend, and I don't want to piss him off with third-degree police questioning. So I pass him his pint, and tuck into my ham, egg and chips, which appear at the same time, and we chat about the more mundane happenings in our town.

I get home, a little the worse for beer, to find that the small posse of journalists has decamped for the night. The dog and I go to our separate beds, and sleep comes easily to me. But I wake in the middle of the night, my mind

159

buzzing with a memory of the most wanted man in America I once read about. He was discovered living quite openly on the west coast – his walls displaying his stolen art, for over twenty years.

I suddenly want to find out more about the art on the walls of these houses, and why Brian was so interested. If I went up to London, I would be able to reacquaint myself with all that wonderful art that resided in the great city, and maybe even do more research into any paintings that might be missing. I feel like a teenager – eager and hopeful. Tintin on the trail. Then I collapse into the pillows with a yawn: 'no Arnold, you're too old. Your memory's going, and you're suspended from duty. You're in a mess. Stop now, before you get into a worse one.'

9.05 am, Monday 28th September

I wake up to the sound of my landline and the doorbell ringing at the same time. I plump for the phone as being closer and grab it just in time to hear the dial tone. Pulling my bedroom curtains back an inch, I look out onto the balding head of a man I don't recognize. The doorbell goes again, a long ring – insistent, hectoring, and I look down to the pavement to see a group of journalists standing outside my house. Well they can wait, but the phone?

I pick it up again to hear the message-tone, and dial 1571.

It's from the memory clinic in London: "We can see you this afternoon, at 3.30. Please let us know if you can attend this appointment." The voice is clipped, but friendly.

3.30? I look at my watch. It is already after nine. No wonder the journalists are out there. They'll have had their breakfasts and all. I go to the bathroom, to the further sound of ringing doorbell, and have a shower. Choose some shabby but robust clothes. Pack a rucksack, with pyjamas and a change of clothes. The rucksack will give me both hands to handle the dog.

The dog! I've forgotten all about him. He must be bursting and hungry. I dash down the stairs to the kitchen to find a puddle on the kitchen floor, and the dog looking guilty – ears down, tail wagging meekly between legs.

"Poor old thing. Not your fault. We're both getting old." I pat him and let him out of the kitchen door, having looked to see if any journalists have come round the back. All clear for the time being. Mop up the puddle as best I can. I put on the kettle, but then think better of it – I could leave now and pick up something on the train.

I call the dog in and give him his breakfast. Phone the clinic to confirm, and let myself out of the back door. The idiot journalist has started banging on the front door as well as ringing.

I pause in the back garden, and look over at Betty's house. Should I take a quick look? See if she's left any clues as to where she's gone, and who with? Part of me is very reluctant to go anywhere near her house and her belongings. For a moment anger wells up inside me. She betrayed me, she cheated on me.

But another part of me is saying, 'Calm down Arnold. You know it was all finished years ago. Stop pretending and feeling all justified, and be thankful she's set you free.'

Her backdoor key's on my key-ring in case of emergencies, and I let myself in cautiously – I don't want any journalists catching sight of me from the front.

Fortunately she had drawn the front curtains before she left – for her own reasons, I suspect, and I am able to wander through her domain, glancing around in the gloom to see if anything is out of place. I get my mobile phone out, and use the torch to look more carefully. The dog's whimpering softly by the back door – he evidently doesn't like being in here, and I wonder what neglect or cruelty might have happened while Betty was supposed to be looking after him.

This place, that used to be my home, seems strange now. Nothing of me remains – no photos, no memories. Like I've been obliterated from her life. No pictures of

Malcolm either though, which gives me some satisfaction. I guess she wanted to conceal that part of her life to the end.

The kitchen sink gives me an idea. I cautiously ease open the cupboard underneath, and find some rubber gloves. A bit small, but useable for my search. Now I can open cupboards and drawers without leaving my prints everywhere. Funny that – mustn't leave my fingerprints in my own wife's house.

There isn't much to see downstairs, so I go up. The bathroom shows signs of a hasty exit – cupboards left open, a toothbrush on its side in the sink, a towel on the floor.

I go into her bedroom – somewhere I haven't been for so many years. On the bed lies a rejected dress with a petticoat poking out from underneath. Pretty, sexy clothes. Not meant for me, but for Malcolm. I rampage through her bedroom, searching for clues, tearing out drawers and flinging her underwear all over the room. Pretty lingerie worn, not for me, but for him. Pretty dresses in the wardrobe. I scatter her clothes round the room, fury building up in me. All these years of not seeing her in these. Just trogging on faithfully next door, paying the mortgage. I ball both cold rubber gloves into my eyes, and sit on her bed, convulsed with grief.

The dog barks, taking me out of my self-pity, and I come to, realising where I am. I go to the top of the stairs, and talk gently down to him.

"Just a minute. I'll just check one more thing."

The bedside table. I pull open the drawer to find a pile of hotel leaflets. London. Paris. Vienna. Buenos Aires. Her dreams, or were they? I pick them up and shove them in my pocket.

I can't clear up my mess. I don't want to, in fact I can't bear to touch those sullied clothes now. Let her or my so-

163

called colleagues find this. They can make of it what they will. My grief has turned to energy and I'm off, away from the journalists and my pathetic past. I run down the stairs, stuffing the gloves into my rucksack. Picking up the dog's lead, I leave the house with the door locked, and run down the common, leaving the posse of journalists to hammer on my front door.

10.30 am, Monday 28th September

The dog and I head for London. Waifs and strays – fugitives in fact. Running from the press, and Forester, who will not be pleased to know that I've left town. He'll probably have me put under lock and key if he catches up with me.

The train is half empty – half clean. We find a seat by the window, where the dog can be out of the way. You don't get many dogs on trains. People look, make comments, want to touch. I don't want to get noticed, but I am bound to be – man and dog on train. Fortunately the journey is only half an hour, and by the time I've bought and consumed a cold bacon sandwich, and attempted to turn a bag, drifting around in tepid water, into a cup of tea, the train is slowing into St Pancras.

Why do we always have to walk fast on train platforms? Why the urgency? I am in London, hours before my appointment. I have no train to catch. Am I afraid that I'll be caught, and put on the next train home?

I get pulled into the stream of humanity that bustles and hammers its way through the turnstiles, find a wide one for me and the dog, and I'm out on the teaming street before I have a chance to wonder which direction I should be going in.

The dog cocks his leg against a lamp post. At least it's just a wee, but oh shit! Literally. I have no dog poo bags, and no idea what to do with the poo when I've picked one up.

I imagine going up to a policeman: 'Excuse me officer, what do I do with this?' Swinging the black bag of poo around nonchalantly. The officer looks at me with an ''allo 'allo wot 'ave we 'ere' expression on his large benevolent face. "Nearest deposit box would be in Hyde Park. Sir." He puts the 'sir' in reluctantly as an afterthought. Probably would have said 'my lad' in times gone past. Hyde Park! That's miles away. "Dogs don't do it in this part of London," he says, reading my mind. And I imagine showing him my Inspector Rackham card and saying, "Mine does," and handing him the bag, as I wander off to inspect the underworld of crime that so besets London's streets.

The dog finishes his wee, and treading delicately over the stream of urine that is making its way across the pavement, I walk along the great arterial dual-carriageway that still grinds through the city. Looking at my watch, it's not even eleven o'clock, so I've got plenty of time to kill before my appointment at the clinic. A coffee first, I think, there's bound to be good coffee to be had in London. Then Mothercare for nappy bags, unless I see a pet shop first.

Eventually finding a place that looks less like a slow moving M1, I try to cross over. It seems to take about half an hour for the lights to change in the favour of pedestrians. No dogs off the lead here, I think. They'd be dead in a minute. I walk down more promising side streets, past offices, milliners, travel agents, clothes boutiques, and finally find what looks like an Italian café. There are still tables outside, but it's a chilly day for September, and there's a snug little place inside for me and the dog.

"No dogs in here." The accent is definitely not Italian, and the coffee, when I sit outside on a cold metal chair, is tepid and bitter. Still, there is definitely caffeine in there somewhere, and charged up, I go on my way towards the West End, with a vague idea about future food and poo bags.

People just don't walk their dogs around Central London, and I can see why. Negotiating the dog through throngs of tourists, office workers, shoppers, and anyone who wants to bustle and rush about a busy city is a nightmare. He doesn't get trodden on, but I do. I feel like an ant with a wooden leg.

After a while of struggling against the human tide, we manage to get off the main thoroughfare and down a side alley. It's quiet with tall buildings on either side cutting out the sun. A service road, I guess. It seems like the back of everything. No windows, just doorways set back in red brick walls.

As I gaze at this peaceful, if bleak, place I notice a pair of legs sticking out into the street from one of the doorways. The dog tugs at his lead, and I follow, intrigued. As we get nearer, a brown snout pokes out from the doorway, and the dog tugs harder as he detects a friendly face in this city of knees.

"Red," barks a grumpy female voice that must belong to the legs. The snout disappears, and I slow down, pulling my usually obedient dog back, as we near the doorway.

The sight that meets our eyes is definitely red in colour. The dog is smaller than my Lab, and of indeterminate origin. His fur is a reddish brown, but he's eclipsed by his owner who wears red from tip to toe. Red wellies, red skirt, red anorak, red scarf, and bright red hair. She's old, but how old is hard to tell. She's got a few years on me, I'm sure, but she doesn't look like she's dying. Far from it. There's a ruggedness about her face. Resolute lines in the face of adversity make her complexion a map of smiles and frowns. I find it hard to tell what expression she is giving me, but the dogs are definitely getting on. Wagging tails, and not a growl anywhere.

"Er, sorry. My dog…"

We look at each other. This is not love at first sight, but there is something of a camaraderie between us. The transformer lines in her face form themselves into what is definitely a smile, and I find myself smiling back.

"Do you fancy a cup of something hot?" Her accent is surprising – something between East End and BBC. Very dark brown eyes look at me from this canvas of red.

"I'd love one." I shiver. "Is there somewhere that lets dogs in?"

"There's something round the corner that's not all health-and-safety. Lets me in – can't be." She chuckles in a wheezy smoker's way, and gets to her feet slowly and painfully. I offer her a hand but she waves it off, pulling herself upright with the help of the doorway. It is then that I realise she is bent almost double with some sort of spinal problem – it makes her body short compared to her legs and she barely comes up to my shoulder.

Coughing and grumbling to herself, she totters off down the alley, her dog now obedient by her side, held by a piece of string, to whatever holds up her red skirt. Wondering what I am getting myself into, I follow – my dog is less obedient than hers, and keeps tugging at his lead, trying to get level with 'Red', his newfound friend.

The 'something round the corner' turns out to be a real 'greasy spoon' of the kind that have got increasingly rare with the advent of healthy eating, or unhealthy burger chains. We find a table by the door – my companion seems keen to be close to the fresh air. The dogs settle comfortably, nose to nose under the table.

"You want your usual, Lilly?" The waitress is with us almost immediately. She sounds Polish and smiles down on us two naughty doggy people.

"Yes, dear."

"And you?" She turns her smile on me.

"Tea, please." I don't want to chance the coffee.

"Something to eat?" Ah, I am expected to eat. I smell bacon. Irresistible.

"Bacon and eggs, please."

"White or brown?" I feel confused for a moment. Oh, toast.

"White, please." Good and unhealthy.

The waitress goes off, leaving us to find a way to start a conversation.

"So what you doing here? Up in the big city." She gets there first. Anyway, I have a good idea what she's doing – surviving.

"Came up for an appointment."

"With your dog?" She looks at me quizzically.

"Well I…"

"And what do you do?"

"For a living you mean? I'm a policeman." It comes out before I've thought how it might seem to her.

"A policeman, eh?" She rumbles and coughs. "I thought you were familiar with the streets."

"I'm not very familiar with London. Never brought the dog along before."

"So," she looks at me shrewdly, "are you running away from something or running after it?"

"A bit of both really." The truth has a funny way of finding you sometimes. There's something about her that makes me want to talk.

"So?"

"I'm keeping away from the press. I got involved in a case – nearly got murdered." What am I doing, telling her this?

"Murdered?" Her voice drops to a whisper.

"There was this old woman. She tried to poison me. We found lots of bodies in the garden."

"What sort of bodies?" She's unhealthily interested.

"Girls. Probably been there since the sixties."

"The sixties? They'd be skeletons now." She has a strange far-away look in her eyes.

"We think she brought them back from London. Her charity work with the homeless." I wonder how long Lilly's been on the streets. Maybe decades. Could she have known any of them? She would have been the right age, but the chances of her being involved… she just likes a good story.

"And she murdered them? And then she tried to murder you?" She focuses intently on me.

"I knew her when I was a boy. Matron at my school. Used to go round to tea. Then this…" I can't go on. I'm not going to tell her about the abuse. Enough.

"So is she in prison? This…"

"Cornelia Witherspoon." I take a risk – it's all over the papers anyway.

She stiffens. Looks away, and for the first time I notice how her hands tremble.

"Here you are." The waitress returns with our food. My bacon and eggs look sparse alongside her full English. I wonder if I am providing her meal for the day – I assume I'm paying. Her coffee smells delicious. But she just looks at it. "Is everything OK? Do you want your usual sauces? Lilly?"

Lilly just looks.

"Are you alright?" I lean forward.

She shakes her head. "Be alright in a minute," she wheezes.

The waitress goes away, and I decide to carry on as though nothing has happened. "So the press want to hear my story. All the gruesome details of how I knew her when

I was young. And I'm in trouble with my bosses." I smile, hoping she will pick this up. "I argued with them too much."

She sits there in silence as though she hasn't even heard me.

"Err... Lilly, are you OK?"

"I knew her," Lilly whispers.

I stare at her. Is she having me on? She's the right age, but what are the chances of bumping into the first street person I've met in London, and finding she knew Cornelia Witherspoon? Maybe she's hoping for a nice big hand-out, but she's a bloody good actress, I'll give her that.

The waitress comes back with the sauces. "Oh, she's having one of her turns. She'll come out of it in a minute." She puts her hand on Lilly's shoulder. "Alright, dear?"

Lilly continues to stare straight ahead. "She's in prison. Right?"

"She does come out with these funny stories when she's not quite..." The waitress points at her own head, and does a little circle with her finger.

"It's alright. I can take care of this. I'm a... social worker."

"With a dog?" The waitress looks me up and down and leaves.

"Yes, she's in custody. You knew her?"

Lilly nods, then starts to eat. She chops her bacon and sausages up small, and chews carefully on each mouthful. I wonder if her teeth are her own. Her teeth. I suddenly have images of the forensics going through all those teeth and checking dental records. Where did all these girls come from, and why were they on the street in the first place? And was she one of them?

I start on my bacon and eggs. The bacon seems salty and, unlike Lilly, I've lost my appetite. I struggle on, looking at her from time to time, but she just eats her way steadily through her vast plate of food.

Is she going to spin me a yarn? Is this what she does – a way of gaining company and a free meal? The waitress seemed to hint at it. But my policeman's instinct tells me different. I have interviewed so many people who don't want to tell me the truth, I hope I might be able to tell the difference.

Eventually she stops eating. There is nothing left to eat. She looks down, burps softly, and then turns her penetrating eyes straight at me.

"How do I know you're who you say you are? How do I know you're not going to trick me, and lock me up?"

I get out my police identity.

She looks at it, wrinkling her nose up as if it smells bad.

"So you're police. But why should I trust you?"

"But you trusted me earlier."

"This is different. I don't want to get into trouble… like before." She looks forlorn at this moment – a frightened old lady in red.

I have an idea. "It'll be in the papers. There'll be my photo." If the press were hammering on my door this morning, they must be running the story. "Have you finished?" I call the waitress over and pay the bill. I look at Lilly. "Coming?"

Reluctantly she gets up. My dog tries to follow hers and gets entangled in a table leg. By the time I've sorted him out, she's disappearing down the street at a pace. I catch her up as she turns the corner.

"Just down 'ere," she mutters.

We stop by a small newsagent's. "You go in. I'll take care of the dogs."

I walk in, hoping she doesn't nick my dog, and look at the papers on the stand. My picture hasn't made the front page on any of them, thank God. A tabloid is more likely to be running this story. I pick one up and leaf through. It doesn't take long. There is the picture of me, tears streaming down my face, with the caption 'Poor old Inspector Arnold'. I look back to the front page, and there is the story with a photo of the house looking appropriately spooky. I pay the Asian man behind the counter, worrying all the time that he will recognize me from the photo in the newspaper. He looks bored as he takes my money. I am in London. Anonymous .

Out on the street, Lilly is much more interested. She looks at the photo. Looks at me. And then smiles. "You poor thing. You were so upset."

"Actually, I was crying with laughter." She looks at me sharply. " No, no, it wasn't to do with the murders. I'd just had a spat with a fearsome old cop, and come out of it rather well. It struck me as very funny at the time." Not so funny now, though.

"Fancy a walk?" For all her creaking bones and wrinkles, this woman's got energy. "We can talk." She's off down Oxford Street, dodging the crowds with expertise, and I stumble along behind trying to keep up. Suddenly the dog goes into a spasm. I know what that means. Back arched, legs stiff. Oh no, a poo is descending onto the pavement. No bag. No means of taking it out of the way of some unsuspecting pedestrian. As I stand there helpless, I feel a nudge at my elbow. Lilly is offering me a bag, bless her. She's on top of all this.

"Thanks. I was going to pick some up at Mothercare," I say scooping up the offending sausage and tying it into an unattractive bundle.

"You can get them at Boots. There's loads of Boots." The expert speaks. "You can dump that at Hyde Park. Come on." And I follow her through the crowds, swinging my little bag, self-consciously.

Hyde Park. A blessed oasis in this overcrowded city. We can walk and talk freely.

1pm, Monday 28th September

"She used to come up every couple of weeks. She was so much younger than the others." Lilly makes a face. "Help. That's what they called it. 'Find you a nice place off the streets, dear'." Lilly's posh accent comes out bitterly. "What if we didn't want a 'nice place' – just wanted to be left alone with a bit of extra help with clothing and food? I'd heard of those 'nice places'. They didn't sound very nice to me."

"So you kept out of it." Our dogs are wandering amiably together, looking at trees and lamp posts, in the way dogs have. I am keeping a beady eye out for any little messages they might want to leave, my newly-acquired packet of scented salmon-pink nappy bags at the ready.

"Yes, I just hung around on the edge of things, trying to get food and the odd blanket. But I didn't want to be inside anywhere. Can't stand it for long." She shivers – the cold fear of containment, her deep claustrophobia showing through.

"And Cornelia Witherspoon?"

"Well, she was different. Much younger than the others. Girls used to like to hang around with her and talk."

"What about?"

"She said she had this dream. She would be able to help us by finding a place to live, and work to do, and it would be wonderful, and get us out of London. She wanted to

175

know about us and our pasts, and why we left home. She said that if there was no hope of us ever going back, or our family finding us, then she would provide the solution. Her 'permanent solution', she called it. We weren't to talk to the other helpers about it, because they wouldn't approve, and would try to stop her. Anyway, none of us wanted to talk to them because they were... you know... in a different world to us. She was the only one we trusted."

Rank evil, I reflect. It reminds me of how the Nazis lured the Jews onto trains, saying how they were going to take them to a better place. "It's a shame you didn't trust the other helpers," I say.

She turns on me. "You weren't there. And you don't know the whole story. How do you think you can judge?" She spits the words out in sudden fury, and turns away in silence.

I catch her arm, and at first she tries to pull away, and then I feel her shake. As I look into her face she's crying. "I'm sorry, that was a stupid thing to say."

"You're the first person who's listened to me in a long time. They've always thought I was mad. Mad old Lilly. But I was there. I knew."

I think back to the waitress and her 'she comes out with these funny stories'. She could be making it all up. There's nothing she's said so far that proves she knew Witherspoon. It could have been some other young helper, but I decide to bury my mistrust. "I'm sorry," I say. "I believe you completely. I've been there too, you know."

"I need to sit down. Not feeling too good." We find a bench, well apart from others, where we can watch the dogs while we talk.

"So how did it all start?" I ask.

"Well, one day after she'd left we couldn't find Jane. Plain Jane we called her, but she was really very pretty.

176

Hated her family and her past. Wanted nothing to do with them. Girls were coming and going all the time, but I used to talk to Jane, and I wouldn't expect her just to go. Say nothing and just leave. We didn't talk to anyone about it. Jane didn't want her family to find her, so she kept out of the way of the helpers, all except…"

"Cornelia Witherspoon."

"Right. So when she came the next weekend, we all grouped round her, and asked if she knew where Jane was. She didn't say anything to start with, but when she could see the other helpers were out of hearing, she said that she had found Jane a nice home and a job out of London, but she was having to be very careful, because Jane didn't want to be found by her family, and if we told, then she would get into trouble with the authorities, and she wouldn't be able to help any of us like she helped Jane. Well, we liked having a secret. Our own big secret. And we were used to keeping things to ourselves, so we all kept very quiet about it."

"Still, I'm amazed she got away with it. All those girls disappearing. Surely someone would have noticed."

"Like I said, girls came and went all the time, and after that conversation with her we were very careful not to be seen in a group round her. She didn't take someone every weekend – just every now and then. And of course we covered up for her so she wouldn't get found out, and whoever went with her would have a good chance of a future life." Lilly breaks down and cries bitterly.

I sit holding her arm and staring out into the park. The dogs are ferreting about in a bush, and I wonder whether I will have to rush out with a nappy bag at any moment. I hope I won't – Lilly is telling her story, and I want to work out if it's true.

"How many of you?"

"There were ten in our group, and one by one, the other girls left with her to find a better life."

"Ten? But we dug up twenty bodies."

"Twenty bodies? Twenty? I thought we were the only ones. Twenty." Lilly stares into the middle distance. She just sits there. Silent.

"So how come you are still here?"

"I was the last one of our group left. I don't think she liked me as much as the others. I was always on the fringe of things, and I wasn't pretty at all. Always looked like I'd swallowed a lemon. Anyway, when all my friends had gone, I started to shadow her, and she noticed that. I don't think she liked it. 'Don't keep following me round Lilly. You don't want your friends to lose their jobs and homes, do you?' But I said I would like a chance too, so she told me to wait, and she'd see what she could do."

The dogs have met a couple of spaniels. All very friendly – sniffing bums, wagging tails. No problem there.

"It was only a couple of weeks later when she found me on my own and she said, 'see you outside the ladies' at St Pancras. 4.30. Don't be late, if you're not there you'll have missed your chance.' She bustled off to help in the soup queue. I couldn't wait. I joined the queue, and waited for my bowl of watery soup and slice of bread. I just wanted to see her and exchange secret glances. When I got opposite to her she ignored me completely. I could have been invisible.

"In those days I used to wear dirty brown clothes. It all went with my wish to go unnoticed – creep around on the fringes of life. Like most of the girls, I was terrified of being found. I didn't want to go back to my family. Not ever.

"Anyway, I was outside the ladies' loos at quarter past four. Didn't want to be late, did I? I remember I was clutching a small bag containing a few treasures. I'd dumped most of my stash in a doorway. Wouldn't be needing it any more, or so I thought.

"She appeared, just before half past, looking angry. 'How long have you been hanging around here?' she hissed. 'Don't want to draw attention to ourselves, do we?' And she was off at a pace heading for a train that was already getting up steam. All the carriages had separate compartments in those days. No corridor. She chose an empty one, and I clambered in after her.

"She signalled for me to sit opposite to her and looked me up and down, wrinkling her nose. 'God you stink'. She got up – I thought she was going to leave me there, but she just moved over to the window and opened it, letting in the smell of smoke and steam from the engine at the front. We started to move then, and I remember being so excited. I was off to a new life. Never been on a train before. The chug-chug of the engine. The squeal of the rails. Then the regular clunkity-clunk, as I made my way to a new life.

"She didn't talk to me at all. Just looked out of the window and scowled. There were only a couple of stops and then we were there.

"'Get out. Come on,' she said. She had lost her gentle warm side, and was all impatient and harsh. I stood on the platform feeling lost, and suddenly afraid. There was no one on the platform. Just me and her. The train started to move away, and I realised I'd left my little bag of treasures on the seat. She saw me turn back to try and get on the train.

'No you don't.' She grabbed my arm and pulled me back.

'But I left…'

'Stupid girl. You'll just have to do without it now.' She was even angrier now. Kept muttering about leaving things for people to find.

"We walked out of the station and saw a porter coming towards us. 'Don't say a word,' she hissed. I was so scared then, I couldn't of anyway.

"'Hi Bob,' she said, all smiles. 'Brought her back for a clean-up and a bit of food. Needs it, poor dear.'

"He looked at me and held his breath. 'You're a saint, Miss Witherspoon, and no mistake.'

"She walked me quickly to a waiting car. 'He's never here at this time,' she muttered under her breath. 'Bloody man.' She opened the rear door of the car and shoved me in. The seats and floor were covered in newspaper. I thought it must be because we were all so dirty, and she wanted to protect her car. It was quite a posh car. All black and shiny, but I shook there, in that enclosed space. She got in the other side and pulled me down so I was lying on the seat. 'Home mother', was all she said, and we rolled off gently down the road in the gloom of the evening."

"So her mother drove the car?" I never saw Witherspoon's mother move from her chair.

"Yes," Lilly goes on impatiently. "Everything seemed dark then, and I was wondering how she was going to find me a home and a job. Would it be straight away? What would the people be like? How could all this work? The more I thought, the more terrified I felt. I used to get dizzy fits at that time, especially when I hadn't eaten anything, and I felt everything going round and round, but I didn't say anything.

"The car stopped and she let me get up. My head was still spinning, but I pretended I was alright. I put my hand on the outside of the car to support myself getting out, but she pulled me away, whipping out a hanky to wipe where my hand had been. She hissed at me, 'Can't have you leaving your dirty hand prints on my nice clean car, can we.'

"She half dragged me into the house. I remember it had a funny smell. In spite of me being a bit pongy from being on the streets, I've got a good sense of smell, and there was something there that wasn't right. Something dead. The house looked tidy in a fussy kind of way, but it was a house, and I realised that I didn't want to be in it. I didn't want to be inside at all. I began to panic as she pulled me into the kitchen.

"'Sit down there, and I'll get you something to drink,' she said. She went over to a cupboard and poured something out. 'A bit of cordial. That should do it. Make you feel better. Down in one.' There was a rustle from the other side of the room, and she was distracted for a moment. I sniffed the drink. It didn't smell right, so I poured it down the inside of my dress.

"'It's a rat. Mother, we've got a rat in the kitchen. Mother!'

"Mother came shuffling in. She looked like a zombie. White as a sheet. All her movements were stiff. It was all too much for me – the room swam before my eyes, and I fell off the chair, dropping my glass which smashed on the tile floor.

"I felt someone nudge me with there foot. I remember Cornelia laughed and it wasn't a nice laugh. 'Well, that worked quickly,' she said. 'Mother, come and give me a hand.'

"I saw their shadows stooping over me, but I must have passed out, because the next thing I knew I was in the dark on a cold floor. The smell was terrible.

"I got myself up feeling bruised all over, and felt my way along a wall until I found a light switch. What I saw when the light went on nearly made me pass out again. A girl was lying naked on a table in the middle of the room – her head turned away as though she was asleep. I went round the table to look at her face. It was Fran – the last of us to disappear before I begged Witherspoon to let me come. She was a funny colour and she stank. She must have been dead for quite a long time. So this was the future – her 'permanent solution.' No home, no job. Just death.

"I realised I was in a cellar. I had to get out, but there was no way, except the door in the corner at the top of the stairs. They must have dragged me down there, which was why I was so bruised. I could feel myself beginning to panic, and I knew that once I let that take over, I would collapse and give up. Survive, I thought. I looked around for a weapon, but all I could find was an old broom. I got hold of it, and cautiously made my way up the stairs. As I reached the top I heard her voice. 'Did we leave the light on mother?'

"There was a grunt.

"'I'd better check.' A key turned in the door and it began to open. I was squeezed behind it, hoping she wouldn't feel my presence . As she came past me down the stairs I made a desperate swipe at her with the broom handle. I caught her on the shoulder and she turned around. I raised the broom again but she caught hold of it and started to drag me down towards her. I could feel myself slipping and being pulled towards her, but I shoved the broom at her letting go of it and turned to run out of the door.

"'Mother! Stop her!' she cried as she staggered back.

"But I was too fast for the stiff old crone, and I dodged past her and ran down a passage, I'd no idea of where I was going. I saw the kitchen on my left – the hall with the front door was straight ahead of me. I could hear Witherspoon running up the corridor behind me as I reached to open the front door. Locked.

"'Got her!' she shouted.

"But I dodged to the side of her and ran into what must have been the sitting room. I remember seeing those

French windows, and thinking, this is it. I grabbed a paperweight off the table as I went in, hurled it at one of the windows, smashing the glass, and ran straight through it and out into the garden – I could feel the broken glass catching my legs and head.

"It was dark outside. I wondered whether I should scream – whether anyone would hear me. I thought better of it, and ran into the darkness round the side of the house, away from the light coming from the windows. She didn't follow me out of the broken window, but as I crept round with my hand against the wall, I saw a light moving, picking out the trees to my right. As I peered round the corner of the house, I could see her with a torch, searching the garden. Beyond her was the road, with street lights and freedom. I pulled back and froze against the wall, hoping she wouldn't see me, and that I could run into the road when she'd gone past me.

"The light got nearer, and I could hear her muttering, 'Where are you, you little rat? Think you can escape from me?'

"Then I heard her sniffing. 'I can smell you, you dirty…'

"She came round the corner. The light was full in my face, and I hit at it, knocking it out of her hand. She made a grab at me, but desperation made me too fast for her, and I ran past her and out of the front drive onto the road.

"I thought I was free then, but she came after me so I ran down the road, looking for somewhere to hide. Hoping there'd be someone about. It was silent – it was the middle of the night. There were no lights on in the houses. I didn't know where I was, and she was behind me. Eventually she would catch me, and that would be that. One more dead street girl.

"I managed to keep ahead of her, in spite of I was gasping for breath, and I put on a sudden burst of speed

183

and turned into the front drive of a large house. There was a sloping track down to the right and I raced down there, hoping I wouldn't collide with anything in the dark. I could hear her feet crunching on the gravel behind me, but she'd run after me without picking up her torch so we were both in the dark now.

"I slowed down and looked for somewhere to hide. As I felt along the wall to my left, I found a small window, low enough for me to climb in. It was a sash window, and I lifted the lower part which gave me just enough room to clamber inside. The floor was lower than I expected, and I stumbled forward into the room. The sash window banged closed behind me, and I was in, sheltering in the dark, hoping she would go past, but she must have heard the noise and she stopped by the window. She pulled it up and I just could make out her shadow as she started to climb in.

"'I can smell you, you little rat,' she whispered as she squeezed her bulk through the small gap. It was totally dark, so she couldn't see me as I felt my way along the walls and out of a door into a bigger space. I could smell apples coming from my left. I thought if I got near them, they would cover up my smell, and she'd never find me. I felt my way through a doorway into a small space with shelves covered with apples. I crept into the back corner, and curled up into a ball. I could hear her breathing as she came closer to the apple store.

"'Clever eh? Well I've got you now.' She must have been at the entrance to the store, and as I pressed back trying to get away from her, the wall behind me gave way, and I found myself in an open space that smelt of earth.

"'I don't know why you didn't die from the poison I gave you, but you'll be dead meat once I've got you back. You'll never escape from me. Not from Cornelia Witherspoon. I will find you and take you back, and then we'll see. Then we'll see.' Her mad whispering covered up my stealthy movements as I slipped back into the space I'd discovered and quietly closed the little door that I'd fallen through, holding it firmly shut with my feet. She went on and on about how she was going to find me, and how she could smell me, but I just remained in my dark hiding place as still as a mouse."

"Eventually the sounds went away, but I didn't move. I must have stayed there for hours, cooped up in the dark."

2.15 pm, Monday 28th September

The dogs have gone. Completely disappeared.

"Oh bugger!" Lilly curses. "Red! Red, come here!"

I feel panic rising. My dog has no experience of this kind of traffic. Roads cross Hyde Park. Roads border it. And they're all busy. I'm standing up now – looking around wildly. I put my fingers to my lips and whistle so piercingly that people look round and stare at us. We'd got so immersed in Lilly's story – the horror of it is still rebounding in my mind. Calm down, Arnold. Calm down.

A bush to the left of us erupts and out fly our two dogs, bits of foliage jettisoned in all directions. They are pursued by a large Alsatian, and three tiny King Charles spaniels.

Before I have time to consider whether they are about to be eaten, or it's just a game, a large beefy woman in tweeds appears and shouts at us, "I say, can you call your dogs off. They won't leave mine alone." She is followed by a diminutive man in what looks like a diving suit, who calls out in a plaintive high pitched voice, "Sonja darling. Sonja dear, come here sweetie."

The Alsatian turns, and trots obediently towards her eccentric owner.

"That's Oscar," Lilly whispers to me. "He always goes out running with Sonja at this time. He's very sweet really."

The tweedy lady on the other hand is far from sweet. She has no control over her dogs, who will not give up the game, and insist on following ours round and round our seat.

"Sit," I command. My dog sits, facing its tormentors. So does Red, and so do we.

"Right," says the tweedy horror. "Right, er right."

She is fighting something inside her. I can't work out what her problem is. Then she says, "Jootsie, Wootsie, Tootsie! Come!"

I feel a smile spreading over my face – what ridiculous names, and they take not the blindest bit of notice of her. "Yap, yap, yap," they go, and she has to pin each one down to get its lead on.

"Now, don't do that again," she says, and I'm not sure whether it's meant for us or her ménage à trois. She gives Lilly a scornful look and drags her little 'ootsies' off, leaving us to pick up the pieces of Lilly's story.

"How did you get out of there? And how on earth did you get back to London?" I'm still scared for this young waif who so nearly got murdered by the psychotic Cornelia. I'm beginning to believe her story, even though it sounds like she's been making it up all her life. The dogs have settled down after their little escapade, and are sitting peacefully at our feet.

"I don't know how long it was I waited there, but when I finally crept out and found my way through the little window onto the drive it was beginning to get light."

"Weren't you afraid?"

"I was scared alright, but I had to get away. I didn't trust anyone in that horrible town. I thought that any one of them could of taken me back to her. So anyway, I crept along the wall of the big house, and up towards the gate onto the road."

"Can you remember if there was a name? If the house had a name by the gate?"

I was sure it had to be...

"'Hazelbank.'"

Bingo. She couldn't have made that up. Now I know how you find a needle in a haystack – you sit on it.

"I remember it 'cos my mother was called Hazel, and I was glad to leave her too. Anyway, as I made for the gate I heard a voice shouting, 'What do you think you're doing?' So I ran as fast as I could, and went and hid in another garden until the coast was clear.

"It was a nightmare getting out of that horrible town. Everybody looked at me, and I was sure someone would grab me and take me back to her. But they just turned their noses up and got on with whatever, while I tried to find the train station. Luckily the town wasn't that big, so after a while I found Station Road, which had to be the way to the station. But would she be there, waiting for me? With her porter friend? 'You're such a saint'. But the platform was empty. No-one was waiting 'cept me."

"How do you remember all this? Why haven't you told anybody before?"

"Oh, I've told this story before... loads of times. Don't tell me you don't believe me either!"

"Yes, but before? But I thought I was... sorry, sorry." She looks so angry, I shut up.

"You'll see. You'll see." She looks down, and grasping her knobbly hands together, she starts to rock backwards and forwards. Red looks up, and places his muzzle on her knee. This seems to bring her back to herself, and she continues with her story.

"So there I was, alone on the station. This creepy feeling that at any moment someone would come and grab me. But nobody did, an' a train came, and I got on it and went to London. There was a ticket barrier at St Pancras.

Of course I didn't have a ticket, so I thought I'd make myself invisible and sneak past the blokes at the barrier, but just as I thought I'd got through, someone grabs me and says, 'What do you think you're doing?'

"'I got to go. Got an appointment.' I says.

"'Oh no you haven't.' He says.

"'My poor old gran's dying.' I put my saddest face on.

"'Oh no she isn't,' and he grabbed me and took me to the station master, who called the police. So I told them. Told them everything. All about how I was nearly murdered, and how I got away. There I was, covered in cuts and bruises. The police, I thought. They'll do something."

"And did they?" I think I know what's coming.

"Yes, they took me to the loony bin."

I didn't see that coming. "A mental hospital?"

"Yes, and I was treated for delusions. Pa-ra-noi-yah!" She spits it out. "They thought I was fucking mad."

"How long?" I'm dreading the answer.

"I'm not saying." She is suddenly incandescent with anger. "It was that woman who got me out."

"What, Cornelia?"

"No. Thatcher. Care in the fucking community. I was one of the lucky ones."

"So you were in there…?" I want to calculate, but I can't bear it.

"But there was someone," she says.

"Someone?"

"Someone who believed me while I was stuck in there. A nurse. She was different. She listened."

"And?" I ask.

"And it was no good. No one took any notice of her, and she left. Don't know what became of her." Lilly looks gentle for a moment. "But that is why I can remember it all so clearly. I held on to it. To my story. It was my truth.

190

I didn't want to lose it, and give in to them and their drugs. Do you still believe me – do you think I'm mad?"

"I just can't believe I found you. A survivor." Like me, I think. "No, I know you're not mad. I've been there, remember." I look down at my hands. My wrist. My watch. "Shit. I've got my appointment."

"Appointment? Oh yeah, I remember. What's it for?'

She's opened up to me, I have to tell her. "Memory clinic," I mutter.

"What?"

"I think I've got dementia."

"You kidding? There's nothing wrong with your mind." She looks at me with such venom. "You be careful. Don't let them mess with it."

"Look, I've got to go. Can you help me? I don't know London, I know it's near here." I tell her the address.

"A doddle. How long have we got?"

I look at my watch again. "Fifteen minutes."

She whistles. "Better get going then."

3.30 pm, Monday 28ᵗʰ September

We're there on the dot of 3.30. Hallowed portals greet me. Marble steps and clean glass doors.

"Look, I'll need your help to put Witherspoon away for ever. Will you make a…?"

"I'll wait here with the dogs," Lilly says abruptly. I know she'd rather die than go in that building. 'You hold onto your soul,' I think as I enter. Do I mean her or me? I walk across a marble floor, and pause, uncertain what to do, halfway to the dark oak counter that protects the pretty young receptionist from the old and crazy like me.

"Mr Rackham?" The receptionist has the edge on me here. I'm used to giving my name and seeing a lot of shuffling through diaries, but this lady is expecting me. Ah, the private sector. Mmm. I think I recognise her voice from the phone call this morning. Odd thing that so often it's hard to tell people's ages from their voices. I had imagined a Mrs Moneypenny in her forties.

I repress the urge to say 'Inspector Rackham' and, after allowing her to swipe my credit card, accept her invitation to sit down with a list of questions that I don't know how to answer.

The problem is that the questions say things like, 'do you ever forget this or that?' Mostly I would say I remember things pretty well, except names, and where I put my keys – which is just a lifetime problem that has got a bit worse over the years. But if I take 'ever' literally, then when I have one of my memory blackouts, I forget everything. So if I fill it in one way it will look as though I'm completely OK. But if I take it literally then I'm just a hopeless case. The form really doesn't seem to apply to me, and I stare at it hopelessly until I am called to go and see the clinical neuropsychologist, Gillian Granger, who shakes my hand as I walk into her spacious consulting room. She introduces Dr Jones the consultant physician – an extremely tall gangly man who has developed a stoop from having to get down to other people's levels.

"Have you filled in the form?" he asks in a husky voice, holding out his hand to take it.

"Er, no. I don't know how to fill it in." I notice a swift glance from him to Dr Granger. Is it saying 'what have we here?' or 'oh God we'll have to help him fill in the bloody form.'

Stumped for the moment, Dr Jones walks to the back of the room, leaving Dr Granger to interview me.

"So, Mr Rackham, can tell me about your memory problems?" She smiles to reassure me, but I know that smile. It means nothing. This is professional time. We are here to look at a problem. My problem.

I describe what happens when I forget where I am. How it seems like a devastating attack, and then how I find my way back. My use of visual memory to recover information. Dr Jones twitches and fidgets in the background, stroking an imaginary beard.

"So this is why I couldn't fill out the questionnaire. One way I look fine, the other looks terrible." My voice is gruff from talking. I sound close to tears, but I don't feel upset. It's like I'm at a distance from myself, looking at the phenomenon that is me.

She asks some more questions about my general health. "We need to take a blood sample and do a cardiac reading, if you're OK with that?"

I'm surprised and show it.

"It's in the information leaflet," she says, simply.

I haven't had a chance to read them. I haven't even seen them – it's all happened so fast.

"You're a policeman."

I nod. Did I say? Did my counsellor say?

"Are you involved in any particularly difficult cases?"

I nod. What can I tell them? I decide to give a brief outline of what I'm having to cope with. I notice another exchange of glances between the two doctors.

"It sounds like you've been under a lot of stress Mr er…"

"Inspector…"

"Inspector Rackham. After the two tests here, I recommend you go next door for a brain scan. This will give us a chance to assess whether your condition is specifically neurological." She pauses. "The scan will need to be paid for separately. Are you alright with that?"

I think of my overdraft. Am I into it already? I clear my throat. "How much?"

"The charge will be £400."

I blanch, wondering how much I am already paying. My card is on their system, the die is cast. Well, in for a penny…

They help me fill in the questionnaire, and Dr Granger gives me some pen and paper tests. The blood and heart tests don't take long – no NHS queues here – and before long I head next door for the scan. I notice that Lilly and the two dogs are no longer outside the entrance, and feel a twinge of anxiety, but reassure myself that she's just gone off for a walk, and will be back by the time all this has finished.

The brain scan takes longer than I expect.

"Having trouble finding it?" I joke to the technician.

She's heard it all before, but still finds it in her to smile. "We had to do it twice to get a clear image. If you would like to go back to the consulting room, Dr Jones will see you when he's had a look at the images."

I glance up and down the road as I return to the main entrance. No sign of Lilly. Stop worrying Arnold, I tell myself. She'll be there. But I am uneasy now, and it's not helped by the fact that I have to wait for Dr Jones to come to his conclusions having looked at pictures of my brain. I sit outside the consulting room in the corridor. The schoolboy outside the headmaster's study waiting to be caned. And the longer it goes on the more anxious I become. The pain of a demented future so much more excruciating than a few swift blows to the behind.

By the time he opens the door and invites me in, I'm shaking and wondering whether I'll have one of my lapses there and then.

"Sit down, Inspector." The words unravel out of his long throat like a strip of sandpaper. I see why he doesn't talk unless he has to, and it doesn't sound as though his vocal chords get much use.

"I've looked at your scan very carefully, and I may have found something, but I need a second opinion."

Stay of execution.

"The scan is inconclusive. There are signs that there may be a neurological reason for your memory loss, but I can't be sure. There is also the stress factor due to your work, and there may be an underlying depression."

Hello, this is me you're talking about. Still, an emotional reason would be infinitely preferable to a physical one.

"It may take some days. I'm sorry. We hope to give you a diagnosis and suggested treatment on the same day, but this time…"

"It will take longer." I can't bear the unravelling-gravelling any more. "I'm planning to stay in London for a bit anyway, so I can come back when you have… consulted."

"Good." Now he can stop.

I get up to go.

"Mr… Inspector Rackham, do you have anyone with you?" he grates.

"I have my dog. Why?"

He looks worried. "If you have one of these lapses… it… er… may be a good thing to have someone there. But…" He brightens up. "Research has shown that dogs can be very useful on these occasions."

"Thank you." I heard that somewhere before.

"Good… er…" he holds out his hand "…bye. We'll call you when we… er…"

I shake his bony hand with its impossibly long fingers, and walk back to reception.

"I'm coming back. Dr Jones needs…"

"That's right," she looks at her computer screen. "Mr Rackham. We will need a deposit of five hundred pounds. The rest is payable when you have your diagnosis and we can start your treatment. Is that alright?"

Five hundred pounds. I give her my card wondering what the rest might be, and how far into my credit limit this will take me. And I walk out of the doors to find my dog who will look after me and keep me from harm.

But Lilly and the dogs are gone.

6 pm, Monday 28th September

I find the dog tied to railings, outside a betting shop, a hundred yards down the road. One whistle suffices. I hear him bark in response, and I'm down there at a run.

"Wondered 'oose that was. Been 'ere for hours. No bovver – just sittin' waitin' for you." The man outside the betting shop looks at me disapprovingly – leaving a lovely dog like that for so long.

"He was being looked after by a friend. She was dressed in red, and had a dog too. Did you see her?"

He shakes his head. "Jus' came out for a fag, and 'ere he was, good as gold. Talked to you, din' I?" The dog wags his tail and looks up at the man, and as he does so I notice a scrap of paper tied to his collar.

'SORY CARNT DOO IT. L', it reads in scrawly uneven block capitals.

Lilly's gone, and taken her Witherspoon story with her. Would she ever have told it in court?

Bugger – what am I supposed to do now? I haven't thought past my bloody appointment at the memory clinic. We need some food and somewhere to stay, but this is London, not some rural town with nice dog-friendly B&Bs.

"Do you know if there's somewhere to eat where I can take my dog?" I ask the man.

"Not much good around 'ere, mate. It's all posh places. Could try up the Edgware Road," he gestures vaguely to the right, "or down on the Embankment," he gestures vaguely to the left. "Plenty of cafes down there." Cafes rhymes with waifs the way he says it. Sounds appropriate, so I decide to go in that direction.

It's a long walk, and we're both starving. I haven't eaten since the greasy-spoon brunch, and I gave half of that to the dog. I start thinking I should just give up and go home – I could come up again for the diagnosis, but then I remember the press, and Forester, and my determination to stay in London comes back. We'll find something. There's a club, I remember, that does good simple accommodation. But does it take dogs? I wish Lilly hadn't disappeared. I need her now – she would know where to go.

We find a café by the river, and set about getting enough food down us to satisfy the huge hole that has appeared in our stomachs. The owner, a kindly West Indian, brings out a bowl for the dog, and I give him some of my meal. Better get some proper dogfood soon, I reflect. All this rich food will upset his tummy, and… I shudder at the thought.

Finding somewhere to stay is easy if you have plenty of money. I do a search online on my mobile and find that the posher hotels will accommodate your pooch no problem, but at the cheaper end, where I'm looking, it's more difficult. I make for the club I knew of, but find it full. Enquiries take me into the city, and at last there's a pub that will put me and the dog up. We go and find a 'Metro' shop and get him the right food, and then settle in the bar for a final noggin before turning in.

As I sit there with a fine pint from an old brewery, I feel the return of my spirit of adventure. Here we are in the great capital, with some of the richest art collections in the world. All that enthusiasm from my youth returns to me. As an art student, with digs up in London, I would tour the galleries to learn from the masters that hung on the walls. Well, I'll go back to that time now. Be a young man on the threshold of life, and search for the clue that will bring meaning to what happened in The Avenues: the Seurat that concealed a safe – so out of place in that Arabic house, Brian's sudden uncharacteristic interest in art, and all those 'copies' of masterpieces hanging up in the houses of the rich. I will dive into the splendour and opulence of London's art world. I will find out.

10 am, Tuesday 29th September

One problem.

The dog.

It's ten o'clock and I'm at the hallowed portals of the National Gallery. A notice says 'Assistance dogs are welcome.' What about my dog? Well, strictly speaking, he is an 'assistance dog' if Dr Jones is to be believed. I remember now where I heard about dogs and neurology. They can be trained to recognize the first signs of an epileptic fit. Is that what Jones was hinting at? My dog is not trained for that, but he has brought me back, with his gentle muzzle nudging at me – reminding me who I am. But is that the same thing? I decide to brave it. I'm not leaving him outside for hours while I do my research. I would worry all the time. He's such a lovely trusting dog – somebody could just walk off with him.

The man at the door beckons me over. "The dog, sir."

"He's an assistance dog." I say, summoning up all my respectable police-inspectoriness.

He shrugs and waves me on. I wonder whether they'll all be like that.

The gallery is vast. A bewildering mass of images confronts me, and I feel almost agoraphobic. Masterpiece follows masterpiece and I can't just stop and examine anything – I am propelled by an unseen force through one great room after another. Eventually instinct takes me to

Level 2 and the Impressionists. I feel more at home here. These are my early heroes: Cézanne, Van Gogh, and Monet – the giant who spanned so many decades with his developing style. I sit and look. My head spinning. I take long slow breaths. Calm down.

Now get up, and look at one painting at a time. Give each one your full attention. I feel the cold of 'Lavacourt under Snow'. How does Monet get that visceral sense of winter? I need to stand back to look at 'The Gare St-Lazare' – the steam, best seen as though through a tunnel.

"Excuse me, sir, is that your dog?"

I jump, a uniformed attendant is standing just behind me, speaking very quietly.

"Yes."

"Are you blind or hard of hearing?"

"Er… no."

"Then I'm afraid I shall have to ask you to leave the building."

"But…"

"This way sir, if you'll follow me."

"But he is an assistance dog."

The attendant stops. "And how is he assisting you sir?"

"I… I…" I stumble to a halt.

"This way sir."

And I'm out before I know it.

Damn. I need to see art, and I can't leave my dog.

I phone the memory clinic and explain my predicament to the receptionist. After a pause, she comes back to me. "Dr Jones will write you a supporting letter. You can pick it up this afternoon."

Another walk in Hyde Park, with the vain hope that I'll come across Lilly. Two doggy bags and a baguette from a stall later I am at the clinic for my letter.

"Dr Jones says it will be a few days before he can get the results of a second opinion," says the receptionist. "He has left this letter for you."

Dr Jones is as good as his word, and will go the extra mile. The headed notepaper looks impressive.

To whom it may concern,

Arnold Rackham is a patient of mine, and may be liable to have a neurological episode. His dog should be with him at all times to provide warning and support.

Dr J. Jones Consultant Physician MA, PhD etc, etc.

Thank you, Dr Jones. I offer my warm thought to the ether, and walk out of the door to access the world of art. Unfortunately, by the time I get back to that part of London, the world of art is mostly closed for the day. There is the Tate Modern on the South Bank, but I've run out of energy, so we make our way back to our pub, and take up residence in the bar.

I start far too early, and drink far too much. The dog slumbers at my feet. He's getting a bit old for all this tramping the streets. Stiff and tired I go to the bar to pay off my food and drinks tab. My card works, but I wonder for how long before I reach my credit limit. As I lie back in bed, the room starts to go round. I'm drunk, I think, silly old me. But it doesn't feel like alcohol – no sense of sickness, and I wonder what Dr Jones will come up with in his search into my neurology.

I must have blanked out, because I wake in the night fighting to find my way back. Nothing feels familiar. An animal stirs uneasily in its sleep by my bed. Who am I? How did I get here? These thoughts pass through my mind in a haze, and I slump back, giving up, and descend into the black hole of sleep.

7.30 am, Wednesday 30th September

I can remember.

The first thing when I wake up is that I can remember having a memory loss in the night. I didn't know where I was, I didn't know what the dog was, but I can remember that it happened. Now that I come to think of it, I can remember all my memory losses. I'm sure I can, and the thought gives me comfort. If I can remember my loss of memory, then surely that must mean something.

Something positive.

Armed with this increase in self-assurance, I get out of bed. My head doesn't spin. The dog wags his tail from his B&B basket, and slowly stretches out a paw with a wide toothy yawn.

We're going places today, dog.

We're going to look at art, and nobody's going to stop us.

A full English breakfast. Probably no better than the one at Lilly's greasy spoon, and a damn sight more expensive. I don't care – I'm off to look at what I love the most.

The day turns out to be a bit of an experiment in accessibility. Some galleries are easier than others. It varies from a casual wave in, to a lot of beard-stroking and consultation with Security staff. In the two largest museums I repeatedly have to explain myself to Gallery

207

Assistants and show them Dr Jones' letter – if only he could have provided one of those little green jackets for the dog.

On the first day I manage four, which is going some, considering the treasures that are held in these galleries. The last, the Somerset, is easiest to get into, though I have to pay. It's near the Embankment and much smaller than the others, but with an amazing collection of Impressionist and Post-Impressionist paintings, all beautifully hung.

The following day, I'm back there, and I slow right down – looking at the brushwork and detail of each painting with great care. It's a wonderful way to spend time – just looking, looking, and getting inside the artist's mind. How did he do this? Why did he do that? Henri Rousseau – a gatekeeper. His painting lures me in. It's small, dark, and slightly spooky. The people in it seem to stand and stare back at me, but when I look closely, their faces are blank. Public servants dressed in black. It will haunt my dreams. Maybe it already has – those strange tall chimneys. The very Frenchness of it.

I tear myself away from this eerie image, to find light and space in a painting of London when it was a series of villages. Pissarro is the painter of Upper Norwood, where he lived for a while – all sludge and snow. I can almost smell that English smoky cold.

Seurat pulls me in next with his Pointillism, and it's then that a curious idea begins to form in my mind. I'm worshipping this brushwork, this genius of understanding how colour is made up from so many tiny facets. But suddenly I wonder whether I'm worshipping a false god. How do I know this was really painted by Seurat? How can I be sure that it's not just a brilliant imitation. True, I did study this technique in detail before I became a policeman, but that was a long time ago. Is my gut reaction to be trusted?

Then I turn a corner and see it: the very painting of the woman powdering herself by Seurat, that I so admired at the house in The Avenues a couple of weeks ago. It can't be – I must be wrong. Is this a fake? Or was the other one? I feel like the ground has been taken from under my feet. I need air. Space. Clutching my ticket, I quickly walk down the stairs, the dog clattering along behind me, and out into the courtyard. Sunshine greets me, and I sit down a little too fast on a stone bench – my head reeling.

Do I really suspect the gallery would put up fakes? If so - why? Would it be to protect the longevity of the painting? Keep it from the light hidden in some cellar? Things are creaking round my mind, making connections. The Pollocks found in a storage bin after twenty years, which turned out to be fakes. The Matisse that hung in a South American art museum for two years before it was discovered to be a fake – the genuine version recovered by the FBI, after the thieves tried to sell it to a couple of their agents, who were masquerading as art collectors. Fake, genuine, fake. Who can tell?

But this doesn't take me any further with The Avenues, and their rich art collectors. They are buying copies, and they know they are copies. Nobody's being duped, unless they are crap copies sold at an extortionate price.

And there's Brian in the middle of all this. Giving talks about prints and copies, rubbing shoulders with murdered ex-headmasters. A friend from the past appearing like a genie in the story, but never to be seen by me.

And bang in the centre – 'Young Woman Powdering Herself' by Seurat. A painting I was so sure was genuine at the start of all this trouble.

One thing becomes clear to me – I must brush up on my understanding of art. Hah! But joking apart, there must be someone I can talk to about this – I can't tell fake from genuine. Here I am in the middle of one of the art capitals of the world. Someone must be just a phone call away.

I reach for my mobile. Two messages – both from Forester. I shudder, I'm not even going to go there.

Holding the gallery guide, I see that there is the contact number for the curator of paintings. A good place to start.

A woman's voice answers. Yes, she can see me tomorrow at 10.30.

Other ideas about people I can contact come into my head. Auction houses would know all about spotting a fake, but I don't want to make a thing about being a policeman. I don't want the likes of Forester to find me. Not yet, anyway.

The dog and I take a walk down by the river. I buy a hot dog, and give my warm dog a drink out of the plastic bowl I have bought for the purpose. Even the bowl attracts my attention with its attempt to be fake pottery.

My mind full of doubts, I go back to the gallery, and up into the Impressionist area to look even more closely at those paintings. Particularly that Seurat – it feels genuine to me, as do the others. There's something about memory. I studied some of these paintings when I was young, sucking in every detail with my fresh uncluttered mind. Nothing jars with that memory. I know I have a good eye for visual detail, and that it's the one part of my memory unaffected by these recent attacks. Yes, I will trust that memory for now, and enjoy making contact again with these old friends. This link with my distant past gives me hope. Surely that past is intact, somewhere in my mind?

As I look round the room, to refresh my eyes from close scrutiny of a much-loved Cezanne, I notice a familiar figure looking at a Matisse in the far corner. It's just his back I'm seeing, he's wearing a smart grey suit, but I could swear it's him – the man I most want to see, is here in the same room.

I walk over to him. "Brian?" The figure turns and breaks the spell. He looks completely different from the front. He stares at me and my dog with an air of puzzlement.

"Sorry. Do I know you?" he says with an Italian accent

"Sorry. I thought you were... someone different." Embarrassing. I have broken his spell, and mine, in one crass moment.

As I turn I see him – the real Brian, coming into the room. He sees me too, and his eyes widen with recognition. He turns and disappears round the corner. I walk rapidly, not wanting to run and draw attention to myself. Brian is nowhere to be seen. The stairs go down, and up, from this point. I opt for down, reasoning that he will want to get out of the building. We go down as fast as is decent, come out into the entrance hall to see the doors to the outside still swinging. I follow through them looking left and right as I come out. Nothing. He could be hiding in a doorway in either direction. I plump for the way out onto a busy street, expecting to come across him at any moment, but I must have made the wrong choice. There is no sign of him. Vanished.

10.30 am, Thursday 1st October

"Forensics, history, the pigments in the paint." Emma Robinson, the curator, is a lively lady in her fifties with steel-grey glasses, and matching long grey hair. "That's how the Jackson Pollock fakes were discovered. Paint is changing all the time – even in the twentieth century, and what artists used in the nineteenth century, for instance, would not be easy to replicate now for your forger. The most successful forger would be the one from the same period, and who would have wanted to forge an Impressionist painting at that time? Nobody was earning any money out of them – the artists were mostly living in garrets, or with their parents."

I risk a cheeky question. "So how can I be sure that you are showing the genuine article here, in this gallery?"

"Come and have a look." She smiles – I can see she enjoys this sort of thing.

As we walk down the long beautiful corridor from her office, I find myself envying her and the rich environment she works in. Maybe I could have been a curator of art, instead of a rather unsuccessful curator of people. I think she does a better job of protecting her charges. Mind you, they tend to stay in one place unless somebody nicks them.

Up the stairs that I ran down as I chased Brian yesterday, and into the Impressionist and Post-Impressionist area.

"Forgers seem to prefer this period, I guess it's the most popular, and the untutored eye would find it more difficult to spot the fake than with, say, a Rembrandt." She looks wistful for a moment. "What a pity some of these talented forgers don't just paint their own pictures. Take the risk, be part of the history. Who knows what might happen."

We stand in front of the very Seurat that caused my sudden panic yesterday. She shows me the detail of the brushwork – every dot slightly different. "True, a good artist could give an impression of this painting – excuse the pun – but the detail? I don't think so. Now, you told me you were a detective. Have a look through this, Sherlock Holmes."

She hands me a magnifying glass, and I look at the paint as though I'm in the world of giants. Tiny cracks become apparent – age shows itself to me, like the wrinkles on an old man's face.

"Now, use your nose. Try not to breathe on the painting, but smell it."

I smell something old, slightly decrepit. A whiff of oil, but not like the oils I would use on my paintings. The dog would be good at this, I reflect. "It smells, I don't know, old?"

"You see?" she continues. "The only forgery that would work would have to be from the same period. True, forgers do try to age their paintings, but the cracks will look new under a microscope, and they'll never get the pigments completely right, and it won't smell right either. And then we have all the other ways of testing. Checking the age of the canvas, shining UV light to expose changes, and X-ray to look right into the canvas."

Seurat's world of colour. What an amazing universe. I pull myself back from the painting, and view the whole with different eyes. It's like being able to see right into the painting, rather than just the exterior facade.

"I see." An obvious thing to say. I could say so much more, but words elude me.

"You spotted the genuine work with very little help. We get experts coming in to view the collection every day. Imagine the cry that would go up if we were hanging copies. Speaking of which, I think we have an example in the basement. Would you like to see it?"

Of course I would. "Thank you for giving me so much of your time."

"Not at all. I don't usually get to show a policeman round. There are a lot of stolen art and forgeries moving around in the art world, and the more someone like you knows..." I don't tell her that I'm suspended for insubordination, and commanded to be in my home town, not in London playing art detective.

The dog and I clatter down the stairs behind her. She is used to these stairs – my knees are feeling it, but she descends nimbly, bobbing down ahead of me into the darkness.

"There." A light turns on automatically as we enter the ancient cellars under the gallery. Stone arches make it like a crypt, but it doesn't have that musty smell that I would expect from a neglected space. This place is visited regularly. We turn down a side tunnel, and set up on an easel is the very Rousseau that I was enjoying upstairs in the gallery, yesterday.

"The Customs Post, I looked at this yesterday."

"Did you study it carefully?" She scrutinizes me closely, like a teacher on a school trip.

"As a matter of fact I did, and this looks incredibly close to the original. What amazing brushwork."

"Can you spot anything? Anything that leaps out at you straight away?"

"Well, it's difficult to be sure, because the light must be different, but I'd say this is lighter in colour."

I have a sniff. "It smells completely different. New," and I cough, "and very chemical."

"Quite right. The pigments are too fresh for a painting that's well over a hundred years old, and it smells new."

"Still, it's very good. I wouldn't mind having this hanging on my wall, except…"

"Except?" She looks at me quizzically, head on one side.

"It's not genuine. Rousseau never went near this. I'd rather have a good photo of his actual work."

"People do go for this sort of thing though. A copy like this is available to buy online. The firm that did this does all the major masterpieces. The cost is generally between £1000 and £3000, depending on size – though you can get one for way less than £100 if you know where to go. We keep some down here, for our students to study."

"Your students?" I hadn't thought of this as a teaching facility.

"We run courses on how to be a curator here. Very popular. People come from all over the world – we have a reputation for being good at that sort of thing." So she is a teacher. At least in one respect. But my mind turns to Brian – he was interested in good copies of art masters. What was he up to? He was here only yesterday.

I take a gamble. "I think an old friend of mine might have been on one of your courses. Brian O'Connell? I saw him here yesterday. Didn't manage to catch him." So far I haven't lied to her. I don't want to lie to this woman. I'm tired of lies.

"No, I don't recognize that name."

I describe him, and as I do so, she watches me with that spotting-a-fraud look on her face.

"Old friend, you say?"

"Yes." I say truthfully.

"Well, a man answering that description came to see me yesterday, but I don't think he was your friend." She looks at me very directly as she says the word 'friend'. "John Collins – I think that was the name. Oddly, he did the opposite to you – looked at this Rousseau copy in the basement, and then went up to look at the real thing. He never came back to tell me what he thought."

No, he didn't, he saw me and ran.

I clear my throat. "You've been most helpful." The dog has that 'I need to get out for a pee' look. "I'd better take the dog out for a walk. But I'll come back and look at things with new eyes."

She looks at me. For a moment I wonder whether she's taken a bit of a fancy to me. Then with a wry smile she says, "We have a lecture this afternoon on the provenance of Impressionist paintings. It would help with your understanding of where they come from in history. You are very welcome to attend." Then she pauses and looks down, "and your dog."

$2^{nd} - 8^{th}$ October

The next period of time is like a renaissance for me. I'm a student again, studying art – not to paint, but to understand. Emma is as good as her word, and offers me the chance to sit at the back of her classes with my dog, soaking in the information like a brand new sponge. How come there's room in my poor old faulty brain, I just don't know, but I learn a lot very fast.

The dark side of this is that I have a shadow. I am sure that someone is following me – every policeman instinct in me shouts this out, but I never seem to catch sight of my stalker. If it is my police colleagues, surely they would just grab me and take me back to face the wrath of Forester. My mobile proliferates with unanswered calls from his office. And part of me feels guilty, very guilty. Maybe it is just my conscience looking over my shoulder.

For over a week, there has been no phone call from the memory clinic, but they have taken my deposit, and my credit card must be reaching its limit. My bank account doesn't look too healthy either.

Life is squashing me between several need-to-knows – my brain, art, Lilly. And there's something else – someone else. For all my new-found student life, I'm missing someone. I decide to take the risk and text her:

'Peggy, I'm up in London. Will be back soon. Please don't pass this on. Ax.' I risk the x – it means more to me than it usually means in a text.

She texts back:

'Coming up to London to stay with Hannah. Much better. Can we meet up? X.'

Hannah – staying with Hannah. What does that mean? Meet up? Be a gooseberry with Hannah? And what if she brings some other company along? Company that wants to take me back. I decide not to text back for the time being.

Proceed with caution, Arnold. Proceed with caution.

In the meantime, I am making the best use of my time. Visiting the gallery some afternoons, and studying. Looking at other galleries, auction houses. Asking questions about art thefts in the past, about famous forgeries. And then there must be the fakes that aren't famous, because nobody's found them out. My brain is teeming with facts, and it likes it. No lapses. Maybe it will go away – my little problem. I walk the dog every day. Sometimes on the Embankment, sometimes I get as far as Hyde Park – always in the hope of catching sight of Lilly – so visible in her red. But she has disappeared. London's a big place, and she could have decamped to another area, so I'd never find her. Anyway, whoever is following me is doing plenty of leg work.

Thinking, sketching, making checklists, and drinking. I could do with less drinking – it's bad for my bank account at over £4 a pint, and it must be bad for me. But I can't stop. A warning image flashes up in my brain, of a meths addict sitting on filthy sacking on the street – that could be me.

A giant juggernaut passes in front of me as I wait to cross the Embankment road to get to my afternoon lecture.

It feels like it will swallow me up, this mass of moving metal. Even the dog flinches at the rush of air and fumes.

I cross over to the safety of quadrangles and ancient stone. The noise of traffic is abruptly subdued by this safe haven, and I make my way to the lecture room for the last in the series on 'The Provenance of Impressionist Paintings'.

There seem to be a lot more police about than usual and I begin to feel uncomfortable, as though everyone in the force is out looking for me. People are standing about in groups, talking in low voices, when I arrive at the lecture room. Nobody takes any notice of me, except a balding man that I've never seen before, who is standing by the lecture rostrum. He gives the dog a hard stare.

We settle down, me and the dog in our usual place at the back, but Emma doesn't appear.

The balding man clears his throat, looking rather pompous in his suit and tie. "Mrs Robinson can't take the lecture this afternoon, due to the circumstances. She has asked me to take her place, and has given me her notes, so I can pick up where she left off yesterday. But first, I'd better take your names – check my list." He looks round the room and pointedly stares in my direction.

He starts at the front, and one by one, people give their names, zigzagging across the room, until he gets to me.

"Arnold Rackham," I say in a rather huskier voice than I intended. Did she put me on the list?

"I can't see your name here," he says. "And we don't allow dogs into lectures." He looks down at his list again, pausing for dramatic effect. "Can you leave. Now, please."

Everyone turns round. They've all seen me coming to the odd lecture over the past week, but will anyone say anything? Someone murmurs something about dogs, but he just replies. "We don't allow dogs. An attendant will escort you off the premises, Mr…?"

"Rackham."

They all turn back round to the front, and look down at their papers, like a herd of brainless sheep. I walk stiffly to the front of the lecture room, and a uniformed attendant leads me out of the building and into the quadrangle. There are a lot of police about, and I'm feeling even more conspicuous, now that I'm being led out like a naughty dog walker.

"There's been an incident," the attendant informs me, as I show him my letter in an attempt to regain my acceptable dog-owner status in this institution. "Unless you have good reason to be here you will have to leave." Thus the list. My temptation to show him my police identity is almost overpowering, but the realization that my name would get back to the wrong people, as quick as lightning, makes me grit my teeth, look down, and walk with him towards the exit without making any further fuss.

Just as I am passing the main entrance to the gallery, I hear a familiar voice.

"Just the man." Emma comes clattering down the steps. "You could help us, couldn't you? Leave him to me, Gary." And she takes my arm and leads me into the gallery, dog in tow. "You've got such a good instinct," she says in a lower voice, as we go into the entrance hall.

On the other side of the hall, I see a table laid out with papers on it, and a number of plainclothes standing round listening to a tall man who has his back to me. I recognize him immediately – bald head like an old crow, long bony fingers stabbing at the papers in front of him. Oh bugger, it's Grimwode. What's he doing here? I need to leave. Fast. My safe haven – gone.

"Sorry, I've got to go. Please don't say anything." I look at her, pleading, before turning and making out of the doors as quickly as I can. Nobody seems to notice as the dog and I leave the buildings, and turn onto the main road. Instinct makes me want to go straight back to my pub, and I walk rapidly through the crowded streets and up to the north of the city, feeling safe for once, in the anonymity of London crowds, and putting as much distance as I can between Grimwode and me.

The pub is closed when I arrive, so I ring on a bell that is at the side door for residents who need to get in out of hours.

A woman appears looking slightly dishevelled. "What do you want?" she says sharply.

"I'm staying here. Can I get to my room?"

"Jim, there's a man down here, says he wants to get to his room." She blocks the way in, while Jim comes down grumbling and coughing.

"Second time we've been woken. What is it now?"

"He says he's staying here."

Jim appears at the door looking bleary eyed. "You," he says rudely. "Some friends of yours came half an hour ago and woke us up. Wanted to get in and see where you were staying. I told them we weren't open. They looked a tough bunch. Wondered whether to call the police, but they went away."

They probably were the police, I think. "Can I pay up now? I need to leave. I've just come to get my things."

"So you don't want to see your friends? They said they'd be back."

I bet they did. "No, I don't think they were my friends."

"Ah, right." He gives me a sardonic smile, "I don't know what you're into, but you'd better come through." He leads the way to the bar, and opens up the till grumbling slightly. Much to my horror and embarrassment, my debit card is refused. He hands it back to me without a word, clenching his jaw and staring hard

223

at me as I fumble in my wallet for my credit card. There is a tense silence as he tries it in the machine and I try to remember my pin code, fumbling it the first time. Thank God, it goes through. I shoulder my rucksack and head for the exit as fast as I can.

"Don't come back," he mutters as I leave, and I feel his eyes burning into the back of my neck as I walk hastily out of the door.

No money. I've got no money, and I don't have the faintest idea how much credit I have on my card. I won't be able to pay the memory clinic. I'll never find out what's wrong with me. My world is crumbling inwards – no escape.

4 pm, Thursday 8th October

I look down the street as the door slams behind me. Then I see him, and I realise who my shadow has been.

Brian. But what does he want? Why follow me for a week? Does he think I know something? Questions rattle round my head as I walk briskly towards him. I get close enough to see the look of indecision on his face, then he turns and runs. I give chase, but I'm hampered by the dog on his lead and the rucksack on my back. He doesn't run fast – just lopes ahead of me, allowing me to keep him in view.

We run into the crowds leaving work in the city – already there are groups of drinkers outside the pubs, spilling all over the pavements. Self-consciously the pursued and the pursuer slow down to a fast walk. We don't want these tipsy bankers cheering us on. Brian leads the way down through the city towards the Embankment. We are getting perilously close to the Somerset Gallery and the swarms of police that must be surrounding it, but he takes a right and we're heading towards Trafalgar Square. His shiny grey suit bobs ahead of me, like he's always trying to make sure I can see him. Fortunately, I'm relatively fit from the past week of walking and I keep up, though I feel the sweat dribbling down the inside of my shirt. The dog trots along easily, as we dodge our way through the crowds and down again towards the Embankment.

It's less crowded on the super-modern pedestrian bridge across the river, and I wonder whether he'll stop here, and we can talk, looking down at the Thames as the pleasure boats float past. Something makes me look round, and I'm disorientated for a moment, as I see what looks like a hotel from Budapest behind me – grey turrets and decorative brickwork standing out against the darker buildings that surround it. Never noticed that before. Have I left London by some magic and ended up in Hungary? I turn back to post-millennial Britain, to see Brian disappearing down the steps at the other end of the bridge. I run to catch him up, nearly knocking over a beggar's beaker, and avoiding an outstretched hand holding heather. "Good luck? Want a bit of good luck, dear?"

I get to the stairs to find he's vanished. I look both ways, but can see no sign of his grey suit in the groups of tourists that saunter round the different world that is the South Bank. As I descend the steps from the bridge, looking around me, I find myself in a temporary village of stalls selling food and crafts. It feels like Terry Pratchett's Ankh Morpork – you could probably get anything here in this fairground.

Foreign languages, foreign faces, foreign food. It all comes to me how sheltered and limited my life has been in my small provincial town. This is London – cosmopolitan, scary, exciting, vital, and relentless. I turn and glimpse the shiny grey suit. Look again and it's gone. What game is he playing with me?

"Can I help you, sir?" A Chinese beauty leans over her counter towards me. No prices anywhere. I think of what I might have in my wallet. Not much cash to see me through while I sort myself out.

"No thanks," I mutter.

With the dog at my side, I wander through the maze of elegant sellers, hoping to catch a glimpse of my quarry – or am I his quarry?

"What are you onto, Rackham?"

Brian's voice is just behind me. I feel a steely grip on my elbow as he steers me away from the stalls to a dank corner of concrete and stone, by some steps. People walk up and down them, in the heedless haste that is London.

"Brian. What are you doing?" I hiss.

"No, what the fuck are you doing?" He thrusts his face up close to mine. "What's all this art stuff? You're onto something, aren't you."

I realise he is very fit and strong, and for all my police-killer-machine training, I doubt whether I can overpower him. He was always the stronger when we were kids. The dog just wags his tail amiably, not picking up the aggressive tension that's building between us. He saved me from an old woman, but will he protect me from an old ex-friend?

"I could ask the same of you. What was that talk in The Avenues all about?" I'm backed up against a wall, and he is uncomfortably close. "I heard about it from Charles – copies of art masterpieces, wasn't it?"

"Fuck Charles," he hisses. "You and me, we did art at school, didn't we. I'm still interested – is that a fucking crime? And why did you chase me?" He's so close, he's spitting in my face.

"So why did you run away, Brian? You're up to something, aren't you. Up to your neck in it. Betty said she met you sometimes when she was with Malcolm." I have to grit my teeth to get this out.

"Oh, so that's it. Your faithful wife Betty, and Malcolm. I knew them. So what?" A look of fear crosses his face for a moment. "We didn't think they'd do that, the buggers."

227

"Do what? Murder Malcolm – is that it? Whatever you're into, it's gone deeper than you thought, hasn't it."

Brian's eyes widen as he stares at me. "I can't believe it – you don't know." He takes a step back and looks round as though he's going to leave. "So what are you on to? Have I been wasting my time? Oh fuck. We… I know you're on your own. Suspended." More spit in my face. "Going round London pretending to be a fucking art expert."

"It's not quite like that. I am onto something." Careful Arnold. "We could help each other – find out what this is all about."

"Oh I could tell you… but you… you know fuck all. Just leave me alone." He starts prodding me in the chest with a finger. "You fucking waste of time."

The dog is beginning to growl. He doesn't like this man being so close to me, and sounding so bitter and angry.

Brian looks down. "Oh fuck. Your dog." He turns and aims a kick at him, but he's too close. My instinct is to protect the dog, and I grab his arm and hold him in a lock – pushing his wrist up between his shoulder blades. He tries to move, and he's strong, but I'm experienced with this particular move and I've got him – for the moment, at any rate. The dog continues to growl.

"Now let's calm down shall we? It's you that's been following me. What's that all about? Eh? Are you going to tell me?" He struggles, so I whisper in his ear. "Someone might notice and call the police, and you don't want that, do you?" Neither do I.

He sags, and I let my grip go. My mistake – he turns and punches me in the stomach. And then walks away leaving me doubled up, gasping for breath. The dog's barking furiously now, tugging at the lead. He wants to protect his master – get the man who hit him, but all he succeeds in doing is pulling me over. I look up from my

228

kneeling position to see Brian's grey suit disappearing in the distance.

I stagger to my feet, and let the dog lead me in a wobbly pursuit, dodging through the ambling groups of tourists. It strikes me that nobody noticed my confrontation with Brian. It was right under their noses, but this is London, and everybody just minds their own business – just like they did in the time of Cornelia and Lilly. The dog, turned bloodhound, has got scent of something. Is it Brian? Do I want to confront him again? I let the dog decide, and he leads me in a wild chase through the crowds, across roads, and into an underground station. We get though the barrier, with the help of my warrant card, and down to a northbound platform just as a train leaves – the ascending hoover-like noise blocking out the dog's barking. Did I see the grey suit? It's too late anyway, and all I want to do is sit down. I drag the dog away from the edge of the platform, and find a metal seat by the wall. I'd like to lie down, but the seat is divided by armrests – no doubt to stop vagrants from sleeping there.

Vagrants? What am I saying? Lilly was a vagrant. All those murdered girls were vagrants. Is that how I think of them? Worthless, a nuisance, to be pushed by – ignored? Even Forester thinks more of them than that.

I sit in this soulless place watching the passengers come and go, and contemplate that every one of them has a soul burning bright inside them, their hidden universes passing me by, each one a life of innumerable possibilities. I want my universe to continue to have possibilities. Not to shrink – the walls of dementia closing in, pushing me to one single thought, 'Who am I? I don't know. I don't know who I am. I don't know who I am. I don't know…'

"You alright, mate? We're closing the station now. You'll have to go." A man in a dusty blue uniform. Is he black? Is he white? I'm confused. I must have fallen asleep, and now everything seems odd – different.

He helps me onto my feet, and taking my elbow, steers me up the stairs and out of the station. The mesh gate grinds closed behind me, and I'm out on the streets. It's dark. There are a few people about, but me and my dog have nowhere to go. Dog. I know he's my dog. This isn't as bad as it can get, but I still can't get my head round what's happening. I'm terribly hungry. The dog must be too. There's something on my back. Maybe there's food in there. It feels heavy.

I find shelter against a wall. I don't want to sit down, because it's wet on the ground. Leaning against the wall I burrow into the bag that was on my back – a ruck…a ruck-thingy. I feel a bag of something, crunchy in my hand. I pull it out. Food. The dog whines and wags his tail.

"Food, dog. We've got food." I smile down at him and scoop out a handful of brown crunchy things. "Here you are." I put them on the ground in front of him and he gobbles them up quickly. I've got a second handful out for myself. They taste stale, and they are very tough to chew, but I get them down, and they fill the space in me that was shouting 'food, food!'

I'm thirsty now, and notice that the dog has found a puddle and is drinking in great big slurps. Could I do that? Could I get down on the ground and drink like the dog? Something tells me this won't work, and I feel in the bag to see if there's anything else. Something cold and hard is in there. I pull it out. A… a b… well I don't care what it's called, I think there's a drink in there. But how to get to it. There's something in the way. It stops the drink coming out. It's blue and I try to pull it off. That doesn't work so I grip it and try turning it. It's stuck – it won't turn. Try the other way. At last it's turning. The blue thing comes off and falls to the ground. With a shaking hand, I lift it to my lips and sip the blessed liquid.

Midnight

I walk in the cold, cold half-light. Hard beneath me. Hard all around me. Everything is grey or black. Some rough surfaces, some shiny, tower above me and disappear into the gloom. There's a noise that I half recognise. A sound that grinds and whines, and then settles into a quiet roar. I nearly trip over a small step down onto a lower place. I see two glowing eyes coming towards me and the roar gets louder. I look round to see the dog has stayed back, has not gone down the little step. The monster with the glowing eyes makes a sudden hooting noise and I stagger back, catching my heel on the step and falling over, hitting the ground hard.

My hip hurts. My hand stings and feels wet, and there's a cold damp sensation in my ear. It's the dog sniffing me to check I'm alright. But I'm not alright. I'm caught in this world that I don't understand. These platforms and lights, with darkness all around. Where are all the people?

There's something about wanting to find someone, and something else about not wanting to be found by 'them'. Is 'them' the same as the person I want to find? No, I think 'them' is a group of people I want to avoid at all costs. But I need help. I don't know where I am. I'm tired and hungry, and I'm in danger because I don't understand things.

I get up and limp on, avoiding stepping off onto the lower level – don't want any more monsters. But as I walk on, I start to recognize things. That picture of a lady with very little on – I'm sure I've seen it before. And then there's the bit where I turn to avoid stepping off my safe platform, and I nearly bump into that tall thin thing with a light high up on the top of it. I've definitely seen it before.

Ideas begin to come into my head. *'Whatsit'*. Am I hunting a *'Whatsit'*? And who made that word? Was it the same person who made up a little song about going round and round following my own footsteps.

Then I laugh: '*The Singing Detective*', hah hah! I'm the singing detective. He was ill and having delusions. Is that what I am? Ill? Deluded? It feels like I'm very close to reality, but just can't name it.

If you go down...

Oh no. A massive chill of fear goes right through my body. Something I don't want to remember. I tried so hard to forget. I practised so hard, and I almost succeeded. Then she came along. Tried to kill me.

There is someone. Someone's following me. I turn round quickly, almost falling over on the slippery wet, and see a flash of white. Perhaps it's my angel. Must be my guardian angel. But there's nothing now. Just me and my dog.

I can't go on walking round and round like this. Eventually I'll run out of... I stop, and look out over the danger zone. It looks better on the other side, or at least, different.

Why did the chicken cross the road?

That's it. It's a road. That's why the dog stopped. Because I taught him to. Now I've got a name for it, maybe I can understand it and it won't be so dangerous. I remember that when I was young, I was told not to cross the road without an… an… adult? Am I an adult? Not sure. Doesn't feel like it. But I taught the dog so I must be…

Look left, right, and left again.

Let's try this. Listen. No roaring noise. All quiet. Careful how you step down. Miss the puddle. Dog's coming too. Now WALK FAST.

I almost trip over again as I come to the other side, and step up to safety. I look around. Light shines, reflected on the wet ground like silver. Like gold.

Streets of London paved with gold.

But it's more like hard steel, and there's nobody here either. No-one to help me. Then the dog starts tugging so I follow his lead, and we walk fast. Up steps. Over water. Over another road. On and on. My mind is dead now – I just follow.

After a while, we stop at some more steps. Great pillars and walls in front of me. A friendly voice inviting me in.

The dog turns away, and I do too – retreating from that friendly voice. Something inside my head says I don't want to be found.

Down yet more steps, across roads, in an endless twilight journey. My mind is trying to engage with what is happening, but is split off somewhere on another journey. I begin to understand things like roads and cars, and then I shut it all down again and just exist.

There are other people now. Some walk fast and silently, others slowly and noisily wandering from side to side, so that I have to go into the road to avoid them.

The owl and the pussycat went to sea.

I'm in a boat with my dog. We are sailing down the street, the floodlights showing up the cracks in the pavement. The cracks. I must avoid treading on the cracks. But the dog doesn't seem to know this. Carrying on, unaware of the danger we are in.

Bears! We'll get eaten by bears!

And the dog is leading me straight towards them.

Oh no, they're not dangerous at all, they're just teddy bears. Silly Arnold. I stop, and there, right in front of me, is a group of teddies sitting round a picnic basket. I try to join them and simply succeed in bashing my hand against the glass. They don't move, they sit there with their glassy eyes, looking at me. Or looking past me.

I feel a shove from behind, and my face is pressed against the hard glass. The dog growls. Somebody's tugging at the bag on my back. I freeze like a boy of ten, terror making me dizzy. It hurts my hands as the bag is torn off me.

"I won't tell," I manage to gasp.

"Don't give a fuck mate," says the voice behind me. "Got what I want."

I hear running footsteps getting quieter, and dare to look round. The street is empty. I don't want to go further, I want to sleep. I sink down with my back to the window, no bag on my back any more, and the dog curls up easily at my side, as though he does this all the time. The hard pavement digs into me, and I shift uncomfortably. I doze off, but am woken by small hard things hitting me. I pick them off my clothes. Pennies – they threw pennies at me.

Pennies from heaven.

It's that singing detective again. Somewhere in my mind I remember that I'm a detective. I'm trying to find out something. I'm going down into the dark places that I tried to forget. I'm so good at forgetting now, that if I keep practising I'll forget everything, and then I won't have to go down into the dark any more.

"I don't know what your game is, Rackham, but I'm watching you." There's a man in metal talking to me. He's bending over me. "You do know something, don't you, and I'm going to find out what it is."

The dog growls, and the apparition goes away, leaving me puzzled and afraid. What do I know? Something important, obviously. So here I sit – a memory locked inside a lost room. I look at some small hard flat round things that are on the ground beside me. I am baffled. I don't know what they are. I am so tired from trying to work things out. So tired... so tired...

9 am, Friday 9th October

The noise hits me. I've been asleep. I'm sitting on something hard. Everything's higher than me, and I don't know how I got here. Legs flash past my eyes, and behind them a blur of red and black shapes moves from right to left. Red, black, red, red, black, black, black, red, and so on – the pattern never repeated. I don't know how long I've been here. I can't remember how I came to be here, or what happened before.

There's something beside me. Warm and gently breathing. I've no idea what it's doing there.

The endless patterns go on, as if I'm on a carousel, and I'm the one that's moving. These mindless objects stationary – floating past my eyes as my world whirls round.

The pattern is broken by a wheel. Spoked and large it comes to a halt right in front of my face. The warm thing beside me uncurls itself – a head appears out of the furry mass. Not for me this head, but looking up over the wheel.

"Arne?"

That sounds familiar. A song comes into my mind:

'I know that name,
Like I know my Rose'

No. Wait. I've got the words mixed up.

"Arne?"

I'm sitting on something hard.

"Arne?"

And cold.

"Arnold?"

Arnold? That's my name.

I dare to look up. The endless pattern continues – now flowing behind the wheel. There's a face above that wheel. I know that face.

"Betty?" I rasp, finding vocal muscles I don't seem to have used for a while.

"It's me Arnold. Peggy."

"Peggy?" I begin to move, stiffly raising myself from my recumbent position and kneeling up on the hard ground. My trousers are damp, and chafe the inside of my thighs. She's sitting in a wheelchair with something metal on her lap, and crowds of people are pushing past her. A lock of hair has fallen over her face – the rest is tied up. She has a crumpled expression I've never seen before.

"Arne, Arnold what's happened to you?" She sounds on the edge of tears.

"I don't know. I don't know." I wave my arms to indicate my place of residence on the street. "I don't know how I got here."

Peggy shifts in her wheelchair and looks up. "Hannah, can we take him back to your place?"

I look up too, and take in Hannah's craggy squaw-like beauty. She looks down at me and holds her breath. The bundle of fur that was sitting beside me moves quickly round the wheelchair to nuzzle into her side.

"Is this your dog?" she says reaching out to stroke his head.

"Er, yes." That's right, he's my dog.

"What's his name?"

"He doesn't have one. He's just 'the dog'."

Hannah looks at me, wrinkling up her nose – searching my face. I can see she doesn't believe me – she thinks I've forgotten his name.

"No, really, I've always called him 'the dog'. Never found the right name for him." It's all coming back to me.

"He's right, Hannah," Peggy says.

Hannah smiles, and it's like the sun coming out over glaciers. Like a new day has dawned in the Arctic waste. "Come on, let's get you back to my place."

Hannah helps me up off the pavement and I follow her as she pushes Peggy through the crowds, in what I now realise is London's Oxford Street.

'Her place' turns out to be a beautiful ground-floor flat in a Georgian house looking out onto Regent's Park. We have to negotiate Peggy's wheelchair up the four steps to the front door – Hannah pulls her up backwards and I take the frame at the front. I look into Peggy's face as I do so, and see troubled eyes looking back at me. 'Where were you?' they ask. 'Why didn't you keep in contact?'

The doorway is negotiated, and we are quickly through the small communal hall and into Hannah's flat. The large Georgian windows let in light from every direction. To the front there is the leafiness of the park, at the back, a large garden with trees. The noise of London is shut out and we are in a private paradise.

"I'm very lucky." Hannah is defensive in her eagerness to disclaim untold wealth. "This belongs to a friend of my parents, and she lets me have it for a low rent."

In the sitting room a Bösendorfer grand piano looks perfectly in place. There is music on it, spread out in an untidy display of black and white. This piano is no ornament.

I look at Hannah. "Are you… a musician?"

"You must be starving, and your dog," she interrupts. "Come into the kitchen."

I look down at my damp trousers, all saggy at the knees. My scuffed unpolished brown shoes, and suddenly I feel shaky. Taking a deep breath, I follow her into the kitchen which feels modern, after the Georgian elegance of the sitting room. Shiny surfaces everywhere, and I am reluctant to put my grubby body down in this hallowed place of cleanliness.

"Here, sit down." She offers me a chair by the table, and busies herself giving the dog a drink and getting the coffee on. Same machine as mine – it seems an age since I was in my cottage.

"Toast? Oh, and I can warm up some beans."

Beans on toast. Not what I expected, but sounds perfect.

The dog gets a raw egg. Hannah knows about dogs, evidently.

I sit amidst the aroma of coffee and beans. Peggy is at my side. There is a tension in the kitchen that is not wholly unpleasant. What is going on between the three of us? Perhaps Hannah is just a mother figure to Peggy. Envious of any other person in her life, but just that. I would be envious about Peggy.

"You look gorgeous." It slips out without me meaning to.

She looks at me, slightly bemused. "You look like you need a bath, and a couple of days' sleep."

I become aware of another aroma that is not entirely pleasant – the acrid smell of urine has been covered up by more desirable scents, but now breaks through making me wish I'd asked for a bath first. I tuck into the beans on toast, eager to get to the self-cleaning stage, and then realise – I've only got the clothes I'm wearing. Where is everything else? What can I wear after a bath? I feel dizzy again. Eat. Get strength. Then sort this out.

"A bath would be great." I look at Hannah to check it's OK. "But I've lost my bag with my spare clothes."

"We'll find something. Look, I've got a gig tonight. Must do some practice." Hannah glances at Peggy, unsure whether to leave us to it.

"It's alright. You go. Inspector... Arne can have a bath, and then we'll talk."

"Bathroom's just up the corridor on the left. There should be a big white dressing-gown in the cupboard, and plenty of towels." Hannah bends down and gives Peggy a tender peck on the cheek, and is gone.

We look at each other. "Well, I'd better..."

"Yes, you had. See you when you get out."

I get up stiffly, and head down the corridor. On the left she said, or was it right? I look through a half-open door on the right, and stop just in time, as I glimpse Hannah getting a cello out of its case. It must have been on the left.

The bathroom is large with a grand old bath in the middle, standing on clawed feet. Everything is white. I run the bath, and wonder what the time is. I haven't checked. My watch says quarter to three, but it has stopped. Absent-mindedly I wind it up, but there is no clock to check, so I take off my clothes, feel the water, and sink into the healing warmth of the bath. Strange sounds start to come from across the corridor. I thought she was going to play the cello, but this sounds more like she's dragging her nails across a blackboard. I sink my head into the water until only my face is above the surface. The sound is blocked out, and I hear the gentle gurgle of the water flowing round my ears – so soothing I could fall asleep.

I wake with a jerk. There is a knocking coming from somewhere and I feel cold.

"Are you alright? You been in there for ages." Peggy's voice comes through the door.

"Fine. I'll be out in a minute." I pour some more hot water into the tepid mixture and reach for the soap, giving myself a good scrub and rinse before getting out. The sounds coming from across the corridor are definitely cello now. Scales up and down, up and down. I go to the cupboard leaving pools of water all over the floor, and find a towel and a white towelling dressing gown that's big enough to cover me decently. My clothes lie in an untidy pile near the door, and I don't want to touch them. They smell of my lost memory. I don't want to know them, but they're all I've got. I emerge from the bathroom holding them at arm's length.

Peggy peers at me from the end of the corridor – her face shows a mixture of concern and amusement. "The washing machine's just out here. What were you up to? It's almost lunchtime."

So now I know where I am in time. "Fell asleep, didn't I." I smile apologetically, and follow Peggy to the washing machine with my unholy load.

"Lunch? Then we'll talk."

"Yes."

And as if by magic, the sound of the cello stops and Hannah sticks her head out into the corridor. "There's soup in the fridge, and bread in the bin. I'll be there in a minute."

2 pm, Friday 9th October

Peggy is lying on a sofa, and I've drawn an armchair up close, so I can talk quietly to her. Behind her I catch the reflection of my face squashed into the curve of the gleaming Bösendorfer.

As I try to pull my thoughts together to tell Peggy what I've been doing, I realise that I've been living on a knife edge – one moment I'm a respectable local policeman, the next a nobody lost on the streets in the big city. It's our minds that hold us where we are in place and time.

In the next room Hannah is playing Bach. I recognize it because, in his more lucid moments, my father used to play records of Casals – one of the great cellists of the past. I loved that music then – it made me feel safe because I knew he wasn't getting blind drunk. It makes me feel safe now, because something in this music encircles my sadness and holds it in an ever-changing embrace. I've been so lost. I need to be held by someone, to stop me floating off again like an unanchored dinghy on a rough wind-swept sea.

Peggy shifts to try to get comfortable. Hannah has helped her out of her wheelchair and onto the sofa, and made us a pot of tea. But I wanted to help her out of her wheelchair – to hold her, and be close. I wanted to make the tea and look after us.

"You look so much better," I say.

"Yes, things are coming back. I can move much more than I could. Maybe it will keep getting better. Hannah's looked after me since I left hospital, and she's managing to work as well. I don't know where she gets the energy from. She's such an amazing cellist – I'd swear her music is helping me mend, as much as any therapy."

The dog, who is sitting at my feet, beats his agreement on the rug with his tail.

"Anyway, enough about me. Come on, tell me what happened to you. I've been wondering what's been going on for the last fortnight. Why didn't you keep in touch?" She looks at me with such intensity. I lean forward – I want to hold her hands, but I don't know how she'd react. I've only got this borrowed dressing gown on, and I still feel dirty – street-stained, in this beautiful room.

"I went to see the counsellor the day after Betty's interview. The day after I'd been suspended." I look at her. "After seeing you with Hannah... Sorry, I'm finding it hard to pull it all together."

"No." Peggy looks me full in the face. "Tell me any way you like. The counsellor?"

I tell her.

Peggy reaches out a hand to touch me. The room is silent. Hannah has stopped playing, and there is no shelter from my thoughts. No music. No comforting Bach.

Hannah appears. "Tea break. I'm making one, would you like?"

Peggy withdraws her hand quickly. Does Hannah see? And what would it mean anyway? Comforting an old police colleague.

I start to get up. "Let me."

"No, I need the break. You stay there."

I slump back into the armchair. Relieved to be able to just relax and take in the sight of Peggy on the sofa. I will draw her like this. Her face pensive, her body draped on the cushions – trying to find rest, but so sore. I want to heal her. A magic touch on her spine – just there. The blessing of pure love. Hah, so you think you're Jesus. Not. But I make up my mind, right now, that I will help her recover in any way I can. That will be my future. Not lonely demented oblivion.

Hannah returns with mugs of tea. Colourful, chunky afternoon mugs.

"I'll get back to it," she says, leaving us to our silence, and we hear her start straight into something that sounds more Romantic. She creates a big warm tone as she glides through the slow opening. Brahms? I wonder. It feels like it should have a piano part with it. She stops. Re-tunes, and starts again, the notes lifting in a bridge of sound. And I start to tell Peggy more of my story.

It's all coming back – I am fascinated by the detail that my mind can recall, after having seemingly lost everything. I don't tell her about Betty's bedroom, and as I skip to leaving my cottage and the train journey to London, I notice she looks troubled.

"Look, Arne…"

The room next door is silent. Suddenly everything feels awkward. The silence goes on a bit too long, but then to our relief a new music starts up. Sparse, melodic, clown-like. Her thick warm tone has changed to light and edgy. She stops. Starts again – this time very slowly. Obviously a difficult opening. What does it make me think of? The cello plays the clown, but it's not Don Quixote. Some other clown.

"I love this." Peggy's eyes light up. She looks relieved.
I look at her and smile. "What is it?"
"Debussy."

We listen for a couple of minutes, but she keeps stopping and going over the beginning – never quite satisfied.

"She always finds this hard to play after the Brahms. Fortunately there's an interval." Peggy shifts uncomfortably, and I wonder if she needs some help.

"Can I do anything?"

"Could you just help me get into a different position?"

I kneel by the sofa and put my arms around her and lift her gently so that she can sit differently on the cushions. I don't want to let go. Our eyes meet.

"Thank you," she whispers, and I retreat into my chair.

I look out of the window onto Regent's Park, thinking back to that time of uncertainty and discovery. I was so sure that my memory problems had gone away. So optimistic.

I continue with my story – the words flow as the light outside fades – the music next door.

I tell her about Lilly – her eyes widen at the description of the basement at 'Hazelbank'.

I tell her about the art, and my discoveries about what is genuine and what is fake.

I tell her about Brian, and then I stumble to a halt as I reach a blank place in my memory – it's like an empty hole, and I can't find anything in it. After an agonizing pause, I look at her, troubled.

"Arne," she says. "Come over here." She strokes the space on the sofa beside her, and I go over and sit next to her, not quite sure where to put my arm. We are so close, but we don't touch.

"Arne, I've got to tell you this. You never asked, never asked how I found you."

"I thought it was luck, pure luck." I am intrigued now, but Peggy looks embarrassed.

"No, it wasn't luck, it was your mobile phone."

"But how did you..?" I am baffled. I'd switched it off after I had contacted her. I didn't want to be found.

"I had your computer. I went to the 'Find my iPhone' app and we tracked you down, eventually, in Oxford Street."

"So it works, even if it's been switched off? But then how come Grimwode or Forester didn't track me down? They have all the gear."

"Maybe they didn't want to."

"But what about those guys who came round to my B&B? If they were police they'd have found me through my phone." So they weren't police.

Peggy and I look at each other, then, strangely, she blushes.

"And how did you come to have my computer in the first place?" I can't help smiling.

Peggy pauses and looks down. "I thought something must have happened to you. I hadn't heard from you – didn't know where you were. Why didn't you keep in contact? "

"I texted you, it must have been a few days ago."

"It was over a week ago. And after I texted you back, I heard nothing more. I got worried. When I got out of hospital we went round to your house. We... broke in. I had to find out what had happened to you."

"You broke in? Who were you with?" I don't know whether to be angry or amused.

"Hannah."

"What?"

"Hannah and I went to see if you'd come home, but you weren't there. I felt a bit... desperate. Look, since the shooting, I feel so bloody helpless. I've always been so... independent. It made me angry, and I wanted to find you. So we broke in."

"Broke in? You and Hannah?" It strikes me as ludicrous. Peggy in a wheelchair with a musician. Burglars!

"It was easy. Honestly Arne – you're a policeman and you don't even have a mortice lock on your front door. Hannah's got very thin wrists – she just put her hand through the letterbox and turned the latch."

Hah! Musician turned burglar in times of need. She would have the necessary manual dexterity, of course.

"Everything seemed undisturbed – it looked like you'd just left." Her face looks sad – she's remembering. "You have so little. Not much to know you by. A tiny house for a man who's…" She stops again, then suddenly laughs. "There was a funny smell in the kitchen - a bit doggy. But I loved your drawings on the wall – I didn't know you could draw like that, Arne. Grimwode looked evil, Forester like a pompous banker, and that woman…" She shivers. " Your drawing of me – can I have it?" She's carried away with her story now – no longer the guilty thief.

"Peggy. Of course you can have it. I hope I'll never have to do another one."

"What? Why?" She looks a bit taken aback.

"That is my memory gallery. When I start losing it I can look at those drawings to find my way back – the people I know." I suddenly realise where this is going.

"That's amazing. But wouldn't you want to remember me? Wouldn't you want my drawing?"

Bugger, I'm stuffed. I'll have to say it. "Not if you were there."

"There? Arne, you're a married man."

"She's gone, Peggy. Disappeared. And she's been with another man for years. You know that."

She looks away, and then hurries on with her story. "Anyway, we found your laptop, which was luckily plugged in and switched on. Honestly Arne, secure – you're not. I found the 'Find my iPhone' app, and we were able to track you down – though it took time. Wish we'd found you sooner."

"I'm amazed at how you found me at all. It must have been tricky with the wheelchair." I've put my foot in it again.

"Oh, London Transport does its best, but in the end we gave up and just walked. Hannah's very fit."

And she did this for me. But I say: "Yes, I was wondering about Hannah." I stop, not sure how to ask, and anyway I've said too much already. The drawing thing is sitting there between us, and Peggy is not going to touch on it.

"Look, Peggy, I..."

"Yes?"

"I may have made a fool of myself."

"Why?"

"Thinking that I... that we... and there's Hannah."

"What about Hannah?" She looks distracted.

"You and Hannah?"

"Oh Arne, she's my friend. We're very close, and she's very possessive. Cares a lot about who I see. Doesn't trust men... had a bad experience. She's not what you think. She puts it all into her music."

Hannah stops playing, her door opens and she comes into the sitting room. Her face is suffused with the joy of her music-making. Her eyes glisten and glint, as though seeing things we cannot.

"Tea break?" She's not looking at Peggy, and has no idea what's been going on between us. "I'll stop now. Don't want to overdo it before I play this evening."

"Hannah?" something in Peggy's voice makes her pause and look at us. "I've told him about breaking into his house."

"Oh." Hannah looks uncertain for the first time in my recent experience. "So…?"

"So it's fine. It's alright. Really." I smile at her. "I mean, what would have happened if you hadn't broken into my house and nicked my computer?"

They look at each other.

"There's supper and then we can go to Hannah's concert," Peggy says a little too brightly.

6 pm, Friday 9th October

"That space Lilly found, could that be where they're hiding something?" Peggy's voice is steadier now.

We've eaten in a state of uneasy camaraderie – nobody's quite sure what to say. We are all smiling at each other, but there are questions behind our smiles.

Hannah leaves us to get ready. She's been fidgety all the time – bad enough having pre-concert nerves, without my stuff to contend with.

"I'm sure of it, and I don't think it's arms or explosives, I think it's stolen art. That's why the dogs couldn't smell anything. It was hard enough with all that grime everywhere. No, I think there are some very valuable paintings there."

"Have you said anything… before?" She's in policewoman-mode now – well away from my kitchen gallery.

"No, this idea has been growing ever since I came to London. I wouldn't be surprised if Grimwode is thinking the same thing now. My guess is that something's been nicked from the Somerset Gallery." Things dropped from my whirling mind are falling into place.

"It's ever since IS started taking antiquities out of Syria, isn't it? There must be a market for stolen art."

"A much bigger one than we anticipated…"

"Arne?" Peggy looks at me.

"Yes?"

"About the drawing."

"Yes?"

"I'd still like to have it. Can I?"

Hannah reappears. "We'd better get going. I want to warm up before the concert." She looks brisk and in control, adrenaline coursing through her veins and making her positively sparkle. "I've called a taxi."

"I'll take Peggy," I say. "You must look after your hands."

Hannah looks unwilling to let go of her Peggy-support-role, so we do the getting-out thing together, and are in the taxi and off to St Martin's.

Our arrival catches me out. The pillars. I remember pillars. Are they the same? Was I here last night? Did someone speak to me? As we get out of the taxi, I don't recognize anything else – just the pillars. We get Peggy up the steps, and Hannah disappears down the far end of the church to 'warm up'. No-one has arrived for the concert yet – we are very early, and we sit at the back.

"Hannah doesn't like me to be at the front, it puts her off," Peggy informs me.

All very still. Very quiet. We are together. Close but not touching. I want to hold her hand. The electricity between us feels palpable to me. As the audience begins to filter in, I am sure they can see it too – sparks and colours flashing between us like a miniature Northern Lights. Time seems to stand still – I want it to last for ever, but eventually Hannah comes out, and sits down at the front of the church and plays her Bach. She plays with ease, as if my problems and Peggy's had not touched her. She's in her own world with Bach, and then Brahms, her cello warm against the fiery piano. And all the while Peggy and I are caught in our own world of wonder. Not looking at each other, not touching, but each knowing the other is there. The interval comes, and people go off for their drinks in the crypt, but we stay, caught in our magic web.

After the interval, the Debussy tells me the story of the clown. The clown who loves a girl hopelessly. Is that me?

At the end of the concert we go down the church to find Hannah, flushed with happiness, talking to enthusiastic members of her audience. The pianist Clarke is close by. Tall, dark, with the long fingers of a young Horowitz.

In the taxi going back to her flat, Hannah talks animatedly about how it went, and Peggy gives her a rapturous report of how it all sounded from our end of the church. I am mute as the lights of London glide by. There is nothing I can say.

So this is love. I never knew it before. I accepted something less, thinking that was all. But now I know what it is. Maybe I'm suffering from exhausted delusion after being out all night on Oxford Street. If that's so, I'll gladly go and do it all again. I look at Peggy, and wonder if she feels the same as me – an inexpressible joy at being in the same space.

The taxi drive is over too soon. Everything's over too soon, and before I know it I'm in bed in a spare room. She said goodnight. We parted without a kiss, and now I'm alone, and my brain won't go to sleep. The buzz of being in love is gradually giving way to a feeling of urgency. I must solve this mystery. I've got to get back home and find that space at the back of the apple store. The space that Lilly hid in, all those years ago. What is hidden in there now? Paintings?

I try to sleep and go off for what seems like a minute, then I wake up and find it's half past two. I am completely alert. Ready to go. Now's the time, something tells me. Quietly I put on my clothes and creep out of my room. Money is a problem. I lost all my money when my rucksack was stolen. I'm living off the kindness of Hannah and Peggy, and now I'm going to have to abuse it. Peggy's bag is in the sitting room, and with a horrible feeling of betrayal I open it, find her purse and take out a £20 note. Will she notice? Of course she will. She's a policewoman and she's trained to notice things like that. I find a pen, and a till receipt, and write on it: IOU £20 A X – my first message of love.

The dog looks up quizzically as I go past his makeshift bed in the hall. Wags tail, but no bark – this is the middle of the night. We don't go walkies in the middle of the night. He puts his head back down and returns to whatever he was dreaming about, and I sneak out of the front door, hearing the final click of the lock behind me.

The street is quiet – nobody walks in Regent's Park at this time of night. I head down to the main road which still has a steady flow of traffic, but as I do so I am sure there is someone following me. I turn suddenly, hoping to catch them out. Nothing. Just empty middle-of-the-night pavements. A cat walks along a wall and jumps effortlessly down onto the pavement, on cushioned nine-life paws.

There are quite a few people around at St Pancras, as I buy my single from a machine that mercifully takes notes. I get straight on a train, and there are a couple of people in my carriage, talking animatedly about scuba diving. I sit back and learn about gear, wetsuits, drysuits, flippers, diving off Lundy Island, and so on until the train arrives at my station.

I look out cautiously before stepping onto the platform. I'm the only one who gets off. The station is empty – no waiting police reception for me. Just an empty crisp packet skating along the platform aided by a cold wind. I shiver – somewhere in my bones I haven't warmed up from the previous night's sleep on the street.

Should I have contacted my police colleagues? Trouble is, I don't trust them, and I don't think they will believe me. So go it alone, Arnold. Be the maverick, be the outsider, and take the risk.

Compared to the great metropolis, my town is completely silent. No cars on the road, no people on the streets at four o'clock. It makes me feel even more exposed – the only living, moving creature in this sleeping town. There is a sudden crash behind me and I spin round, almost falling over in my attempt to see my pursuer. A fox struts across the road, bold as brass in the streetlight. Stops and stares straight at me – he makes me feel that I'm the intruder, not him. He turns and trots on into the shadows of someone's front garden.

I walk down through the town towards my destination, my ultimate discovery, the thing that will rescue my self-esteem, not to say my reputation, in the police force. My heart beats louder in my ears as I walk up past the church and turn into The Avenues. Don't be an idiot, my alter ego says. Contact the station now – tell them you're about to enter the house, and that you need backup. Backup for what? I look around – the avenue is completely empty. No-one about, no-one following me – not even the moon, which is hiding its face tonight.

It's nearly pitch black when I turn into the drive of 'Hazelbank', but I can see that there is no police tape any more. Grimwode and his terrorist squad have given up and gone.

I find my mobile, which I had the foresight to charge up using Hannah's charger. Switching the torch on, I turn down the side drive that descends to the back of the house, and true to Lilly's description, about three quarters of the way down there is a small window quite close to the ground.

I try pushing up the sash – at first it seems stuck, but then gives way with a small protesting squeal of swollen wood. I manage to ease myself through the small gap, and as I do so I have a horror-image of Cornelia Witherspoon easing her plump body through the same space like an evil spider. Shuddering with sudden fear of the dark, I drop down into the room where Sergeant Brown had watched me examining the back wall with such scorn. Well, now I'm going to show them – all my childish fantasies about being a great detective come to the fore as I shine my light to see the way to the apple store and the great works of art that I will discover there.

Round the corner, up a couple of steps, into the small room lined with shelves, and down to the end – right in the dark corner where Lilly hid fifty odd years ago. There must be a door here, just big enough to squeeze through. I push against the wall at the back, but find nothing but resistance. If it had been easy, I reflect, then my colleagues would have found it weeks ago, but I feel around the edge of where I think the door must be, hoping for a catch. It does occur to me that the terrorist group may have made it much more secure, and that it will need a lot of force to open it now. Maybe I should call for assistance, but I am reluctant – I don't trust my police colleagues anymore. They'll just grab hold of me and drag me away – mad Rackham, that's what I am to them. And anyway, what a coup it will be if I turn up at the station with millions of pounds worth of stolen paintings.

As I have these thoughts, I feel a small movement under my fingers. Something gives way, and the wall begins to slide back revealing a tiny room. This is it. I shine my light into the darkness and can see four painting-shaped packages in bubble wrap. I carefully pull out the nearest one, and ease my hands round the tape that holds the bubble wrap on. Once again, I realise, I'm failing to follow procedure.

I pull the bubble wrap off to reveal a painting covered in tissue paper.

Tissue paper? That rings a bell. Someone asked me about a piece of tissue paper, stuck to a bit of bubble wrap.

This is all starting to make sense.

I gently pull away the tissue paper, turn the painting towards me and shine my light on it. Manet, I'm sure it's a Manet. I look closely at the brushwork, using all I have learnt to work out if this is genuine. I could do with a magnifying glass. I get a bit closer to try and catch the smell of the paint, instead of the aroma of rotten apples.

Closer, so close, I'm almost touching the surface with my nose.

I hold my breath.

It smells old, it must be…

Somebody pulls me backwards by my collar and my head explodes in a fantastic show of fireworks. There is a terrible pain on the back of my skull before everything goes dark.

7 am, Saturday 10th October

"Koo yana piktoorat? Koo yemmy piktoora nooha?"

I can't work out where I am. Sounds somewhere foreign – exotic even. But I have this terrible headache, and I am lying on a hard floor that smells of coal and petrol. There is some light, I think it must be daylight, shining through from somewhere above my head.

"Koo yana piktoorat?" The voice is insistent, and as I raise my head slightly to see who is talking, I feel a sudden pain in my thigh – the man standing above me has just kicked me.

"Painteengs, where painteengs?" Another kick.

I scramble up onto all fours – my head is spinning and aching, but now I can see my assailant. It's our young Albanian gunman, and true to form he is holding a gun, and speaking in what I guess is Albanian.

"Koo yemmy piktoora nooha? Now!" He gets me by my collar, and pulls me up. His gun is pressed against my temple, and he leads me to the apple store where a single bulb is suspended from the ceiling, illuminating the back wall. I can see that where before there was my suspected cache of priceless paintings wrapped in bubble wrap, there is nothing now. Just a hole going back into the foundations of the house.

He drags me back into the main basement, and presses his gun harder against my temple. "Who take painteengs?"

261

Who hit me on the head? Brian? If I tell the gunman he will certainly try to track him down and kill him. Do I care?

"Who? I count – zen…" He is going to shoot me in the head if I don't tell him. He is going to shoot me anyway. I close my eyes.

"Nya, doo, tre" – fuck, he's counting in Albanian – "katar, pesa," five - keep count, "jashta, shtata, teta, nanta" - nearly there, tell him it's Brian – argh…

There's a shattering explosion. But I don't feel a thing – no earth-shattering pain then oblivion.

I don't feel any different.

"Inspector Rackham? Sir? Are you alright?" I don't recognize this voice. Am I dead?

I open my eyes. A police marksman is walking towards me, looking down at the ground beside me with his gun pointing just by my right knee. I follow his gaze, and there, lying in a spreading pool of blood, is my would-be executioner. He's got a hole in his head – looks dead enough to me.

Another officer, wearing bulletproof gear, comes in quickly and kneels beside the gunman feeling for a pulse on his neck.

"Dead. We won't get anything out of this one."

My rescuer takes his helmet off. His expression is grim as he looks down at the dead terrorist. He shakes his head, but at this moment all I want to do is hug him – he saved my life.

"Good work, Harry," Forester walks into view. "You hadn't got much choice. We had no time to do anything except react, and we've got our police inspector back, safe and sound eh, Rackham?" He looks at me with a wry expression. "We'd better get you mopped up, and then you can let us in on what you've been up to. You were lucky McDonald raised the alarm, we only just got here in time."

So Peggy alerted them. My head aches, my thigh aches, and I feel a complete idiot. If I'd called the squad in, we could have retrieved the paintings. Now they've gone, and I have a very good idea who took them.

"Brian O'Connell sir. I'm sure he's taken them. He's been following me for days. I thought he'd given up."

"Taken what?"

"The paintings, sir. I saw one. It was a Manet... I'm sure it was genuine though..." I can see by the look on his face that he thinks I'm just babbling. Concussed.

"Well it's not my case," he shrugs. "I'll pass this straight on to Commander Grimwode. Get him on the radio, will you." He turns to someone, then back to me. "Please don't ever think of going it alone again. You might not be so lucky next time." He actually chuckles, and smiles at me. I don't suppose Grimwode will smile at me.

I stagger forward and nearly fall, but am caught by the marksman. I whisper, "Thank you, you saved my life."

"All in the course of duty sir," he says, but I bet it meant more than 'duty' at that moment.

I'm led out by a posse of my fellow police, grateful to have them there, for a change. The air is fresh on my face – it's a cool autumn dawn as I am led out into the courtyard. An ambulance has been driven down. The squad cars will have been parked out of earshot. I feel looked after and supported after my time in the wilderness, though God knows what awaits me after I've been 'mopped up'.

1.30 pm, Saturday 24th October

Some 'star' TV presenters could do with minders, I reflect, as I sit in my chair in my office, twiddling my pen and awaiting the next development in my future. The minder could protect the public and fellow TV workers from the 'star's' megalomaniac outbursts, he or she could save the people around the 'star' from getting injured. I could be a minder, but I'm probably not the man for the job. Probably not strong enough.

Look for another job. And I am looking for another job. The trust between me and my fellow force members has been fatally punctured. I'm needed for the Witherspoon case, but after that…

I have a minder now, though I am not a threat to myself or the public. He is called Trev and he is large and fast. He's very likeable, is Trev. Witness protection is what he specializes in, and I'm a witness. Trev has a sense of humour, and knows when to be quiet – good company, and to be frank, I'm grateful for it. But I know they don't trust me anymore, and once my usefulness is over I'll be out of the force as fast as they can throw me.

Can I blame them? If I'd kept in contact instead of going AWOL we'd probably have millions of pounds' worth of reclaimed masterpieces, instead of having to scour the ports of the world for Brian, and his little stash. The painting thing still bugs me though. I told Grimwode in one of our far-from-amicable interviews that I had suspicions about collections of copies in The Avenues. But he ignored me as usual, which made me reflect that it wasn't all my fault that we lost the paintings in the basement.

Forester, on the other hand, has been friendly, and I regret some of what I said to him about his 'protected life', though I still defend my attitude to witnesses in abuse cases. I would have to be very convinced that Paul would have proper protection from lawyers and media, before I would try and persuade him to come forward and give evidence against Cornelia Witherspoon. I feel differently about Lilly. She never said she didn't want to give evidence. She told her story to me, a policeman, and then ran away. And I wonder whether, in her case, telling her story in court would be cathartic – a way of telling the world of the injustice done to her – all those years shut up in a psychiatric institution. Forester has put out a search for her, but no luck. I'd have thought someone as red as her would be easy to find.

My thoughts wander back to the minder idea, and I imagine the great corporation demanding that young up-and-coming presenters have to sign this agreement that 'the corporation reserves the right to insist that .... has a minder to protect them, and everyone who come into contact with them, if the situation demands it'. Sign under pressure, regret at leisure.

Strangely, no results have come back from the memory clinic yet, but I've pushed that fear to the back of my mind. My mind, by the way, has been behaving itself recently. Maybe it's the company of Trev making me feel secure – knowing someone has their eye on me. Anyway, I'm taken up mainly with wondering what has happened to Peggy, and what to do about it. I haven't seen her. She hasn't contacted me for two weeks. All I've had is my computer back, and an exchange of texts with Hannah about the dog. I'm glad he's with them at least – he's my representative in the world of Peggy, but I don't dare phone. I feel like I must have overstepped the mark somehow, and the longer it goes on the more difficult it gets to break the ice.

I sit in my office wondering what to do. It's more like a crèche really – my nanny sits in the corner reading a newspaper and nurse comes in, in the form of Claire, to offer me a cup of tea.

"How's it going?" I ask pleasantly. "London stuff still proceeding?" I'm not allowed to know about the 'London stuff'. Can't be trusted.

"I don't know sir, it's all…"

"Classified, I know. Sorry."

She smiles apologetically, and hands me my cuppa. Trev gets his too. I think she likes him – maybe there's romance in the air. We could do with a bit of it in this office – I've been missing Peggy terribly since the night I left her.

Claire leaves me to my cuppa and my thoughts. There's meant to be another visit from Grimwode this afternoon, and I am dreading it. I think he'd like to break me into little pieces, and examine each bit for the truth. But the truth is, he should have listened and treated me with more respect in the first place. We're at loggerheads now, armed to the eyebrows like two knights in a jousting competition.

There's a knock at the door. I brace myself. It's Claire again – I notice the way that Trev looks over the top of his paper.

"Commander Grimwode can't see you this afternoon, sir."

I breathe out slowly. "But I've got another visitor for you." Her eyes meet Trev's and she smiles, turns, and mutters something down the corridor. There's a clatter of crutches and Peggy appears at the doorway looking

267

youthful in joggers and a bomber jacket, her long hair tied back in a ponytail.

I catch my breath and stand up too fast, spilling my tea, as she walks awkwardly into the room with the support of her crutches, her legs further apart than normal to give her balance. I bustle round and pull out a chair for her. She says nothing, just looks down, concentrating.

"You're walking," I croak, stating the obvious.

"Yes." She's breathing hard, though with exertion or emotion I can't tell.

I help her into the chair. Go round to mine behind the desk in silence, finding a tissue to mop up the spilt tea.

I don't know what to say. Maybe two words will do: "Thank you."

"For what?" She won't look at me.

"For telling them. I'd be dead if you hadn't."

"Why didn't you tell me?"

"What? That I was going? I…"

"You're a bloody fool. You nearly got yourself killed." She looks straight at me.

"Sorry."

There's a shuffling sound in the corner. Trev pulls his newspaper together and stands up.

"I'll be just outside." And he goes out closing the door behind him.

"Look." We say it together. "I don't know…"

"You go first," I manage to get in.

"Look, I don't know if it's because I broke into your house, don't you trust me now? We've always worked things out together."

"I know I should have trusted you. If I'd told you what I was doing I wouldn't be in the mess I'm in now." I speak low and urgently. I don't want us to be overheard.

"You worked it out with me, remember. All that stuff with Lilly – her story about the basement. I could have…

268

I don't know… sorted out some cover for you. You shouldn't have gone on your own after what happened to you in London."

"It was Brian O'Connell. It must have been. He attacked me in London. He knew I was onto something. He knew the paintings were hidden somewhere, so he followed me the other night. I felt it but I never spotted him."

"But why paintings?" Peggy is being pulled away from the emotional and into police-mode.

"Brian was obviously onto something about the paintings. He held that spoof meeting about copies of great works of art. I think he was just fishing to see if he could find out where they were. He and Malcolm Smith-Rogers and their mates were all in on it, trying to put pressure on our terrorists to get a share of the hoard. You saw where Smith-Rogers ended up. I wouldn't be surprised if Brian ends up the same way. Silly bugger – playing with fire."

"So the paintings are lost."

"No." I'm lost, I think. If I lose you now – I'm lost. "Brian will have a difficult job selling them. The terrorists on the other hand, will have connections with IS, and all their customers who are buying artefacts taken from Syria. I wouldn't be in his shoes for all the tea in China."

"All the tea in where?" Peggy looks at me with a puzzled smile. She's a different generation, I realise.

"China. Just a term us oldies use for…"

"You're not that old," she says warmly.

"Look Peggy," I say her name – it's like passing a boundary, "can we meet up somewhere?"

"Yes, OK, but where?"

"I don't know yet. You know I'm being mindered, so we may have a chaperone." I think of Hannah – she was a chaperone. "How's Hannah? How's the dog?"

Peggy smiles in a solemn kind of way. I love that smile. I'd like to bottle it and carry it around with me. "The dog's fine, but Hannah's not very happy with you. She'll get over it… she loves having the dog."

10 am, Saturday 31st October

Our 'meet up somewhere' turns out to be a café exclusively for those involved in a trial at The Old Bailey. Peggy is allowed to sit with me while we wait for the trial of Cornelia Witherspoon to begin. Trev sits discretely at the table next to us. We don't know what to say – perhaps the Old Bailey isn't the most romantic meeting place. My mind dreams up stories of love affairs started in this café, a bit like 'Brief Encounter'. All very stilted and proper: 'catching a train', except it's 'going to prison'.

I feel strange and rattled – uncomfortable, as though I'm about to perform in the Albert Hall. This was not helped by the awesome hallways, with their domes and arches inlaid with marble, that I walked through as I entered this place of trial and tribulation. Witherspoon has somehow managed to get a very good legal team behind her, and I have the feeling I'm in for a rough ride. The trial has been brought forward, the defence claiming that poor Cornelia is too frail to be kept in custody for long. Go for bail? I don't think so with teams of forensic scientists still poring through her house and garden. How long does it take? I wonder. It's obvious to me, but then I know stuff that the court doesn't so I shouldn't be surprised by the machinations of the law. So far the forensic evidence is inconclusive. I'm on my own.

I need to go to the toilet again. Off we go, Trev and I – inseparable. He must be thinking, 'Poor old Arnold with his poor old bladder'.

I return to hear our case being called. Peggy stands up with difficulty, and we slowly make our way through the grand halls to the courtroom. Stand firm, Arnold, stand firm. Shoulders back like a soldier, head up. Look them straight in the eye.

Not so easy as it happens, as my anger with Cornelia Witherspoon evaporates into fear when I actually see her sitting there in the dock, and I find myself towering over the miniscule lawyer who now interrogates me. The forensic witness has failed to sound convincing, and now I'm under the cosh.

"Lost her? Lost your chief witness? That's not the only thing you lost in London, is it Inspector. You lost your wallet." Someone laughs, and then stops abruptly remembering where they are. "And you were seen begging on the street. Oxford Street, I believe. Needed the money, did you?"

"I wasn't begging."

"Speak up," the judge can't hear my husky whisper. "So the court can hear you."

"I wasn't begging, your Honour." My voice sounds feeble and whining in the great and hallowed courtroom.

"What were you doing, then?"

It was all going well until I told them about Lilly's disappearance. The court heard how I came across Cornelia Witherspoon in her garden, how I was poisoned by her and chased into the garden and saved by my dog. How I came across Lilly and she told me her story. But now… it all sounds so unlikely. Like some fabrication from my own imagination.

"I was tired. I went to sleep." Sounds completely mad.

"You went to sleep on the pavement in Oxford Street."
He says this slowly as though he wants to check every
word.

"Yes," I mumble.

"Speak up," barks the judge.

"Yes, your Honour." The whine is back.

"Is this what you normally do? Sleep on the street?"
The lawyer asks.

"No." I shake my head to emphasize for the hard-of-
hearing. I notice a movement up in the gallery. A man
walks in. He looks like Paul.

"And what were you doing in London?" the lawyer
asks.

Oh my God it *is* Paul – what is he doing here? No Paul,
let me hang myself. Don't get involved.

"Sorry?" I'm distracted.

"In London. What were you doing in London?" His
voice gets even more piercing, I'm surprised that's
possible.

"Art."

"Art?"

"I was looking at art."

There's another burst of laughter from the uncontained
source. This time it's picked up by others and turns into a
general rumble.

"Silence!" He's a right Tartar, this judge.

"You – were – looking – at – art."

"Yes."

"And why were you looking at art?"

"I needed to find something out that's to do with
another investigation."

"Another investigation, eh? And since when were you
a police art expert?" He smirks at me in a way that makes
me want to hit him. This kind of boy was the worst kind
of bully at school – a jeerleader.

273

"Well, I paint."

"You paint."

"And I draw."

"You draw."

"I was an artist before I became a policeman."

"I don't see where this is going," interrupts the judge.

"Sorry, your Honour." He turns obsequiously to the judge. He turns back to me. "Isn't it true that you've been suspended from duty?"

"Yes."

"And that you were suspended from duty for in-su-bor-di-na-tion?" How he likes that word.

"Yes."

"So you went off to London to look at art. And this was off your own bat without the knowledge of your senior officers. And so, as you wandered round London, looking at art, you came across this Lilly person who just happened to be sitting on the street. And she told you all about the defendant and how she tried to murder her, and gave you proof. Did she give you any proof? No, I don't think she did. In fact, I don't think she existed."

There's movement up in the public gallery. A flash of white.

He turns to the jury. "Ladies and gentlemen of the jury. We have heard that the evidence from the forensics has been inconclusive so far, and I put it to you that what Inspector Rackham has been telling us is entirely the product of his lively artistic imagination. Indeed, it is a pack of lies from beginning to end. He is the prosecution's only witness in the case, and his claims are denied by the defendant who says that he walked into her garden demanding to interview her about the terrorist incident. Walked into her house, and when she gave him a cup of tea, she became so confused that she put the wrong thing in his cup, thinking it was sugar. Her eyesight is very poor…"

I can hear someone talking urgently in the gallery. There's something going on up there. I look up. I see Paul standing up.

"Her eyesight is very poor," the lawyer repeats over the increasing disturbance at the back of the court.

"It wasn't very poor when she tried to murder me forty-five years ago," a voice shouts from the gallery. I recognize that voice.

"We must have order," shouts the judge. "Clear the gallery, and what's that dog doing in here?"

Everyone is looking up at the gallery at the sight of an old woman dressed in white, with her dog on a lead, being hauled out by two policemen.

Undeterred, as though this happens every day, the silk for the defence carries on. "Her eyesight is very poor, her health is failing, and it is inhumane for her to be held in custody any longer. The prosecution have shown us… nothing. There is not a shred of evidence to keep her from her home, surrounded by her loved possessions – the comforts of her old age. Your Honour, ladies and gentlemen of the jury, I submit that this trial should be dismissed immediately, and that this innocent and elderly lady be allowed to return home."

There is an urgent consultation on the prosecution bench, and the chief prosecutor heads towards the judge with the defence lawyer in his wake. I try to attract the attention of another member of the prosecution team. She comes over and I whisper. "That's Lilly," gesturing towards the emptying gallery. "For God's sake, don't let her disappear again."

No wonder we couldn't find her – she was in white, and now, back in court after a three day adjournment while we interviewed her and gathered supporting evidence, Lilly is giving a good account of herself. The anger at all those years incarcerated in a mental institution is being vented on the defence lawyer, who is definitely losing the battle. We even have the station master's logbook showing her original arrest, and something of what she claimed at the time.

She's down at his level – he is short but she is shorter. He is vicious but she is viciouser. Here's an old lady who's really been badly treated.

"Just tell me one thing, Miss er… Lilly." Battered and bruised, the lawyer has a final go. "Why did you run away from Inspector Rackham? If you knew all this, why didn't you come forward sooner?"

Lilly pauses and straightens her bent body up as far as she can. She looks round the court – at the gallery, at the jury, at me. "I was locked away for years because they didn't believe me. Given drugs because they said I had hallucinations. Made to keep quiet. Cause no trouble, was the message. Old habits die hard, mister, and it was only when I met the wonderful Inspector Rackham, that I found someone I could trust. He is an amazing policeman. He can spot the truth a mile off, and he's the sort of person that people will talk to…"

"So why run away from him?"

"It wasn't him, it was the rest of 'em. How could I know they would believe me, or him? He was out on his own, I knew that. I figured it wasn't safe, so I ran away. But I had to see that woman," Lilly points a shaking finger at Witherspoon in the dock, "go down, so when I found out this was going on, I came here. And when it looked like nobody was going to believe Inspector Rackham when he told my story, I couldn't stop myself from speaking out, could I?" She spreads her arms wide, embracing her truth, and giving it to the court.

And it's not just her story.

My brother Paul comes forward to give evidence. He risks so much to give his story. But when he has finished, his eyes glow with the release of it. His 'hallucinations' made true.

"No further questions, your Honour," says the defence.

Paul is followed by another, and another, and another. All boys who were abused by their school matron, who now sits like a dreadful old crow in the defendant's box. She never looks at anyone – just stares into the middle distance. She could be dead for all the movement she makes. Like her mother, she says not a word.

But after nearly half a century, these lives are being set free. And mine too. Crushed balls. In those few moments she crushed the ability for real intimacy out of me.

The defence is in disarray. More conclusive evidence has come from the forensics, which along with the witness statements, makes the whole story pretty clear. Why did she do it? How did she get away with it? It's from a period when people did get away with abusing children. And murdering them. Children weren't listened to. Whether anyone will ever understand the distorted workings of Cornelia Witherspoon's mind, I doubt. I think, like her mother, she will never utter another word, and her inner secrets will remain, like her, locked away for ever.

11.45 am, Tuesday 3rd November

We are gathered in the stately hall outside the courtroom. The jury has pronounced her guilty, the sentence of 'life' has been passed, and we are all wondering where we can go and have coffee.

There is a feeling of hilarity amongst us, the victims. The other 'boys' have been offered counselling, but have said 'no thanks – already had some.' A bit like refusing another biscuit at a tea party. Ugh.

So is it Pret, or Costa, or some other?

Jack says his club isn't far. It would be more private for our celebration. Jack must have been one of the last of Witherspoon's victims – he seems much younger than the rest of us, for all his lack of hair.

I feel someone touch my elbow. It's Peggy, standing tall with her crutches. I want to turn and hug her there and then, but something holds me back. Is it the fact we're work colleagues? The fact that I'm so much older than her? The fact that I'm still married?

"Well done. You did it. Did you hear what Lilly said? Wonderful policeman." She hugs me, dropping her crutches on the marble floor. She clings onto me to keep her balance, and buries her face in my shoulder as I put my arms around her. I close my eyes. This is nice, this is very nice. I could hold her all day.

I hear the sound of someone picking up her crutches, and I open my eyes to see Forester looking at us with an amused smile on his face. "Sergeant McDonald, Inspector Rackham, I think you might be needing these," he says. "And er… well done Rackham. A good job." He pats me on the elbow as Peggy extracts herself, and walks away with a spring in his step.

"Do you want to come too?" I don't want to let her out of my sight.

"No, I've got stuff to do. Hannah's got a taxi. See you… soon?" She seems embarrassed now – that sudden show of affection took her over a line she hadn't meant to cross. She clunks off towards Hannah who is waiting by the entrance.

"You coming?" Paul says. He laughs and reaches out to hold my arm and lead me out of my Peggy-induced trance.

We leave the hallowed halls of justice, and amble down the steps into the street. Nobody is taking any notice of us. The press have been mercifully caught out by the sudden turn of events in our case, and are probably off making some unwise celebrity's life a misery.

"So, you and Peggy..?"

Paul is mercifully interrupted by a sudden flash of white, and there is Lilly. Resplendent in a new coat. Somebody gave her a coat. Wow. What about her life back? Still, she has something now. The world knows she was wronged. At least they will, if anybody bothers to report it.

"Coming with us?" I say. "We're going to Jack's club."

Jack looks uneasy about this. Old woman off the streets with her dog? In his squeaky-clean club? What will they say?

"Nah. I just wanted to wish you well. You boys. I'm off down the Embankment for a walk. We need a bit of fresh air, Red and me."

I bend down and scratch Red behind the ears. He looks up at me, and I could swear there's a smile in his eyes. The dog who made the connection through my dog. They understood something at a doggy level. Red wags his tail, and Lilly looks longingly in the direction of her walk. The others have walked on, leaving us alone.

"Thank you," Lilly says. I can't see her face, but there is emotion in her voice.

"Thank you," I say. "It was brave of you to come."

"Nah. Couldn't let the old witch get away with it. Worth the risk."

She walks off, stooped low, her dog by her side. Neither of them in charge really – just going through life together.

I stand, watching her go. Looking round, I realise that the others have disappeared, and I have no idea where they've gone. Jack's club – did he ever say the name?

My phone croaks. It's Grimwode. Grimwode? What mud does he want to drag me through now?

"You'd better come back. There's been a development."

"But I thought I was suspended."

"Never mind about that now. You're still into art, aren't you? See you in a couple of hours."

And that is that. No coffee with 'the boys'.

3.30 pm, Tuesday 3rd November

The Avenues, rid of its local witch, holds more intrigue than fear for me now. The impossibly rich, they seem to me, live here in their Victorian mansions, and one of them has been burgled. Grimwode's interest must be because it was an art theft. He's not here in person, thank God. Too taken up with his investigations in London, along with his art experts there.

His diminutive representative is here to greet me.

"Thank you for coming, sir," says Sergeant Brown.

Sir? I never thought I'd be called that again. It's mid-afternoon, and the autumn light shines low on the front windows of the house.

"Shall we?" I let him lead me to the front door.

"Archibald Rowlinson, sir. He called us in this morning. He has a collection of copies of well-known paintings, which, he says, were very expensive. He came down for breakfast to find that one had gone. Here we are."

A tall rubicund man in his sixties answers the door. I've never seen him before, but then I never mix in such exalted circles. He looks me up and down, taking in my scuffed shoes and rumpled clothes.

"You are?" His voice is surprisingly uncouth for someone who looks like they've stepped out of an Agatha Christie novel.

"Inspector Rackham. Commander Grimwode asked me to come." The urge to say 'sir' is almost overpowering. But I won't say 'sir' to this rude man. Make use of Grimwode's name instead.

"This way." He leads us through the hall to what must be the dining room. I get a flash of 'Cluedo' – *'Mrs Scarlet done it in the dining room with the lead piping.'* Get a hold, Rackham. This is serious, and puzzling.

"Only one painting taken, my colleagues tell me."

"Yeh. It was there." He points to a series of Impressionist paintings displayed along one wall. They are there to show off, rather than for any artistic purpose, judging by the unimaginative way they have been hung. There's a gap where the stolen painting should have been.

"Degas. Never really liked it."

"Then why did you buy it?" I can't resist having a dig at this pompous man who knows nothing about art.

"Oh, the whole collection was offered as a bulk deal. Twenty percent off if I bought the lot, and a good deal on the alarm system to boot."

"Sounds like a bargain." I can't help the sarcasm. "And you didn't hear a thing, or know you'd been burgled till you came down this morning?"

"No. The alarm failed to go off. They told me it would be foolproof. Pah! Load of rubbish. Didn't work, did it." He isn't looking at me. Perhaps in his mind, there is an imaginary burglar alarm seller somewhere in the room.

"Was it a good alarm system?" I'm thinking you pays your money you takes your choice, and this is a man who clearly likes something for nothing.

"Like I said, came with the paintings. Massive reduction. Normally very expensive, or so they told me."

I walk up to a copy of Monet's 'Le Grand Canal'. It's certainly a good-quality copy. Makes me think of that Seurat that covered the safe, in the raid that was the beginning of all this Avenues nightmare. I look closely. Get my magnifier out. Yes, it's a good copy, probably Chinese.

"Only the one taken, you say. How valuable is your collection?"

"The paintings, after the twenty percent off, came to five thousand quid each, and there were twelve in the collection."

Not megabucks for the likes of Archibald but over the odds for a Chinese copy, which could go for anything from £70 to £3000. He's been ripped off.

"Can I see the receipt for all of this?"

"It's in my study. Got it out for the insurance company. I can let you see it but I need it to do my claim," he says grudgingly.

I follow him into his study – *'Rev. Green done it in the study with the revolver.'* This would be such a perfect house for a murder mystery weekend.

I look at the headed notepaper: 'The Riches of Art'. All very elaborate and tasteless. There is a list of the copies, with the artist and the name of the painting. The Degas sets something off in my memory. Quite a few Degas sketches and paintings were stolen in a famous art heist some years ago. I will check to see if Archie's missing Degas had the same name as one of them.

"We will need to make copies of this receipt and any other paperwork you have to do with this 'deal'."

"I…"

"We will get it back to you within the hour, that is unless…"

"I'll copy it for you here. No problem."

Ah, helpful at last. "And can you tell us anything about the people who sold you this, um, bulk deal?" I follow him out of his study to his rather less pretentious office. Very functional indeed – the place where, no doubt, he grinds the bones of us undeserving poor to make the odd extra quid.

"It was all done over the internet, except…"

"Except?"

"There was this local bloke."

"Yes?"

"Wide as he was tall. Laughed a lot."

I bet he did – all the way to the bank.

"Can't remember his name though." Obviously not a friend.

"Well, if you remember anything more about him, and anything else that could help us…" My gentlest tones are used.

"Oh, just one more thing." It's working – he's warming up. "I think there are others."

"Others?'

"Other people who have bought these collections. Not like mine, of course…"

Of course. How could they be like yours?

"It would be very helpful if you could tell us who they are. They might get burgled too. We should warn them."

"I'll have a think about it."

Not all ego then? We'll see.

"And this local er… bloke. Could you identify him?"

"Certainly. If I saw him again. Wide as he was high. Laughed a lot."

That reminds me of someone, but it can't be.

"And what was his part in all this exactly?"

"Put me on to it. In a pub."

"Which pub?" My heart takes a lurch.

"I think it was the Railway Arms."

Not your sort of pub, I'd have thought.

"Funny bloke. Knew a lot."

4.30 pm, Tuesday 3rd November

My home feels strange after recent events. The dog is still being looked after by Hannah, there is no Trev to look after me anymore, now I've done my witnessing. Peggy remains with Hannah still. In fact I wish I was living with her too – the two most important beings in my life are there, in that beautiful flat, and I am here in this dusty cold cottage.

Once it was my home, my retreat. Now it feels empty. My self-deceiving slow-lane life has gone now, leaving this house an empty husk full of the things that kept me going. The little details, the little rituals – now I can't even take the dog for a walk.

And Betty. Where's Betty? I know we're looking for her now – her and her so-called solicitor. But they've vanished. A part of me hopes they'll never be found. I don't want any more crocodile tears and deceptive tales from the wife I never knew. It's a strange relief now, to know that she's not next door, however cold and lonely this place may be. At least it's honest.

I rub my finger despondently on the surface of the kitchen table – it makes a streak across a moorland of dust. I look at my gallery of faces on the wall with their names. Cornelia Witherspoon can come down now, as can Forester. It was all over this morning and now I'm back. On my own.

Pull yourself together, Rackham. The things that have bugged your life, things that you tried to forget, have been brought out into the open. You have laid the ghost – sent her to prison even. And now you've got a case. Something to do with art. Something you know about.

I think of phoning Peggy, but after that sudden closeness, I just want to leave it. Let it soak in. I fact I'm almost afraid to talk to her. Supposing I find out she didn't really mean it – that the hug was just an accident.

I pull myself away from thoughts of Peggy, and turn on my computer to search for 'art thefts'. There're quite a few from years ago. Not so many recently. I look for Manet, Degas and other Impressionists. I find an article about an art heist that happened decades ago – paintings thought to be lost, possibly destroyed. And there's the name of Archie's missing Degas, but it's all so long ago – it seems so useless that I shut it down without bothering to look carefully at the other stolen paintings. I'll do a proper police search tomorrow, down at what's left of the station now that all the invaders have gone, but the idea of these stolen paintings fits with my suspicions about these 'Riches of Art' collections.

The light is fading outside, and I want a walk, so I lock up and go down my garden path and out onto the common. Even this lovely familiar piece of rural England has lost its attraction. No longer a solace – just something to be walked through. The memories of the 'Ups-and-Downs', the sight of my home town in the distance – they mean nothing to me at this moment. I don't seem to be able to shake off this feeling of uselessness – nothing having any meaning. Walking down the common, the grass goes crunch, crunch under my feet. Nothing else. No rich smells, no ear-catching birdsong, no familiar heart-warming shades. Just descending darkness, as the evening draws in. I stagger slightly as I take the root-knobbled path by the old drainage pools, heading back up towards the pub. Maybe I'll find solace there – not just in drink, but in company. Charles, my old friend – wide as he is tall. Propping up the bar. Knowing everything.

The lights glow invitingly out into my darkness. There are pretty lights on the outside too, hung in a string under the eaves of this Edwardian building. Everything says celebrate – 'eat, drink and be merry' – but I wonder. Will I be merry in there? Not sure. Think I might be sad. Think I might be betrayed again.

In the warm bar the specials board declares Steak and Kidney Pud – a welcome break from the takeaways I've been having with Trev.

Charles is looking down at a newspaper – doesn't see me come in. He's on his mobile talking fast and low. I keep a discreet distance, and prop up the other end of the bar, quietly ordering my Steak-and-Kidney-and-a-pint. Looking round to make sure nobody can see, I surreptitiously take out my mobile phone and take a photo of him quickly, before he sees what I'm doing. I can't help noticing that he is unusually animated – his normally calm, benign face looks angry, frightened even. After a couple of minutes, he looks up straight into my face, but it's as if his eyes don't know me for a moment. Then he turns quickly away and finishes his conversation, and turns back to me – his face made up into the normal, urbane, and cheerful Charles.

"Trouble at 't'mill'?" I can't think what else to say.

"Oh, it's just Mother."

Mother? I didn't know he still had a mother.

"Sorry to hear that." What pantomime are we playing?

"Oh… she's causing trouble. Won't listen to anyone. I'd rather not talk about it. How's the returned hero? Heard all about it – gadding about London, putting that

Witherspoon murderer away. I thought you were in deep shit, now you're in clover."

No, I'm just a lonely old cop noticing that you're covering something up. Mother indeed. That was business you were talking on the phone, and something dodgy to boot, or I've really lost my touch. I notice he doesn't ask after the dog either.

"Nice to be back." I lie. "Quite a relief to be rid of the cavalry, and back to normal." Normal? What's normal? Playing with Charles and hiding things?

"So are you on to some other case now? Or are they giving you a rest?" He really doesn't know I've been up The Avenues looking at a burglary? I don't believe it, I think he knows all about it.

"Out to clover? No. Something's come up." I'm not retired yet, Charles.

I've moved up the bar to sit next to him, pint in hand. I notice he's on the whisky already.

"Keeping you out of trouble then." The rumbly laugh follows, and for a moment I hope that Charles is out of trouble, but my instinct says otherwise.

"Charles, you know we talked about Brian and that talk he gave in The Avenues?" I decide to go straight for it.

Charles looks puzzled for a moment – more pantomime? "Er… yes?"

"I remember you mentioning that he talked to a man, and that they went off together?"

"Did I? Oh yes, can't remember his name, though." His acting is being put to the test – it's almost comical, or would be if I hadn't trusted this man so much in the past.

"Well," I lower my voice conspiratorially, "someone called Archibald who lives in The Avenues has been burgled."

"Really." He's keeping up a good front, but did I see his eyes flicker at the name Archibald?

290

"An art theft. They broke in. The alarm didn't go off. And they took one painting. A Degas."

"A Degas?" Blank look now.

"Funny thing is, and I shouldn't be telling you all this," I lower my voice conspiratorially, "there were nine other paintings in the house, but they only took that one. And it's not as if they were very valuable either. They were all copies worth about £3000 pounds a go, if that. So what's all that about?"

I look at Charles wondering what will show in that implacable face of his. There are forty-three muscles in the human face, and it can make thousands of different expressions. Far more than any other animal – in fact the human is the only animal that can tell lies with its face. It's part of what makes us human.

"Must have been worried about being caught. Scarpered with what they could get." Nothing shows.

"But why that one? It wasn't the most convenient place on the wall. If they were going to take more, you'd have thought they'd have started at one end and gathered them up in an orderly fashion. These guys knew what they were doing – they even managed to stop the alarm system going off. It was quite sophisticated. It was sold with the paintings as part of the deal. So what's going on, do you think, Charles?"

I see something behind his eyes. A flicker of uncertainty.

"Well, I think it sounds baffling. Actually, it sounds like a cock-up. What happened there wasn't what they meant at all. They heard something, and panicked, and just took the first painting that came to hand."

A cock-up? Now that's an interesting idea. Thank you Charles.

My Steak and Kidney pud arrives, and I realise I'm starving. The interview is over, and I offer Charles another drink.

"What was the whisky?"

"The Macallan, but I'd love a pint."

"A pint after a malt?" I am surprised, and he hasn't even commented on my Steak-and-Kidney.

"Thanks. Now tell me more about what you were up to in London."

Filtered information, I think. "I spent a lot of time in art galleries. Got to see some old friends – Seurat, Monet, Cézanne, Matisse. Really interesting to look closely at them and see the brushwork," I mumble between mouthfuls of delicious beef and gravy.

"I'm surprised they let you look that close. There's usually an alarm system that gets set off if you get too close to a painting in these galleries."

Gosh, you know a lot about all this for someone who never goes to art galleries, I reflect, as I munch on a particularly juicy bit of kidney.

"I made friends with the curator of one of these galleries. She let me look at the paintings with a sort of microscope. Showed me the difference between a copy and the real thing."

As I look down at my plate, contemplating a nice bit of suet, I notice that Charles' right knee is twitching in a rhythmic way. Almost as if he's about to run out of the pub.

"You mean a fake? I wouldn't have thought they'd have fakes at a London gallery."

"There's quite an interest in copies these days. The Chinese ones are so good. Sometimes it takes a real expert eye to tell the difference." I scoop up some peas inelegantly with my gravy. One way to get greens down. Never been keen on my greens.

"Did you do anything else while you were up there? Wasn't that where you found the old vagrant woman who was such a key witness in the Witherspoon case?"

Vagrant? I'm really going off you, Charles, and you're just trying to change the subject.

"Oh, I bumped into Brian. Literally in fact. He punched me in the stomach."

"He what?" This is news to Charles. He's obviously not in with Brian.

"Yes, he thought I knew something. Not very nice."

"No. I mean I'm sorry to hear that. But also didn't I hear you ended up begging on Oxford Street?"

Touché. "After he assaulted me, I was mugged and my money and everything taken. I collapsed on the street and was found in the morning." I can lie too.

"Well bugger me, Arnold. What a rough time you've had of it. You need a proper break."

I need a different job, I reflect.

"So what's up in Charles's world?" Time to flannel until I show Charles's photo to Archibald Rowlinson.

6.20 am, Wednesday 4th November

Betrayal is a funny business, I reflect, as I lie in bed trying to stir myself to go somewhere – I can't quite remember where yet.

Charles has deceived me, and I am deceiving him. He was one of my only friends, and now I wonder whether I was ever his friend at all, or whether I was his stooge – his useful policeman. I feel dead inside. This creeping disenchantment with my life and where I live has gone right down to my toes, and affected my eyes. Everything looks different now. Cold. Detached. My home is a fridge. I shiver, and get out of bed trying to shake this feeling off, what did they use to call it, 'ennui'?

Then there's Peggy – my hope, my dream. Did she betray me when she told Forester that I'd come back to search the basement? No. She saved my life.

Did I betray Burt by asking about Brian's visit? His wife thought I did.

Judas, with the thousands of concealing expressions in your face. Will I trust anyone ever again?

Do I trust my counsellor?

Oh shit, I'm meant to be there in ten minutes – that's why I had to get up early. I rush to get dressed. No chance to shave, but I will clean my teeth this time. No honky breath invading her consulting room this morning.

"Do you trust your instincts as a policeman?" She's quite an active counsellor, not just a listener.

"I think they've improved in the last month. They were poor before then, like I didn't want to know…" God, the truth. It's good to speak it. "I can read people better now. Charles for instance…" I feel my face crumple. She offers me the box of tissues. "No, thanks."

She lets me sit in silence. I feel a tear coursing down my face, and I cover it up by rubbing my eyes with my balled fists. I'm tired, and that's the truth.

She presses her fingers together and looks at me thoughtfully.

"Do you trust your instincts as an artist?"

Boom. Something resonates deep inside me. A light bulb switches on. All that art, it has fed me – kept me alive. I love that world, I'm passionate about it. Probably I will never paint a masterpiece in my life, but God, do I appreciate the work of others.

"Yes. Yes I do. It's where I started and it's something that has come back since my trip to London." I realise so much has happened since my first session with her. It's taken so long to get another one, what with the court case, and Trev sitting looking over my shoulder – I could hardly have brought him along. 'Is it OK if Trev sits in the front room and waits for me? They don't trust me not to run away.' I can't imagine it, and the thought makes me start to laugh.

She looks at me quizzically.

"Sorry. It was just a thought. I had a minder for a while. They didn't trust me not to go AWOL."

"Do you trust yourself?" She is sticking with the trust thing.

"I'm beginning to. I haven't had…" Then I realise we haven't talked about my memory loss at all. "Since I stopped covering things up – pretending life was hunky-dory. Yes, I think I trust myself a bit more."

I don't want to talk about my memory lapses. They're like a thundercloud approaching and I want to stick with the positive sunshine of my newly rediscovered art appreciation. Art – I love. People – I'm beginning to understand better. All good things. I don't want to talk about my memory.

"Tell me about your trip to London. The art."

I tell her about the discovery of fake and real. The difference. How much I have learnt, but I miss out the visit to the memory clinic, and Lilly, and Brian, and my ending up on Oxford Street, and Peggy. I can choose what to tell her, and I can tell her the bright things that make me happy, and leave out the dark things. I shiver and stop.

"Yes?" That look she has that sees through things.

"I've been leaving out the hard side of what happened in London." I look down, unable to look her in the eye.

"So tell me."

I tell her about Lilly, about chasing Brian, and then I get stuck again.

There's a long silence.

"The memory clinic," I mumble.

She nods.

"I haven't told you about the memory clinic."

"How did that go?"

I suddenly want to go to the loo. I feel my bowels moving.

"Do you have a toilet I can use?"

She shows me through the door to the corridor. The toilet is next door. I sit there with my head in my hands, sweating. I haven't had a memory lapse since Peggy discovered me on Oxford Street, and I don't want to go back there. Life has been a whirl of meetings and court appearances and I've been constantly minded – never been alone since I was clobbered on the head by Brian. If it was Brian. I haven't looked at my post. I haven't had time. There's probably all sorts of bills and life catching up with me, and the one thing I don't want to see – the results of my scan at the memory clinic. And there's the bill – how will I pay that? I don't know how much money I have – that whole part of my life has been left unattended for weeks, and what state is it in now?

I manage to get off the toilet. There isn't much time left for me to tell her the truth. The huge bit I left out.

I stagger a bit as I go back into the room. She half stands to help me, but I'm in the chair before she's got close.

"Sorry." I say. "I'm sorry – I left a whole bit out. I have been hiding it from myself. Doing that thing again. After Brian hit me in the stomach I had a serious memory lapse and that's how I ended up on Oxford Street. Peggy and Hannah found me, and I haven't had another one since.

"But the memory clinic? That was scary – all sorts of questions I couldn't answer, and then they did a scan, and the results were inconclusive so he needed to get a second opinion, and he said I shouldn't be alone so he wrote me a letter saying I should have my dog with me at all times, which is why I was able to take the dog into art galleries. You must have wondered."

I pause for breath.

"Have you seen the results?"

"No, I haven't been able to get near my post. No, that's not exactly true – I haven't wanted to open my post, and now it feels like it's all on top of me." I feel panic rising in my chest. I need to control this. Maybe counselling isn't a good thing after all.

She looks concerned. "You can come back with the letter – we can look at it together. You don't need to be on your own. It's time to finish now, but give me a call and we'll arrange another appointment."

"Thank you." I rise unsteadily from my chair.

"You know, I wonder why you're a policeman, and I wonder if they know how lucky they are." With these strange words she lets me out of the door and into the cool autumn air.

7.45 am, Wednesday 4th November

Breakfast. I scour the cupboards for cereal and find a packet of cornflakes. No idea how long it's been there, and the inner packet hasn't been folded over to keep the contents from going stale. Still, it's all I've got.

Milk. No milk in the fridge. I search cupboards again for UHT, but no success. I begin to feel panic set in. I'm on my own – supposing I start losing my memory again? Just now I would welcome Trev's company. I get out my mobile phone to call Peggy – I don't care whether it's too early, I need her now.

It's in camera mode, and I can't resist looking at the photo I took of Charles last night. He's looking down at his paper, brow furrowed, eyes animated. Not the urbane Charles that I thought I knew so well. Not the Charles who helped me out with a plan of the basements at 'Hazelbank'. That's a point. Where is that plan? I don't remember it showing that extra little room. If he had done up the house, he would have known about it.

Now I no longer feel alone and afraid – I'm back on the case. I search through my desk drawers, not there. Up in my studio, there's so much paper around, but I can't believe it's got buried. Then I remember – my car. I go out into the road, and there's the plan, still on the back seat of the car. It doesn't take me long to see that there is absolutely no sign of the extra space behind the apple store. He deliberately gave me that plan to put me off the scent. It's a photocopy, and as I look closely, I can see signs of where he has cleaned up the tell-tale lines of the extra space with whitener.

Oh Charles. You must know that I've seen that little room, and will put two and two together. To be honest, I'm surprised you haven't disappeared like Betty. I'd better get on with checking your photo with the charming Mr Rowlinson before you decide to scarper.

It's 8.15 when I pick up my phone again to find Sergeant Brown's mobile number.

"Hello Brown, it's Inspector Rackham. Can you put a watch on Charles Hamilton, at number thirty-two Lonsdale Avenue."

"A what… sir?" He sounds startled, as though I've just woken him up. Inspector Rackham giving him orders?

"A watch. You know, send someone round to keep an eye on him."

"I'd better just check…" with Grimwode, no doubt.

"Just do it, Brown. We don't want him slipping away. He definitely knows something about these paintings."

"Right, sir, I'll…" check with Grimwode.

"I've got someone on the other line. Have to go." My phone shows me Peggy is trying to get through.

"Hello." My voice goes down an octave.

"Hello. Are you OK? I mean after yesterday…" She sounds uncharacteristically unsure of herself.

"Yes, I'm fine. Though I hate being on my own. For tuppence I'd be on the train to see you."

"How was the celebration?"

"I missed it. I was called just after you left. Grimwode wants me to investigate an art theft in The Avenues. Are you alright?"

"Yes. No. I don't know." She pauses and takes a breath. "Oh, so Grimwode wants you now does he? Can I come down and see you? And bring the dog?"

"Why? Is he being a nuisance?"

"No, he's fine. I just want to see you, er, make sure you're alright." I hear her mutter something to someone, presumably Hannah.

"Listen. I'd love you to come down. I'm in the thick of this case at the moment, so I don't know where I'll be. I suspect an old friend's involved and I don't know who to trust. Brown is following me around and referring to Grimwode all the time. I could do with your support."

"But I'm still officially off duty."

"I didn't mean that sort of support, I meant moral…emotional…you know…" Why can't I just say it? "Anyway, you already know a lot about all this… we could, you know, discuss it together."

She mumbles something down the phone.

"What?"

Brown comes up on my phone wanting to get through. What's Grimwode said now?

"Got to go. Brown's come back to me. See you soon."

"Bye," is all she says. Her voice sounds very distant.

I press 'accept' feeling like a dog.

"Sir. We've had a call from Mr Rowlinson. He thinks he might be able to help with finding another art collection for us to look at. Doesn't want to tell us. Wants to talk to you directly, apparently."

Well, well, well. I've obviously hit it off with him. Surprising.

"I'll go round there now. I want to show him a photo of Charles… Hamilton."

"He said there's no hurry, sir. He's just having his breakfast."

Breakfast. Lucky man.

"I'll walk. He should be finished by the time I get there. Have you sent someone round to watch Charles Hamilton?"

"Yes, sir." Brown responds just a bit too quickly. He's obviously about to send someone, having got permission from Grimwode.

"I'll be there in half an hour. I'll call you if I need assistance."

"Sir."

I switch off the phone, and sit down in my armchair. I feel light-headed, possibly due to lack of food, but also the rapid succession from police case to love and back to police case again has left me dizzy.

Too early to pick something up at the Café on the Green. No almond slices till ten o'clock.

I go and have a shave, and double-check my appearance which has been tatty of late. Peggy persuaded me to buy a pair of smart trousers and a nice tweed jacket for my court appearances, so I don these. Want to give my new friend Archibald the right impression.

Out of the back door. Down the garden. Onto the common, which has gained its beauty again. Must be love that does it. With a spring in my step, I come to the main road and wait to cross. There's a car coming up on my right some distance away. I'll be most of the way across the road before it gets here. Should be safe. As I cross, it speeds up. I can hear the engine accelerating. I quicken my step to get across, but to my alarm the car veers across to my side of the road. He's trying to run me down. I make a dash for it and run straight into a tree on the other side of the road, just as he zooms past. I turn to see him disappearing round the bend in the road – no chance to get his number.

Cursing, I reach for my phone. "Brown. A car has just tried to run me down. Yes, a black BMW 6 series. Can you put out a call – it was going up the A6. No, didn't get the registration. See you at Rowlinson's. Looks like I might need someone to cover my back."

I look down at my clothes – covered in bits of moss and bark. My knees are all scuffed from contact with the tree. So much for the smart impression. I shakily walk down the path to park, keeping a wary eye out for any signs of pursuit, but none appears. It may just have been a trickster, or someone high on coke, but it does seem a bit of a coincidence.

9 am, Wednesday 4th November

I dust myself down in front of Archibald's front door. He takes his time answering – presumably cleaning his teeth after his sumptuous breakfast.

"Hullo." He looks me up and down, clearly taking in the state of my clothes. "Inspector Rogers…"

"Rackham, sir. Inspector Rackham. You called about another collection."

"Yeh, I did. I didn't expect such a prompt response. Come in. Just had breakfast." I can smell it. The aroma of bacon and eggs makes my stomach rumble. "Can I offer you anything Inspector? Cup of tea?"

Full English would be lovely. "Thank you, sir."

I follow him into the kitchen, where a Filipino maid is tidying up. "Can you make a cup of tea for the Inspector?" She nods and carries on with her tidying up. We go out and into the drawing room. A fake Matisse stares at me at a drunken angle from behind the sofa.

"So, you called about someone else having one of these collections."

"Yeh. Problem is that I only know her first name, and I'm not sure which house it is. Alex. Big in marketing. Met her at that meeting organized by Ben, that we discussed."

"Brian?"

"Brian, that's right."

This spurs me on to do the thing I've been dreading. "Is this the man who put you on to the, um, 'Riches of Art' collection?" I show him the photo of Charles on my phone.

He barely glances at it. "Yeh, that's him. Jonathan, I think his name was."

"Charles?"

"No, definitely not Charles, maybe it was Andrew."

This man has more of a problem with names than I do. I wonder if he's got the name of the woman with the art collection right.

The doorbell goes.

"Can you get that, Lovely?" There's a crash in the kitchen. Lovely must be the maid, but where's my lovely cup of tea?

Lovely brings Sergeant Brown in, raises her eyes to heaven, and walks out.

"Sir?"

Archibald grunts something and turns to me. "Better go and find where Alex lives." He walks out of the door and into the hall. "Coming?"

But my cup of tea!

We follow out into the autumn sunshine. The leafiness of The Avenues has turned to golds and browns. Not many flowers are left, but still some beautiful roses, their red matching the dying leaves of the trees. I think of what has happened to me in The Avenues this autumn and wonder whether this will be the end of it.

"This is it. I'm sure this is it." We have turned into Browning Avenue, and are standing in front of a grand late-Victorian house set back behind a glorious copper beech. All the woodwork is painted that old-fashioned green. A gabled porch leads out onto the carriage drive, and we follow Archibald up three worn stone steps to the large front door, inset with stained glass. The policeman in me says, 'so easy to break in through all that glass. Not secure.'

A square-looking woman in her seventies answers the door. She exudes confidence and cheerfulness.

"Hello. Can I help?"

"Alex, isn't it?" Archibald is all genial.

"Alice. Weren't you at that talk the other week?"

"Yeh. Look, I'm Archibald Rowlinson, and…"

"Archibald. That's it," says Alice.

"I've just been burgled."

"No!"

"And the point is that they only took one of my paintings from my collection."

"Just one? How extraordinary."

"The thing is that I remember you saying you had a collection from the same company. Er…"

"'The Riches of Art'," I pipe in.

"No, that's not me. That would be Alex. She lives next door, but she's away on a marketing trip. I'm keeping an eye on her house for her while she's away." Alice really does love to talk.

"Could you take us round there to have a look at her collection? We're police officers and this may be very helpful to our case." I decide to take the lead before we go down any more blind alleys.

"By all means. I'm sure she wouldn't mind. You are police officers, aren't you? You don't mind showing me some identification do you? Only…"

Brown and I present our cards for her perusal.

"… what with what's been going on in The Avenues recently: there was the shooting and then that terrible discovery at the Witherspoons' house."

She leads us round to the equally splendid house next door.

309

"That poor policeman who got all mixed up in it. Broke down in tears in front of the cameras, and ended up a tramp on Oxford Street. Dreadful."

"Yes, I…" What can I say? Brown keeps a straight face.

"You are Miss…?" Brown has to say something.

"Mrs Harper. My husband's up in the attic doing something dreadful to a spinet."

The mind boggles. Wasn't there that joke about Bach practising on a spinster in the attic?

"Here we are." Alice Harper jangles a bunch of keys, trying to find the right one. In goes the key. She opens the door, but the alarm on the wall to the right starts blinking.

"Oh dear, I'm sure the key is on here somewhere." She rummages and rattles her chain but all to no avail. The warning beep, beep starts to sound. Soon The Avenues will be filled with the cacophony of Alex's alarm.

"Just a minute. Try this." Archibald has a bunch of keys out and has instantly found the key for his alarm. He reaches past Alice and puts it in, it turns, and the noise and flashing stop.

We all look at each other. So that's what they've done. All the alarm system keys are the same.

"So much for security," mutters Archibald. "Must get back now. No doubt hear from you later, Inspector Ramsey."

"Rackham, sir."

"Rackham." He's off. No doubt coffee and croissants call.

Alice shows us into a large room that runs front to back. Once a drawing-room and a dining room, now knocked into one. A pity, I think. The old Victorian proportions were better, but modern living has taken over here. Lots of space, and plenty of wall to show off Alex's new collection.

The bright colours of the Impressionists bring the room to life. One could forgive the owner for creating this perfect gallery of masterpieces, if one didn't know that they were copies. Fakes, some would call them. But these are good copies, so good, that even to a student of art, they look like the genuine article. But they're not. They are a puzzle. Why go to all this trouble to hoodwink the rich in order to break in and steal just one painting? The people who robbed Archibald's house knew the alarm wouldn't go off. They had a key.

I decide to look more closely at the collection, and I get out my magnifying glass for a close look at the brushwork. First up is a Seurat. I know it's a copy, because I saw the original of this painting at the Somerset Gallery a few weeks ago. My head spun then, and I'm beginning to feel a bit woozy now, but I think that's just due to lack of breakfast. Maybe I should send Brown off for a sandwich, but I want company – support even – in case the guys in the black Beemer turn up.

The Seurat is good, but the age of the paint shows up under magnification. It looks new, and smells new, definitely not over a hundred years old.

I glance around. Brown is looking bored and fidgety. He picks up a magazine from the coffee table, and settles down on a sofa to read about cars. My eye catches a work that looks different, just behind his head. It's a sketch by Degas, and it stands out because of its lack of colour. Or is it just that there is something familiar about it? On the face of it, it looks very unfinished. Not the sort of thing your untutored punter would want hanging on the wall. A mixture of images denoting music, the inevitable dancers, and people placed oddly out of perspective. Just a drawing. No title underneath. No clue as to what it's all about.

"Excuse me." I gesture to Brown to move out of my way so that I can get a closer look. He reluctantly gets up, taking his magazine with him, and goes over to sit in an armchair.

"Not that chair, I'm afraid." Alice has come back into the room. "She never lets anyone sit there. That's her special chair." She says it in a way that makes me think that she doesn't quite approve of Alex's chair obsession.

"I'll just be off next door and leave you to it for a bit. Please be careful, Alex would never forgive me if…" She looks at me as if for the first time, scrutinizing my dirtied clothes. Her eyes widen. "You're the…"

"Yes, Mrs Harper, and here I am, back safe and sound."

"It must have been… would you like a cup of tea?" She's sorry for me, but if that means I get a cuppa…

"Oh, yes please, just milk no sugar." I notice she doesn't offer Brown anything.

"I'll bring it round in a minute."

She leaves me to my inspection of the Degas, and I have to say, whoever did this knew what they were doing. I take off my shoes and kneel up on the sofa to get a closer look. Not a late Degas – the signature is quite clear. The paper looks old – could be nineteenth century. The lines have those right angles that forgers so often miss, but then I suppose if the artisan in China was copying carefully… No. This is an amazing copy.

Or is it genuine? Is it from that art heist I found on my computer yesterday?

I lean forward to see if the smell of it will tell me anything, but my head begins to swim. Lack of food and drink. Must be that. I sit down heavily on the sofa and stick my head between my knees to try and stop the dizziness.

"Sir?" Brown is on his feet. "Are you OK?"

"Just need a glass of water. Be alright." Brown scurries off to find the kitchen and I hear the scrunch of gravel

312

outside as a car draws up. I don't need a glass of water, I need a gun. I begin to panic.

The front door slams. "What the..?" A tall Amazonian woman in her forties comes into the room. She has blonde hair with a dark streak and she's got power-dressing off to a tee. "Who are you? And what are you doing in my house?"

Brown returns clutching a glass of water. "Police, Mrs..?"

"Miss Davis. And who gave permission for you to come into my house?"

"Er, your neighbour."

"Oh, Alice. Bloody Alice. I should have known not to trust her with the keys. Well you can get out now." She is furious, and with my head spinning and all, I'm not in a very good position to reason with her.

"Alex?" Alice's voice comes from the hall. "We weren't expecting you back…"

She comes in holding my cup of tea. "I see you've met these policemen, this is the famous Inspector Rackham," she gesticulates towards me. "You know, from the Witherspoon case…"

"I don't know, and I don't want them in my house. Why did you let them in?"

"Archibald thingummy brought them round, he's been burgled and they took a painting and they wanted to see your paintings and his key worked for turning your alarm off, which makes you wonder, doesn't it?" Never at a loss for words, our Alice. She walks over to me and gives me a blessed cup of tea.

"Listen, Alice," Alex hisses at her as if she's talking to a particularly stupid teenager. "You should have contacted me before you let the police into my house."

"Alex, dear," she's completely unfazed. "They seem such nice policemen, and what with the things that have

313

been going on in The Avenues recently, I thought it best…"

"That's precisely why…"

"Excuse me, Miss Davis," the tea has done its job, and I feel the need to take charge before we lose a vital piece of our puzzle. "We were called by Archibald Rowlinson who said that he…"

"Who's bloody Archibald Rowlinson?"

"He said he met you at a talk about art copies, given a few weeks ago."

"No idea. Listen. Can you leave now?"

"I think I may have discovered a genuine Degas here, given to you as part of your collection deal." There. Now it's been said. I can see Brown suddenly taking an interest in proceedings.

"Well, I don't know what that means. A lot of money, I suppose. And since I'm the owner…" What a pleb. Are all people with money like this?

"Miss Davis, I'm afraid you may be in possession of stolen property."

"What do you mean? I bought it. Now get out of my house and come back with a warrant if you want to look at my paintings." She looks like she means it, and I shrug my shoulders as I glance ruefully at Brown. Defeated at the very moment of my glory.

But I hadn't reckoned with the impregnable nature of Brown. He stands a few inches shorter than Amazonian Alex, and a stone or two lighter, but he looks her in the face and whips out his identity card. "Counter-terrorism. I'm afraid we do have the right to be here. Your paintings may be connected with a terrorist incident in which a police officer was shot…"

"I know…"

"Inspector Rackham here has been called in by the squad as an art expert." When did I become one of those?

"And we will have to inspect the entire collection, and call in other experts. Also we may have to secure the site."

"You mean my home?" she wails. "No. This can't be happening. This Degas can't be anything to do…"

"I'm afraid that if you fail to cooperate, you will be seen to be perverting the course of justice which is very serious in the case of terrorism."

"Golly, you'd better do what they say, Alex." Alice is very impressed – her excitement is palpable.

"I'll just make a call to my Commander, and I must ask you to stay here for the moment, Mrs Harper." He turns to Alice, who looks as if wild horses would not drag her away.

Blimey. I'm impressed. This man knows how to turn a situation round. Poor Alex is poleaxed and goes into the kitchen and returns, sipping a huge glass of red wine. Funny, I thought pouring large glasses of wine was reserved for policewomen in TV dramas, and at the end of the day – not at ten o'clock in the morning. She plumps herself down in her special chair, and says not a word more.

I content myself with a careful inspection of the other paintings. Art expert, eh? Well, I'm pretty sure that the rest are all copies. Just the Degas, and I hope I'm right. If I'm wrong, I'll look even sillier than I do already. Poor Inspector Rackham. I catch Alice looking at me, a new interest showing in her face.

An idea of what's going on here is growing in my mind and I'm prompted to ask a question. I turn to Alex – her glass is half empty already.

"Do you know anyone else who has bought one of these er… 'Riches of Art' collections?"

She just looks straight ahead of her, as if she hasn't heard me.

"Toby Williams bought one," Alice butts in irrepressibly from the other end of the room. "My husband says he was very excited about it, so much so, that it's affected his recorder practice. Just spends his time looking at baroque paintings and not playing Handel, or even Purcell for that matter."

"A baroque collection. And you're sure it was from the same firm?"

"'Riches of Art'? Seems such a 'common' name. Fake Art for the Rich would be closer to the truth. But…"

"Mrs Harper..?"

"Alice, please."

"Alice. Do you have the contact details for Terry..?"

"Toby."

"Toby. Do you..?"

The sound of another car on the gravel outside reaches our ears. Brown's hand goes straight to his inside pocket. He's carrying a gun. I'd never have guessed – he just doesn't seem the type.

"Someone's just arrived sir," he says into his phone as he goes to the front window.

I move forward cautiously to see whether it's a black BMW. Hannah's in the driving seat, and Peggy is getting out, complete with dog.

"Mine, I think," I say as I walk to the front door to let them in. The dog rushes up to me, tail wagging, nose against my knee. Then he catches sight of Alex sitting trance-like in her chair, and trots over to her before I can grab hold of him, and puts his muzzle in her lap. Instead of the scream of 'get this beast off me', that I expected, she puts her glass down and holds his face in both hands, gently fondling his ears.

"Randy Collins," she says to the dog. "He's got a collection as well. Quite a lot of Rembrandts – likes that sort of thing." She looks at the dog, shaking her head as though it's a sad business.

I look at her, scarcely able to take this in. I hope the dog's taking notes.

11 am, Wednesday 4th November

"An almond slice and a large cappuccino, please."

Redemption is at hand – at least in terms of my stomach. I see Peggy shake her head in disbelief when I place my order. I imagine my diet is going to change if we get together.

"Decaf latte, please." She's not going to eat. Maybe she's had something already before she sped down from London.

"You should have something more substantial after your fainting fit," she continues. "I see they do salads."

Salad? In the morning? No, I want to feel that heavy almond slice settling into my stomach, and giving me a nice sugar rush.

"We haven't got long – Grimwode will be down from London with the forces of darkness, and then I'll have to go round to the other houses to see if I can spot any more genuine works of art, in these so-called collections. Anyway, how did you find me?"

"I'm still in the force you know. I just asked at the station." She looks flushed.

"Well, here I am." I smile.

"What do you think's going on? Why is Grimwode treating this so seriously?" Her puzzled frown makes me want to pull her towards me over the table. I look round. The Café on the Green is almost empty, but there is a tall man in a dark suit sitting a couple of tables away, and he's looking in our direction.

Instead, I lean forward and talk softly. "I know what's going on. Ever since I found those paintings in the cellar, I've been wondering. Then, after the burglary, the penny began to drop. The houses with the collections are safe houses..." My phone croaks.

"Rackham." It's Grimwode, and for once he sounds excited. "We'll pick you up in five."

"We've got five minutes." I look round for the waitress. She's got our tray but is in conference with the attractive lad behind the counter. "Excuse me, we have to go very soon, can we have our...?"

She shrugs and gives me a poisonous look, then brings our tray over sulkily, plonking my coffee down so it spills into the saucer.

I decide to ignore this. We haven't much time. "Peggy. You seemed, I don't know, quiet when you phoned this morning, and you said something that I didn't catch. Is everything alright?" I put my hand on the table near hers.

"I miss you when you're not there, and Hannah's going off on tour tomorrow. That's all – I used to be so good on my own, but now... I miss your company. All that work we've done together." She looks at me – can I actually see tears in her eyes? She actually misses me when I'm not there. This is a revelation after all those years of a semi-detached marriage.

"I er... you know..." I take a sip of my coffee, looking in her eyes all the time.

"Me too," she says, and grins from ear to ear.

I wolf down the almond slice which settles a little uneasily in my stomach. Maybe I do need someone to look after my eating habits.

There are flashing lights outside the windows – the cavalry has arrived.

"I'll pay," Peggy says. "You go."

I remember how the last time I was in here, I didn't pay and it caused their waiter to get shot down in the graveyard. It seems years ago, but what really worries me is that I never thought to go and find out how the lad was doing. Never cared.

A uniformed policeman opens the door to the café, and I reluctantly get up and leave Peggy. "See you soon. I'll text you."

Grimwode is sitting in the car when I get in. "That painting that was stolen from Rowlinson's, have you checked to see if it's been recently stolen from anywhere else?"

"Not recently. There's something about a heist decades ago, I haven't had the chance to do a thorough check, but I…"

"I thought not. Still, well done for spotting the other Degas, and for putting us on to Charles Hamilton. We've pulled him in. I'll interview him later."

Somehow Grimwode manages to make the word 'interview' sound like a visit to the torture chambers at the Tower of London.

We arrive at Alex Davis's house to find a squad car already there with an armed policeman at the door. Grimwode is not taking any chances. "I heard you were nearly mown down by a black BMW this morning."

"Yes. Ruined my trousers."

"Humph," is all I get as we climb out of the car.

Alex is still in her chair, with the dog in attendance. She's given the address of her fellow collector to an animal who can write. Alice is standing to attention, glee written all over her face, awaiting developments.

"You can go home now, Mrs Harper." Grimwode is in kind mode. "We will need to have a police presence outside your house for your protection."

"Golly." For once she's at a loss for words, as she trots out of the front door to her husband and his poor spinet.

The dog stays with the grateful Alex, who has turned out to be as soft inside as she is hard on the surface. "I'll take care of him while you're gone." No you won't, he'll take care of you, I reflect. Now there's someone I've been able to trust – the dog.

We arrive at Toby Williams' house, to find a police presence already there. His collection of baroque paintings is less familiar to me, but there's a Vermeer that stands out. I look closely and carefully, and it does have all the hallmarks of a genuine masterpiece.

Next, we go to Randy Collins' house. Dark Rembrandts cover the walls of his gloomy dining room. He is a gloomy American living in gloomy England, perhaps wishing for the sunlight of LA. Anyway, I discover another possible genuine masterpiece concealed amongst the very convincing Chinese copies.

There're a couple more addresses given to us, and Grimwode calls in for reinforcements as we drive back to the station. I feel the need to do the same.

"Can I suggest we call up Emma Robinson? She'll have all the latest equipment for …"

"We already have. She's on her way. I must say, you seem to have uncovered a lot of crime in your so-called peaceful neck of the woods. Pity you didn't do it sooner."

Sour bugger. I'll never call him sir, and damn the consequences.

"Still." Is that a grimace or a smile? "There might be a promotion in this for you."

Actually, I don't know whether I care. I'm not sure I want to be in this job any longer.

3 pm, Wednesday 4th November

Poor Charles. He's been in with Grimwode for ages. Solicitor or no solicitor, he's probably been through the mangle. I saw the beginning from the sweaty viewing room, but found I couldn't bear it. So I went to the canteen which was still serving up bacon-and-eggs-fried-bread-two-sausages. A killer – lovely.

But I'm worried now, sitting there with my third cup of tea. The dog's still with Alex Davis. Peggy's off somewhere – maybe at my cottage. Paul is back in Wales recovering from the court appearance. I worry about them all.

And now I have to face the other side of things: Charles, who I thought of as my friend, has taken me for a ride. A very long one. And Brian, a friend from my childhood, has punched me in the stomach and clobbered me over the head. And what have they done it for? Money. Money matters far more to them than friendship, or even common decency. Looking back like this, brings me to Betty and her long term infidelity – my burying my head in the sand – no relationship there at all, just self-deception.

"Sir." Brown appears – his usual worried expression makes me think of a kindly social worker. "Commander Grimwode would like to speak to you." In my office, no doubt.

I leave my tea, and follow him out of the canteen, wondering where my policeman brain has gone. It's all about my life and my relationships now, I realise, so I don't know how much use I'll be to Grimwode anymore. Promotion, huh – I'd rather stick my head in a bucket of sick. That thought pulls me up sharp. Last time I said that to myself was when Cornelia invited me in for tea. Put on your armour, Rackham, and prepare.

Grimwode looks up at me when I walk in. He looks tired. "Tough nut, your friend Charles. I've put the frighteners on him – everything. But he just sits there and sweats like a bag of miserable potatoes, and says bugger all."

He twiddles one of my pens in that irritating way he has, and looks at me – an unusual distant look in his eyes. "You remember when we used to work together?"

Yes, I remember – you were the one who chose to forget.

"Do you remember how we played 'bad cop – good cop'?"

"Yes, Dick, I remember that very well."

He flinches when I say 'Dick', but decides to ignore it. "I think we're going to have to do that with friend Charles."

"But he's been telling me porkies for years. How am I going to get the truth out of him now?" What I dreaded has come to pass – interviewing an old friend turned traitor. How will I behave? Will I be the one to break?

"Just remember the format. I'll loosen him up a bit more, and then we'll send you in and he'll melt. I bet you."

It does feel like the old days. Anyway, what choice do I have?

"OK."

He gets up stiffly, and walks to the door. "Ten minutes, and then it's your turn."

I stand up and walk round my office. Unlike my home, this says nothing about me. No photos, none of my art – that would have been a cause for mockery. Just lists on the wall – Grimwode's now. And a big wall calendar. I walk round and sit in my chair. Chief Inspector Rackham? I don't think so. Police art expert? Never heard of one of those – martial arts, maybe. No. I don't want this anymore. The betrayal and deception of my past life have caught up with me, and I feel a warmer human being than I was. I want my life back, before my memory problems return, and I lose it all anyway. I get up and look out of the window – longing.

There's a knock on the door.

"Sir." It's Brown. "Commander Grimwode is ready for you now."

I feel my bowels wanting to move, but this is no counselling session, so I'll just have to hold onto myself. I feel like I'm in a dream as I follow Brown to the interview room. Grimwode is there by the door.

"I'll be watching."

I feel so strange – I wonder if I'm going to have another memory lapse. Charles is sitting slumped forward, looking down at the table. He looks shrunken. A different Charles to the confident beaming friend that I talked to in the pub over the years. His solicitor is well known locally. A good man who cares for his clients, and makes the police work hard to prove their case.

The tall gangly detective with the Adam's apple sitting across the table from them with his back to me turns round as I come in. 'Waste of time' his face says, then he turns back and switches on the machine. "Interview with Charles Hamilton continued at 3.15 pm. Detective Inspector Rackham has entered the room." He says it in a mechanical voice. He sounds so bored he could be a robot – probably is.

The thought makes me chuckle.

"Well Charles, you've got yourself into a fine pickle." I can act too.

Silence. He doesn't even look at me.

"We have four witnesses who say you introduced them to this dodgy website where they bought their collections which all happened to have one genuine stolen masterpiece concealed as part of the collection. An alarm system was installed for which your criminal friends had the key, and this enabled whoever set this up to pop in and retrieve said masterpiece at their leisure. Were you part of that? Did you pop in and pinch a Degas from Archibald Rowlinson's house? Should we search your house more carefully and look for it? Have you got a concealed basement room?"

He shakes his head, but remains silent.

"Speaking of concealed basements – why did you slip me a photocopied plan of the basement at 'Hazelbank' with the hidden room obviously Tippexed out? That was silly Charles. If you'd thought about it, you must have known I'd rumble that in the end. You did that house up in the first place, so you'd have known about it. You must have thought I was really stupid. Your pet dumb cop."

Silence. He won't look up.

"And all that time I thought you were my friend." I can feel my voice quaver slightly. All the jollity gone out of it for a moment.

"I was your friend." He looks up at me, pleading.

I pause, gathering my thoughts and emotions. I'm good cop, remember.

"As your friend, I must tell you that you're in a very dangerous position. The people you've been working for are terrorists. They don't mind using guns and killing people, and you're a danger to them now…"

"It's nothing to do with terrorism." At last we have a dialogue.

"Ah, but we think it is, which is why you have been interviewed by Commander Grimwode, and why we can keep you for fourteen days – two weeks…"

Charles starts to shake. The thought of Grimwode for two weeks is enough to crack the toughest criminal. And I don't think Charles is that tough. Poor Charles. I feel sorry for him, so I decide to tell him what I've worked out over my bacon and eggs.

"I think the scam is this: the group that you work for needed a lot of money to buy arms. They got wind of a collection of paintings that were stolen decades ago. They tracked down the people who were holding onto them, and unable to sell them to anyone, and now there're probably a few dead art thieves floating around in a river somewhere. Then our terrorist group brought said collection to a house called 'Hazelbank', in the lovely genteel Avenues, and hid them in the basement. But that didn't feel safe enough. So they hatched this plan to conceal them in collections of Chinese copies – they're very good these days – and sell them to innocent rich punters in The Avenues together with a dud alarm system. Right so far?"

Charles shakes his head wearily.

"But then a local group of criminally minded gentlemen, including Brian and Malcolm, get wind of this, and decide to put the squeeze on your friends in order to get a share of the booty. This is very unwise, and Malcolm gets kidnapped. His right hand is cut off – an Arabic punishment for theft – and a finger is sent to Brian and co. to put the frighteners on them. How am I doing?"

He shakes his head again.

Oh dear. Well, I'd better keep going and see if I can pierce his armour.

"At this point, after an anonymous tip-off, I lead a group of officers in a raid on 'Hazelbank', thinking it's small time drugs – no doubt we were tipped off by Brian and co.. We are not armed, and have no idea what we are getting into. We find Malcolm's hand in a safe, concealed behind a very good copy of a Seurat which was so good that I was convinced it was genuine – I know better now, but it set something off in my mind. Something about art, that just wouldn't go away."

I crouch down and look at him from the level of the table, to see if there's any reaction. A flicker of something in his face.

"Then the young Albanian who was meant to be guarding all of this takes flight and shoots P… Sergeant MacDonald, which sets this whole Counter-terrorism investigation in motion. So the group that you work for…"

He shakes his head again.

"…didn't have the chance to complete their plan to conceal all their paintings in the houses of the rich and good."

"But that doesn't make them terrorists." Charles's solicitor butts in. "What right have you to hold my client under the terrorism act?" He's said this before – I can tell by the impatience in his voice.

"That's restricted information." I bet he's heard that before as well, but I say it anyway because I don't actually know what else the squad found in the house, or why they decided it was terrorism, because I lost the report.

I decide to take a chance. "But I can tell you that certain substances were found during the search that related to explosives – the kind that Middle Eastern terrorist groups use – and the gun that shot our policewoman was a certain Russian model which would indicate the same."

That surprised the solicitor – he hasn't heard this before.

"But to get back to what happened, the terrorists decided to kill Malcolm Smith-Rogers, and park his body in a car outside my house. Were they trying to confuse us by doing that? And I wonder how they knew which was my house, Charles?" I nearly go on to say that they stole my report, but manage to stop short. Grimwode is watching.

I look at Charles, sweating away in front of me. How many layers do I have to go through, before I get to the real Charles?

"So to continue, the terrorists sent the Albanian gunman back to retrieve the paintings from the concealed room in the cellar. But that got screwed up because I spotted him outside La C... er... The Café on the Green in his ridiculous disguise, and he ended up shooting an innocent bystander. After that debacle, I guess they decided to leave things and wait for the police activity to die down, but in the meantime Brian, our local opportunist criminal, decides to find out more for himself."

"I don't see where all this is leading," the solicitor chimes in.

"You don't have to. This isn't a court of law, and I am taking the time and trouble to tell my friend Charles how it was.

"Now I went up to London on a completely unconnected case and found Lilly. You remember Lilly, Charles? That old vagrant woman? If you'd taken more interest in that case and what the old vagrant woman said, you'd have had more warning that I would catch up with you. She told me she hid in this basement, in a concealed space at the back of an apple store. The very space you Tippexed out on the plans you gave me, and then I realised that there must be something there. I was guessing of course, but my policeman's nose..."

I tap my nose. Charles looks at me in disgust, and so fuels my desire to nail him.

"So I went there and found the space. There were a number of paintings hidden there including a genuine Manet. Then bang, someone hits me over the head – Brian, who was following me in London, has finally caught up with me, and he makes off with said paintings.

"I wake up to find your Albanian terrorist threatening to shoot me if I don't tell him who took the paintings, but fortunately I am saved by a police marksman."

Maybe not so fortunate for you, Charles.

"You know, Charles, I wonder how that gunman knew I was there. Was it chance do you suppose, Charles? Or did someone local see me come back and alert his terrorist friends that they needed to get a move on?"

He's shaking again. I lower my voice to sound more kindly.

"Now the terrorists are in a right lather. They've lost four paintings worth millions of pounds and in a panic they rush in and grab the Degas off Archibald Rowlinson's wall, but forget, or fail to replace it with a copy. A silly mistake…"

"Bloody fools." Charles can take no more. "If they'd listened…"

"Ah, and who would 'they' be?"

Trapped. Poor Charles looks up at me pleading. "I can't – they'd kill me."

"They'll kill you anyway. You'll need to be kept somewhere secure for the rest of your life. Why did you do it, Charles? You had plenty of money. I can't believe you're an extremist. What made you..?"

"It was money. Good money. This art heist was old. Everyone believed the paintings had been destroyed, but there they were sitting there, in a house in Surrey. It was so easy. Nobody would suspect – there were certain

330

clients, in the less law-abiding parts of the world, who would pay good money for an original Degas, or Rembrandt. Especially if they were sympathetic to the cause. All I had to do was to set up The Avenues end of things, and keep an eye on the local bobby. And for that I was paid good money. Very good. So simple until that idiot shot a bloody policewoman." This is a Charles I don't know – never knew. Local bobby – it makes my blood boil.

"And who were they?"

Silence.

"Listen. Shall I call Commander Grimwode in? You can tell him if you like."

"I don't know their real names," he says, pleading.

"Alright. You can help us identify them. We'll take you through to the computer, and show you faces until you recognize them. The more you help us, the more we can protect you."

I nod at my gangly colleague. I've finished. Job done.

"Interview terminated 3.35 pm." The machine speaks to the machine, and I get up, without looking at Charles, and leave the room.

"Rackham." Grimwode pulls me down the corridor as I come out of the door, so that we are on our own. "That was good work. You know, we really should work as a team again. I loved the bit you made up about the terrorist's explosive substances. I was afraid you'd spill the beans about what we really found." And for the first time I hear Grimwode laugh. It's a strange experience.

6 pm, Wednesday 4th November

It's dark outside as we sit at my kitchen table, and I realise that we are alone for the first time. There's always been someone else around – nurses, Hannah, minders, waiters…Now the only other person is the dog. And he's asleep in his bed after the exertions involved in looking after Alex.

Now we are alone, it feels uncomfortable and uncertain. Each of us waiting for the other to say something. Not wanting to wreck the moment. I've done good. I've been possibly offered promotion. But I haven't got the faintest idea what Grimwode meant by his last comment. I'm out of the loop, and I'm disenchanted with the force. And there's something hanging over me. Something I don't want to look at. I can't relax, I can't just be with Peggy.

Peggy is restless. She shifts in her kitchen chair, and I realise with a jolt that she is probably in some kind of pain. I wish I had nice comfortable furniture like at Hannah's flat. She is finding it hard to look me in the face. Finding it hard to smile.

"Arne I…" She breaks the silence.

"Peggy, there's something…" I want to deal with my sword of Damocles.

"I looked through your post. Sorry. It's private, I know, but there's so much, and I was worried in case there was something…"

I really don't mind. It's good to find someone who actually cares.

"It's OK," I say.

"I found this." She brings out a letter with unfamiliar printing on the front. Not a bill. My stomach clenches, my bowels feel uneasy. Is this it? I try to read it upside down.

"It's from the memory clinic," she goes on. "Do you think it's the…?"

"I was going to read it with my counsellor. She'd know what it meant."

"I think we should read it together. I'm with you on this, Arne. You know that don't you?"

"Yes. You open it." I stand up and come round to her side of the table and kneel down by her as she opens the envelope.

Dear Mr Rackham,

We have examined your ultrasonic scan for signs of shrinkage of the cerebral cortex and hippocampus consistent with Alzheimer's disease, and found none. During our examination, however, we noticed what could be lesions in the parts of the brain associated with memory. These were inconclusive, however, so we consulted Dr. Nambarton of the USA Memory Clinic Association. He agreed that the scan was inconclusive, but suggested you have another one in twelve months' time.

Your blood test came in, and there may be signs of early onset Alzheimer's, but we would suggest you come in for an electroencephalogram, as this could rule this possibility out.

From talking to you we observed that you were under a lot of stress, and that you may be suffering from depression. In some cases this can cause symptoms that can be confused with dementia, and we suggest this may be what has happened in your case.

Because of the uncertainty regarding what is causing you to have these occasions of memory loss, and because of their severity, we would recommend that you avoid driving and being on your own. Your dog, we remember, was a reliable companion, but it would be safer to make sure that some person is with you, or knows where you are, as much as is possible.

We enclose our invoice, and would appreciate early settlement.

Yours sincerely,

Etc. etc....

"Oh my God, that means..." Peggy begins.

"A stay of execution. Yes."

"But you're going to need a reliable companion."

I put my arm round her then, and she hugs my head, and the tears begin to come. The dog barks, and we laugh, and we cry.

Epilogue

We have just passed through a Welsh town with an unpronounceable name that looks like Belch, and are driving down a long straight hill with the mountains and the Beacons opening up on our left.

In my pocket is a letter. A letter I want to share with Paul. It's an offer of a job with a legal company, based in Cardiff, that deals with art fraud and theft.

Alex. Stormy wine-drinking dog-loving Alex told them about me. A real turn-around from the woman who wanted to eject us from her house. Maybe a door opened inside her as well.

I'm on a hinge. One door is closing and another opening. I will be sixty the year after next, and I need a new direction. I can no longer do police. My guts won't stand it anymore. But maybe I can do art – my first love.

I think of money for a moment. I have had to borrow off Peggy to pay for the memory clinic, but I'll be able to pay her back when I start on my new salary. I think of Lilly, and how her life has changed. She got compensation in the end, and she has a caravan somewhere by a river.

Peggy puts Paul's music on. "I'm dying to meet him properly," she says.

'Like the occasional gardener, I let the weeds grow,
Now I look in my garden, and what do you know?
They're everywhere, everywhere, everywhere.
But come the autumn they will die
And I will have the chance to dig them out
And put in bulbs, and watch them grow
When spring comes round again.'

I think back to Grimwode laughing, and I wonder what they actually did find when they searched 'Hazelbank'. I'll probably never know.

Acknowledgements

With special thanks to Shelley Weiner for teaching me, and helping me write the first draft of this book through the Gold Dust scheme. Shelley has had a huge influence on the way I write.

Thanks also to Claire Renshaw for advice on dementia; to Jonathan and Shaun for checking that my police methods weren't too wide of the mark; to Judith Kilby Hunt for advice on art originals and copies; to Becki, Alice and my wife Judith for help with proof reading; to my neighbour Amanda for reading *The Occasional Gardener* in an earlier version and encouraging me to finish it; and to my cousin Ann, brother Jeremy and sister Briony for their constant support of my writing ventures.

About Nick Hooper

Nick Hooper (known as Nicholas Hooper in the film world) is a BAFTA award-winning composer, and has written the music for two of the Harry Potter films. Inspired by working so closely with J K Rowling's stories, he turned in 2012 to writing words as well as music.

Nick published his first novel *Above the Void* in 2017. *The Occasional Gardener* introduces Detective Inspector Arnold Rackham. Its sequel, *The Mirror in the Ice Cream Parlour,* is due for publication in 2019.